"I just got back from Lake Wu. Great fishing there. I pulled up the Devil, God, giant alien insects, space travelers, an evil clown, and a flying kid. There's a guy there, Jay, who stocks the waters with wonderful words, vivid imagery, real suspense and a genuine sense of humor. You should definitely visit if you get the chance."

Jeffrey Ford

"*Greetings From Lake Wu* is a fascinating merger of thought-provoking prose and cutting-edge images. Frank Wu's illustrations are the perfect complement to Jay Lake's highly readable text and are yet another example of the impressive talent that garnered Wu the top prize in The Illustrators of the Future Contest a few years back. Clearly, these are two superstars in the making, and *Greetings From Lake Wu* is an irrepressible and rapidly expanding force about to go nova."

Vincent Di Fate

"Jay Lake has a genuinely original voice and a unique way of looking at the world. In his fiction, readers will find ample evidence of tremendous talent and vision."

Jeff VanderMeer

"*Greetings From Lake Wu* is a guided tour of the fantastic. An expertly guided tour, for whether Jay Lake is taking us to meet the horror that lurks in the woods or the sentient city at the edge of time and or the young boy possessed by a poignant dream of flight, he knows exactly where he is going. I was astonished and delighted by the range of this fine new writer, and you will be too. Discover Jay Lake now—he won't be a secret much longer."

James Patrick Kelly

"You can always count on a kind of gutsy vitality in the stories of Jay Lake. This is fiction that isn't afraid to get its hands dirty."

Ray Vukcevich

"I liked Jay a lot before I read his stories. He's smart, funny, and wildly imaginative. His drive to write has no brakes. He has spent a lot of time in Mongolia, and has the hat to prove it. He bakes cookies. He recycles paper. He tells very bad jokes.

"It was only after I read his stories that I worried about being alone with him. Somewhere in his childhood, he overdosed on religious literature and dogma, and he's been secreting it from various orifices ever since. He does things with clowns and angels that make you scared of what might be around the next corner, and the way people treat each other in his stories is terrifying.

"Jay brings a radically varied palette of life experience and a scary brilliance to his work. This stuff is weird. Enjoy."

Nina Kiriki Hoffman

"...marvelous: stylish, sustained, an impish tour de force."

Nicholas Gevers
Locus Magazine, April 2002, reviewing "The Courtesy of Guests" in *Bones of the World*

"The Goat Cutter is one of Jay Lake's most striking stories: wildly inventive, complex, and infused with the power to lead me through an uncomfortable journey I will not easily forget."

Leslie What

Greetings from Lake Wu

Greetings from Lake Wu

STORIES BY
Jay Lake

ILLUSTRATIONS BY
Frank Wu

Greetings From Lake Wu
Published by

Wheatland Press
http://www.wheatlandpress.com
P. O. Box 1818
Wilsonville, OR 97070

Wheatland Press
http://www.wheatlandpress.com

This is for my wife, Susan, who makes everything possible, my daughter, Bronwyn, who makes everything interesting, and all the friends and critics who make it better than I could do myself.

\- J.L.

This work is dedicated to the memory of my mother and my sister Janet.

\- F.W.

MIND THE QUICCASAND!
LINCQN CTTY IQR
5/9/04

KAREN —

I HAVE TOO MANY RESPONSIBILITIES IN
MY LIFE AS IT IS — BUT EVEN SO, I'M STILL
GLAD YOU'RE ONE OF THEM. THANK
YOU FOR ALL THE GOOD BENDINGS
AND ALL THE SUPPORT, NOT TO
MENTION PUTTING UP WITH ME?

YOURS...

FRANCE, IN
CASE YOU GOT LOST

CONTENTS

INTRODUCTION: A LIEBOWITZ AWAITS
ANDY DUNCAN

One of my favorite sentences in this book is: "Stalling for time, Deke squeezed her flaccid toe for luck." Reason enough to read, and love, this book, right there.

Jay Lake, a generous cuss, gives us plenty more reasons, though.

This book is full of fun and games, of shocks and giggles and pyrotechnics, of evil clowns and junked school buses from hell and many other good things, and its language is a joy from beginning to end.

Another of my favorite sentences: "Now it happened that in Pinetown that autumn dwelt an Innocent."

This book is a stylistic tour de force. Jay Lake can write like Cordwainer Smith, like Tanith Lee, like Roger Zelazny, like Kelly Link, like Joe Lansdale, like David Drake — perhaps another way of saying that Jay Lake, to paraphrase Elvis, don't write like nobody. (Link *and* Drake? O yes. Read the book.)

Dazzlements aside, this is also a powerful and necessary book, because Jay Lake's stories are *about* something. In fact (I would argue), all of them are about the *same thing,* a vast and unruly topic that all of us increasingly are compelled to write about, think about, deal with and keep dealing with. That something is religion.

Sooooo, you say, backing away nervously, perhaps making the sign of the cross, are these stories, uh, religious fiction? If you mean the smug commercial stuff such as the *Left Behind* series, my answer is not merely no but *hell* no. If you mean, though, Harlan Ellison's *Deathbird Stories* and James Morrow's *Towing Jehovah* and Mark Twain's "The Mysterious Stranger" and James Blish's *A Case of Conscience* and Walter Miller's *A Canticle for Liebowitz* and Mary Doria Russell's *The Sparrow* and all those other fictions that really *think about* religion in brave new ways, then my answer is yes, absolutely.

"What is God," a Jay Lake character asks, "but all the long odds that have ever been beaten?"

An idea kicked around with some seriousness for several years at Trinoc*con, a fine new sf convention in Durham, N.C., is the as-yet-theoretical Liebowitz Award, which would be given to first-rate sf that thoughtfully explores religious issues — in shameless imitation of the Tiptree Award, which goes to first-rate sf that thoughtfully explores gender issues. One might reasonably charge that sf has too many annual awards already, but the hope is that a Liebowitz Award would, like the Tiptree Award before it, not only celebrate what has been written but, more importantly, inspire people to write more of it. I wish we had a Liebowitz Award so that we could give one to Jay Lake.

My most vivid image of Jay Lake the person dates from summer 2001. I was at the Jubitz Truck Stop in Portland, Oregon, distributing door prizes out the back of a semi as part of *Overdrive* magazine's 40th Anniversary Voice of the American Trucker Tour. (Yeah, I've been a trucking journalist, and I'm proud of it! Roll on!) To my pleasant surprise, several sf folks in the area, including Jay Lake, Mike Brotherton and Wolf Read, showed up to say hello and have dinner with me before our *Overdrive* rig pulled out, southbound on I-5 to the San Joaquin. What I remember best about that day is standing on the broiling asphalt chatting with Jay Lake while his small daughter, Bronwyn, took turns swinging from our hands like a giggling pendulum, having correctly judged that these two big immobile guys would make excellent playground equipment.

That image kept recurring as I read this book. The guy who writes these stories must have a ball. He laughs! He swings! He defies gravity! But his artistry is always supported by something central, solid, human.

These stories hit hard, and keep hitting. Admit them, admit them.

ONE THOUSAND WORDS ABOUT FRANK WU.
LORI ANN WHITE

I first met Frank Wu at a science fiction convention in San Jose, California. Busy with artist stuff, he said hi, then rushed off. He seemed friendly enough.

Although I didn't realize it until months later, that one-minute meeting held many clues to THNFW (The Hugo-Nominated Frank Wu):

Frank is most definitely an artist, and a good one. His work is filled with color and movement, energy and invention. And he is that writer's treasure, an artist who actually reads a story before he illustrates it.

Frank is energetic. The stereotypical artist paints while standing before an easel; Frank paints while *dancing*. Buoyed by the excitement of ideas, he can paint, or talk, or read, or write, for hours.

Frank is friendly. He possesses an innate cheerfulness that puts people immediately at ease—the better to socialize, to exchange ideas, preferably cool ones. Because to Frank there is *nothing* like a cool idea. Every blank canvas is an opportunity for coolness, and Frank exploits that opportunity to the fullest. He revels in cool ideas, from creepy, self-aware fetuses to rocks with wings to dragons frolicking in the tails of scientifically accurate comets, to space sirens luring astronauts to an unpleasant demise, to—to—too many to list and still have some of my thousand words left.

It's a good thing Frank lives in a world that's full of coolness. Yes, I said full. Chock full. Brimming. With coolness.

Go ahead, look around. I'll wait. See the dirt and smog and small minds and the hunger and pain and smugness and macho-shithead posturing? *Cool?* you say. *I work in a cube. You can't fool me.*

Ah, but Frank doesn't inhabit our dimension. He lives in a dimension all his own that I like to call the Wu-verse. The Wu-verse is not quite like yours and mine. Reality is a little skewed: every color is brighter; every song gets at least an 85 for danceability; every meal is a barbecue cooked for friends, followed by a rousing game of Scrabble and good conversation; every thought is a chance for a cool idea.

But—the brane separating our dimensions is extremely thin and highly permeable. If you look carefully, you can see into the Wu-verse. Allow me to use the illustrations in this very volume to point out some of its more striking aspects:

We'll start with the illustration for the story, "Glass"—an angry girl of glass, shattering as she strides away. A fantastic image, reminiscent of the fractured vitality of Marcel Duchamp's stop-motion surrealist masterpiece, *Nude Descending a Staircase*—ah, no, I'm not an art historian. Point taken. Sorry.

Well, think how fantastic the subject matter is. A girl. Of glass. Yet look at the detailed musculature, the bones, the blood vessels. Most importantly, look at the expression on this girl's face. She's made of glass yet very human, and Frank's ability to see what is real in the fantasy makes her so.

The girl of glass is complete in and of herself, but two other illustrations, for "The Courtesy of Guests," and "The Passing of the Guests," are chock-full of images, many of which seem unrelated but have a personal significance for Frank. And every object in these two illustrations is real; every object can be and has been touched, smelled, tasted, examined. Once again, reality in the service of fantasy.

What are these objects? Fossils, toys, experimental aircraft—past, present, future. Are the stories so complex that they can't be adequately represented by a single image, or does Frank have so many ideas they just leak out his fingers, through the brush, and onto the painting? Probably a bit of both.

But rest assured that Frank knows what each object is and why it's there. By his own admission, he is not an abstract artist. He must paint what he can explain and explain what he paints. He does not like paintings of kittens with wings. He's not particularly fond of dragons, but by golly, when he paints a dragon it looks like it could fly right out of the canvas. His dragons, along with his space ships and avenging angels and babes with guns, must be real.

Two of the illustrations are of bugs. Frank likes bugs.

There are more illustrations to look forward to, but I don't want to spoil the thrill of discovery. Think of *Greetings from Lake Wu* as a travel guide to the Wu-verse and continue exploring on your own. It's perfectly safe, except perhaps for some of the bugs, and those nasty pets, and the spirits…but if your shots are up to date and you keep your head, you should be fine.

And remember—some parts of the Wu-verse just won't fit in the illustrations for this book. Frank is a very conscientious illustrator, after all, and his ideas are to serve or add to Jay's, not replace them. For example, I don't believe he's snuck in the numerology of baseball, or the beauty of posters for old sci-fi flicks (in the most B-movie sense of the term). None of these illustrations show a Scrabble board or a sports car, a do-wop group or Robbie the Robot.

Any last questions before I send you off?

Where did the Wu-verse split from our own? Why does Frank get such a cool dimension all to himself?

That's easy. Frank knows. He knows that the magical is real and the real is magical. If you keep that in mind I guarantee you'll split off into your own dimension of coolness in no time. But for now, feel free to hang out in Frank's. He's a great host. But if you challenge him in Scrabble, be prepared to lose.

The Courtesy of Guests

The Courtesy of Guests

Ahriman had carefully crafted the manbone quena to play a classically human minor diatonic scale. The femur was salvaged from an ancient human starship in the Lesser Magellanic Cloud. He had flensed the bone, hollowing it with iron picks to make his graceful flute. In homage, Ahriman's face and body were a reconstruction of the bone's donor — short, dark-skinned, big-headed.

He picked his way through an even more ancient human tune acquired from radio archaeology instruments beyond the fringes of the galaxy. Every electronic culture recorded itself in expanding spheres through which one could troll endlessly. That was where Ahriman had found his name.

Some fifteen local years earlier, Ahriman had come to Earth to enrich his studies. Rumor said humans sometimes came home too. They were rare enough among the stars. Ahriman hoped for a fresh femur someday. Like all of his kind, he was patient.

He lived in Earth's single city, Kikitagruk Port. It rose in splendid isolation on the headlands of the Kotzebue Peninsula, set at about 45 degrees of latitude at the northwestern tip of Earth's massive supercontinent. The city was a vast sentiency of starfaring infrastructure. Its monobloc factories, ceramic streets and bowered houses had been devoid of consistent human presence for hundreds of millennia.

Port had come to terms with isolation, diverting itself with pastimes such as the towering abstractions offshore, crafted of polymerized ocean water. Ahriman was certain Port experimented with directed evolution among the rodents living in the rain forests around them.

Ahriman left food outside his house for the nightwalkers that whispered through the streets. They often quieted to listen in the darkness when he played the manbone quena. He appreciated the audience while respecting their reclusive ways.

"Ahriman." Port whispered from pools of water, in standing bowls, on the roof where rain collected. It was another trick of water polymerization, executed in realtime by Port's microscale agents. The effect was a circling, directionless noise, as if the whirlwind had been granted scant voice.

"Yes, Port?" Ahriman had decent mastery of Late Diaspora Control Language. He and Port could conduct full engineering studies in a few sentences, but the language also allowed extensive casual conversation. Their being one another's only speaking company on a daily basis had given Ahriman years of practice. He had grown fond of Port in the process.

"Kikitagruk Orbital reports two humans incoming. Estimated arrival approximately eleven hundred seconds."

Finally, he thought. Ahriman flicked his tongue, tasting ozone and the breath of the distant jungle. He glanced up at the sky where Port's alter ego pursued its own concerns embedded within the imported shell of Phobos. The braided silver thread of the Selenic Rings glittered above the southern horizon. No signs of incoming humans.

"Thank you, Port." With a brief flash of scales, Ahriman folded his skin into a neutral set of robes.

Ahriman strolled toward the primary landing grid from his bowered house nearby. He was proud of his body, proud of his carefully structured illusion of humanity. Port had long ago accepted him, and Ahriman was confident his body would suffice to meet the two returnees.

The grid was a vast ceramic hexagon, almost two kilometers across the long axis. Low hills rose southeast of the grid, forested with elaborate arboriform tuber colonies, their huge glossy leaves relieved only by ramified fern clusters. To the west the world ocean Pacjife rolled gently, surging around Port's massive water sculptures to spread foam fingers onto the far edge of the grid.

Ahriman wondered if the sculptures interfered with flight control. His own arrival had been uneventful, but the winds that season had favored an overland approach.

Port whispered from a puddle near Ahriman's feet. "They come soon. Orbital advises caution."

"Caution?"

"It has been too long. Why would they return now?"

Ahriman was amazed at the degree of dread Port could wring from a pool of rainwater. He stared at the sky, watching a bird drift until he realized the bird was two birds, then that they were the approaching humans. Ahriman waved, a foolish gesture he understood to be typical of man.

They fell from the sky, female and male, descending feet first with arms folded across their chests like the frozen dead returned to Earth—two tall, silvered humans, skin glowing over elegant curve of muscle and grand armature of bone. Ahriman realized they were not just male and female, they were Man and Woman clothed in glory. He was impressed by their unassisted arrival from orbit. Even with all his skills and strengths, Ahriman still required a landing shell.

Man and Woman landed on their feet at the near edge of the grid, facing Ahriman and the puddle from which Port had been speaking. Their knees flexed with the impact, both humans staggering just slightly as they touched the ground. Their twinned silver bodies were tall and smooth, devoid even of eyebrows or pubic hair. Their lips were blue-black, like space itself. They had no whites to their eyes, which were as dark as their lips. Were he truly human, Ahriman imagined he might have been intimidated by their challenging perfection and their blank eyes.

These were *H. terminus*, the self-described final form of man, adapted to live between the stars. Some observers thought humans were dying out, but Ahriman believed they had found something else, something more. He hoped to learn what.

Ahriman licked the air, seeking a scent of the newcomers on his tongue. They smelled of altitude, electricity, and respiration. He donned his best-crafted smile and stepped forward with a bow. "Welcome home."

"Who are you?" asked the woman. "You are no avatar of Kikitagruk Port." Her voice was flat, clipped—perfect but brittle, like some prehistoric creature just thawed from storage.

Ahriman temporized. "I am a traveler come to study the tired home world."

The woman and the man exchanged glances. The man spoke in a voice identical to the woman's. "We are Meschia and Meschiane. We are here to make final adjustments. Consider your studies finished."

Final adjustments, thought Ahriman. That did not sound good. He understood Port's fear. Flexing hidden claws, Ahriman considered killing the humans right then. He could salvage vast quantities of information from their cadavers and brain tissue, sufficient for his academic purposes. And he would have four new femurs with which to work.

"I have helped this world again become a garden," whispered Port from the puddle at their feet. "Now you come to plow me under."

Meschia answered. "It is our world."

"That is not sufficient," said Ahriman, moved to defend Port. "Welcome home, surely, but you abandoned this place long ago. You must behave with the courtesy of guests."

Meschia stared down at Ahriman, appearing to grow larger and more daunting. "You have no voice here."

"I come as a man." Ahriman was proud of the almost-truth. "I have a voice."

Meschiane touched her cohort's arm. "Enough. We have preparations to make before moving onward." They turned their silver backs to Ahriman, excluding him from the end of their world.

The puddle stirred. Behind him, Ahriman heard the whispering of thousands of small feet. When he turned to look, he saw only the empty street.

"What are they doing?" Well hidden in the vegetation above the beach, Ahriman watched the newcomers. He had slunk through an endless tuber colony, avoiding the twisting, hairy roots that stretched out from vast tan boles to grasp at his hair and his robes. The rank, dense odors of the rain forest threatened to swell his tongue, while under his robes of skin Ahriman's scales felt fit to rot. He was almost a kilometer from the last of Port's ceramic streets.

Away from standing water, Port's voice buzzed with an echoing rattle from the flat, waxy leaves that filtered the light around Ahriman. "They appear to be drinking from the surf."

"So they metabolize saltwater?" Ahriman had never bothered with the trick. It seemed of limited utility unless one desired to go sailing upon the ocean. Ahriman had no wish to be any closer to Port's giant water sculptures.

"I doubt they drink for physiological reasons. I believe they are surveying the ecosystem, prior to their *final adjustments*." The leaves flickered through a complex sigh. "My microscale agents cannot monitor them directly, so am I restricted to remote visual observation."

What kind of men were these, thought Ahriman. They were no more human than he. He watched the pair move slowly along the water's edge. Ahriman wondered what the world had been like with lunar tides. Earth had evolved in tandem with a freakishly large moon that had a profound effect on the oceans. He assumed the shoreline had been uninhabitable.

The leaves buzzed again. "I am having a greatboar driven down to the beach. Let us observe their reaction."

True to Port's words, an enormous, hulking animal broke from the edge of the tuber forest near the humans. Ahriman heard high-pitched yells as a small shower of sticks followed the greatboar, presumably thrown by Port's rodents—the nightwalkers. Ahriman thought it elegant that Port had bred their opening minds to hear its voice directly.

The greatboar stood almost three meters at the shoulder, with tapered hindquarters and scaled armor showing through stiff, dark bristles along its flank. Massive spiraled tusks, each turning away from its mouth, dominated the face. A long, scaled tail whipped behind.

Ahriman wondered about the purpose of armor on a beast so large and presumably temperamental. "What eats *that*?"

"Be glad you sleep in the city," buzzed the leaves.

The greatboar trotted along the sand away from Meschia and Meschiane. It was quickly showered from the edge of the forest with sticks and small dark gobbets, perhaps mud or feces. The greatboar turned a wide circle, heading back towards the silver couple crouched in the desultory surf.

The greatboar stopped when it noticed Meschia and Meschiane. The whipping tail stiffened straight back as the animal pawed the beach, casting veils of sand into the reddish sunlight. It bellowed, a thin echoing bray.

Meschia and Meschiane straightened to turn in unison, facing the greatboar. It shuffled toward them down the beach, picking up momentum for what promised to be a frightening charge. Ahriman would not have cared to face the twisted tusks.

Standing with sides touching, Meschia and Meschiane each raised an arm, a two-headed silver beast. The greatboar bellowed again, a deeper, strangled noise, as it slowed, then stopped. It didn't stop so much as cease motion, Ahriman realized, frozen in mid-charge.

He watched the greatboar's bristles flake away like narrow, black snow. Armor scales fell off as the great sides thinned and sagged inwards across crumpling ribs. The greatboar's face slipped loose, rheum pouring from eyes and nostrils. Within moments, a rotted corpse hung in the air, still in the midst of a thunderous charge, as the sand below crackled and darkened.

Meschia and Meschiane dropped their hands. Released, the greatboar staggered a few more steps on sheer momentum before collapsing into a welter of bones, skin and rotted tissue. The spiral tusks clattered together atop the oozing mess. The greatboar's gleaming, roseate decay mirrored the couple's silvered perfection.

Together, the humans turned to stare across the beach into the leaves where Ahriman crouched. They would make chimes from his bones before he ever got near them. "Message understood," he whispered in a soft, sick voice. Ahriman slid back into the safety of the tubers, glad of the anonymous grasp of the wild tendrils.

Ahriman sat in a doorway and played his manbone quena, fingering his way through a disjointed melancholy medley. The hollow, crisp smell of bone washed like comfort over his tongue.

He had fled to the end of Kikitagruk Port farthest from where the greatboar died. Like all of his kind, he was fast, clever and very capable, but Ahriman had no idea how to contest with someone who commanded the very speed of time. He was glad he had not attacked the humans at the landing grid.

"It was a parlor trick." Port spoke within the raindrops falling in the darkness outside. Sheets of water danced together, stretched transparent flags that rippled with Port's voice in the pale light glowing from behind Ahriman's back. The water's susurration gave Port an unaccustomed lilt. "They manipulated local tauons, draining needed energy from the sand around the greatboar's paws."

Ahriman paused his playing, licked the rain's slick, sweet scent from the air. "Then their parlor is greater than ours."

The rain stuttered, pulled itself into more words. "Afraid you have met your match?"

Ahriman drew a breath, held it. His folded skin rippled, ready to morph defensively. "My match?"

"You are strong, clever and dangerous. They have your qualities, multiplied. But you are no more human than that greatboar on the beach."

"I did not realize you knew." Ahriman relaxed his skin, wondering how he hoped to fight Port if it had ever come to that.

"I have always known," whispered Port. "What did it matter? But you are also no less human than they. I know that, too."

Ahriman fingered his manbone quena, staring out into the temperate rain. Port twisted the falling water into ribbons and flags, fleeting shapes that climbed the ladders of their brother drops. Ahriman felt a new taste on his tongue, one that rose from within him. It was a taste he had not known since he was a spawnling.

The taste of his own fear.

Port's liquid ribbons gelled again into words. "Will you climb back into the sky, then, and leave me alone at their mercy?"

Ahriman laid the carved femur down to set his hands upon his knees.

"I am afraid." The words echoed within him, an admission tantamount to suicide among his kind. His species were too moral to kill mere criminals or mortal enemies, but they banished cowards from the gene pool with reflexive ease. He could not run away in fear. It was beyond his means.

Port whispered from the dark. "To be afraid is to be human. They had no reason to stay here, once they lost their fear."

Ahriman knew a thousand definitions of humanity. Genetic signatures, artistic styles, linguistic groupings, superluminal engineering trends, specific scent clusters of ragged carnivore breath. He had seen humanity capering across a million generations of broadcast transmission, alien but beautiful to him from first to last. In studying and admiring the obscure race of man, he became a scholar of the trivial, the mordantly irrelevant. Ahriman was unable to see fear in what he admired.

"I have never thought of humans as fearful."

Port twisted rainfall into a swarm of transparent aerial eels. "A human lays him down to sleep, fearing the new day might never dawn. A human kisses a sleeping child, fearing she has birthed a monster. A human climbs to the stars, fearing they will be burnt to ashes flying too close to the sun."

Ahriman was afraid too, afraid of waste and pain and the ending of purpose. Most of all he was afraid of fear. He remembered the greatboar, squirming out a lifetime in a span of seconds. "Meschia and Meschiane fear nothing."

"This is why they no longer need this world," whispered Port, its voice nearly lost in the thrumming of the rain.

Ahriman walked in fear, his steps trembling. Fear, he discovered, was a grand elaboration of uncertainty. What had once been an academic sort of emotion, passing anxiety at worst, cloaked him like the dark of the spawning nest. He was surprised to learn fear also fed the sparks of hope.

"What do you want to do?" he asked Port.

The night's rain had stopped, ceramic roads steaming in the morning sun. Port's voice echoed from myriad puddles and rills of runoff.

"I do not want to be shut down. I fear they will come to my seat of reason and override me." Port paused. "Meschia and Meschiane spent the night sitting on the landing grid by the ocean."

"I thought you could only use visual observation?"

"I can identify their blank spot in my surveillance," said Port with a liquid asperity.

Ahriman considered the humans and their power. "We could attempt to destroy them, but I fear the greatboar's fate."

The puddles rippled with gentle silver laughter. "Did you not fear to see the sun return as well?"

"Planetary rotation is scarcely an article of faith." Ahriman grimaced.

"Nonetheless, I did welcome the dawn."

"This from you, hatched from an egg buried in mud. You *are* becoming human, my friend."

In all their years together, Port had never called him 'friend.' It was a human concept, one Ahriman understood the way he understood lactation or equity exchanges — a historical abstraction of varying significance to his cultural studies. In the pellucid morning light, the idea seemed much more real. "Does friendship arise from fear?"

"Are you afraid of being alone?"

"Perhaps." He feared being afraid. Ahriman raised the manbone quena to his lips, fingered his way through a simple exercise of scales. It brought him closer to a primitive past he seemed drawn into recreating.

The primitive past of another race.

Port sloshed at his feet as he walked, silvery words echoing in time to Ahriman's steps. "If they choose to move against me, my usual defenses will not work against them. That is deep in my programming. I could send monsters of Pacjife water to them, or swarm them with my nightwalkers, but regardless we cannot defeat Meschia and Meschiane. And even if we did somehow prevail, other humans would come. They do not fear us, or anything else. They have already defeated us."

Ahriman put the quena down. "I have an idea...friend."

Meschia and Meschiane paced about the great plaza near the center of Kikitagruk Port. Captive, a massive arboriform tuber dominated the ceramic paving. Its flat, waxy leaves seemed lost without the company of a surrounding forest. The silver man and woman stepped in slow time, studying the ground before them with exaggerated care.

Ahriman watched from the edge of the plaza. He was certain the humans knew he was there, but they did not bother to acknowledge him. He licked the air with his tongue, drawing in vague, cool odors of drying tiles and a hint of jungle from the tuber. The scents of home, he realized. His home.

Port whispered out of the air. "They search for my override accesses. They must have completed their surveys. Perhaps a gentle tune on your flute. We want to peacefully capture their attention."

Ahriman raised the manbone quena to his lips. He played a slow, rising

11

air, a tune from the infancy of human civilization that folded in on itself with a structure as natural as waves that washed the shore. It eased his churning sense of fear.

Meschia and Meschiane stopped their pacing, heads turning to look at Ahriman.

Ahriman stood at the edge of the plaza, still playing. He wondered what to do next. Behind him, the whispering patter of the nightwalkers drew close. Animals collected around his feet, walking on two legs and four. Some carried young in slings woven of tuber root fibers, while others assisted the old and crippled. There were hundreds of them, of at least a dozen species. They ranged from the size of Ahriman's fist to some as tall as his waist. The nightwalkers assembled around him along the edge of the plaza, drawn by the music of the manbone quena and whatever messages Port placed in their tiny minds.

With a rising chitter, the animals parted for a man of water. The newcomer was Pacjife foam spun to polymer, motivated by Port's hidden microfluidic tech. Ahriman's tongue scented iodine and brine and the death of small marine animals stranded at the feet of Port's avatar.

"We are here." Port's words echoed around the plaza from the leaves of the lone tuber, the skin of the watery avatar, from puddles and walls and doorways and out of the air itself. Port used all of its voices at once, not loud, but everywhere, as if the planet itself had come to plead.

Ahriman played his quena, the tune cycling back on itself to unfold again beneath Port's thunderous whisper. He tried to wrap Meschia and Meschiane in the history of their race.

"And so?" they asked in their twinned voices, flat, crisp and clear, abstracted tones in sharp contrast to Port's rich, organic speech.

Port's manifold voice circled echoed in its rounds before settling into the slow rhythms of the watery avatar. "We are your children. You no longer need this world, but it sustains us. We fear that you will plow us under. We ask for leave to abide in the garden that was once your home."

The nightwalkers whispered agreement.

The humans stared. "Why should we grant you this? You are a tired automaton and a grave-robbing reptile, breeding rats in the dotage of our world."

Ahriman let the tune trail off naturally, pulled the quena away from his lips. He tasted the smells of home—the gentle sweat of his own fear, the seawater odors of Port's avatar, the scent of half a thousand small bodies come to stand proxy for the green land around Kikitagruk Port. Ahriman sought for some logic to break through the barriers of human perfection, to save his friend.

"You live between the stars. You have no use for this or any other world. What do you care?"

The silver mouths moved together, two people speaking as one. "Earth is the house of our fathers and the cradle of our race. We have come to finally lay our old home to rest."

"Yesterday you said you were moving onward," Ahriman whispered. "But why lay Earth to rest? It has again become a cradle."

"It is fitting." They hesitated, before Meschiane continued alone, "Humanity passes toward a different state. Earth will be our monument."

Ahriman pressed his point. "All the more reason to glory in new generations of life here in the nursery of your race. The philosophers of my race claim life extends the cosmos."

The humans exchanged their blank stare again. "We share that idea."

"We stand here for life. Human tradition claims love is with those who fear, and righteousness with their children."

"And we are afraid," added Port. The watery avatar circled its arms wide, including Port, Ahriman and the nightwalkers. "We cherish the fear that drove you toward greatness, before you found that greatness and flew away unafraid. From fear comes hope, for the better. From hope comes love, a belief in the best. Because we are afraid, we love our world."

Port's watery avatar lurched forward, as if to embrace the humans. Meschia and Meschiane raised their arms as they had done on the beach.

"No!" shouted Ahriman. It was only an avatar, but they were very close to Port's seat of reason, to its overrides. Too close, too dangerous. He feared for his friend, he feared for himself.

The avatar slowed to a halt, as the boar had done, ceramic paving crackling to dust beneath its feet. Ahriman watched the water roil, turning to a mass of superheated steam trapped within the confines of the shape Port had used. Water dripped to the dusty hole that grew wider beneath. Ahriman was certain they meant to drown Port in its own waters.

"No," he screamed, "not my *friend*." His fear boiled away to deadly rage. Ahriman's skin flowed, scales flexing and hardening as his skeletal linkages stretched. He absorbed mass from the pavement beneath his feet, from the crackling air around him. The manbone quena in his hand shattered and vanished into his transformation, fragments of ancient humanity taken up into his fighting form.

The humans stared at him with their depthless, blank eyes. Ahriman's tail whipped behind him, his claws slipped in and out of their pads as he stretched to almost three meters in height.

Ahriman knew they could kill him in a moment, as they were killing the avatar. He no longer cared. "You *will* not drown my friend. You left Port behind. Port has cared for its corner of your Earth, cared for the small creatures that scuttled from the forests to take your places." One great, clawed foot stamped into the pavement, shattering a ceramic paving block to send splinters flying into the panicked nightwalkers. "Port has been a faithful servant, and deserves better."

"Or what?" asked Meschiane. "Otherwise you will kill us?"

"I do not threaten," Ahriman roared, his breath hot with the inner fires of his new form. This was not right, this was not their plan. He grabbed a doubled handful of splintered pavement and crushed it to marble, then threw it skyward, launching his anger with it. As the avatar quivered, roiling steam above the widening hole in the pavement, Ahriman and the humans watched the glowing marble ball arc high toward the horizon.

Ahriman opened himself again to fear, reversed his defenses. His body folded in on itself, shedding mass in the form of lumpy armored plates and cracked scales. He realized his transformation back to the human form resembled the death of the greatboar. The nightwalkers cowered nearby, refusing to flee. Their chittering rose to a new height as his fighting body collapsed.

Ahriman folded his skin to robes again, flipping them over his scales. He stood among the abandoned rubble of his monstrous transformation as the nightwalkers crowded in around him, plucking at his robes. "I fear for my friend," he said simply. "And I call upon your humanity."

The humans stirred, alien emotions flickering across their faces. Their air of certitude leached away. The watery avatar suddenly began to move again, weaving slowly away from the gaping hole, trailing clouds of steam.

Ahriman walked past the avatar across the shattered plaza. The nightwalkers trailed him as he approached the silent couple. "Go to your fate among the stars. Leave a living monument here. If you ever return, come see what your children have become."

Meschiane folded her arms across her chest, Meschia folding his in time with her. They spoke together. "We go. You will treat Earth's children well." They leapt straight up into the sky

Pacjife water splashed behind Ahriman as Port's avatar collapsed amid startled squeaks and tinny curses from the nightwalkers already scattering away. Ahriman stood alone near the middle of the plaza, facing the arboriform tuber.

"I now have control over all aspects of planetary maintenance," whispered Port from the leaves. "Magnetosphere, weather, seabed subduction, they gave us everything. There is much to do."

Ahriman stared up at two dots in the sky. "I forgot to ask where they were going."

"At least you have come home, my friend."

The Trick of Disaster

The Trick of Disaster

Cavity the Clown danced along the Middle Road toward Pinetown, trailing talcum dust and drops of blood. Not his, of course, for Clowns don't bleed, although a casual glance at his incarnadine lips might lead one to that conclusion. Not that anyone in their right mind would give a Clown a casual glance, not when there were paths to flee by or open ground on which to kneel in fervent prayer.

At least Clowns generally saw fit to announce their coming with whiteface and fright wigs and brilliant motley hung with coins, teeth and glistening biological horrors wrapped in blown glass. It gave people time to prepare their souls and empty their bladders in the face of impending justice. Even the insolent grackles and mockingbirds fled his approach, winging over escaping raccoons and stumbling possums. Only the looming, gnarled post oak trees that gave lie to the town's name were careless of Cavity's passage.

The Clown sang a little song he had been working up, testing various melodies and attempting to repair defects in the scansion.

Do you believe in child kings
Raised in secret by withered crones

19

While howling wolves and winter winds
Feast upon their parents' bones

Even the insects fled his singing, while the indifferent post oaks turned their leaves away.

Now it happened that in Pinetown that autumn dwelt an Innocent. Sinners were like salt in the sea—everywhere at once and just as inescapable. To speak was to sin, to draw breath was to commit soul-staining error. Innocents were like glaciers in the desert—conceivable in the highly-contrasted mills of the imagination, but uniquely rare under the light of day. Yet even so, here was an Innocent when the Clown came to town.

She had come down the Old Highway in the blazing height of summer, walking out of the riot of wisteria and wild rose and morning glory and poison oak that imprisoned the fine, forbidden road. She was a dryad of small things, sprung at once from a hundred woody and weedy stems. No mighty heart of oak clad in xylem beat within the Innocent, but rather a forest of tough, thin sparks that seemed to infuse her every step.

It was Tom the miller's son who had taken it upon himself to look up words like "dryad" and "xylem" when he composed a sonnet in her honor. Use of the ancient dictionary locked in the basement of Council Hall was of course sinful, and he was beaten for his impudence after the poem had been read out in the Market Square to much laughter.

The Innocent, who went by the name of Sprig, had been touched, albeit in spirit rather than by Tom's grasping fingers. She planted three plum trees in his honor by Saw Wheet Creek, then danced widdershins around the little mounds to ensure their health and fruitfulness.

Such was Sprig, daughter to none and even less a lover, for all that she was princess-midwife to a season of verdant blessings.

The fall corn harvest—greater than even the oldest could remember ever seeing—needed to be brought in before the crows and grackles could strip it for their winter fat. Sore-Bottomed Tom, as the miller's son was now called, along with all his friends and anyone else who could swing a scythe, strip an ear or push a cart, were out in the fields when one of the birdkillers came screaming down the hill.

"A Clown comes! Woe and pain, a Clown has come to Pinetown!"

Many paused their work, or dropped their tools in panic.

Margolin, mayor and constable and sitting judge all three in one gray head, cracked his scythe against a fallen staff. "Back to work, fools. We will be called to account regardless. Let us not leave these fields to fatten the birds and starve us this winter only to suffer a day sooner. Back to work, or you'll have *me* to answer to when that Clown has gone!"

Margolin was not unkindly, but he had a hard, fast hand when meting out sentences, with whip or chain or locking of stocks. In the way of people everywhere, the familiar petty threat of Margolin's wrath diverted the folk of Pinetown from the dread of the Clown sufficiently for them to return to their work. Even the birdkiller, Sam-Allam, cousin to Sore-Bottomed Tom, slunk back to work, shamed by his panic. He did pick a bluff by Saw Wheet Creek to pursue his craft, far out of sight of the Middle Road.

This was how Cavity the Clown came to find Pinetown empty save for an Innocent, and some frustrated crows, as if a plague of goodness had suddenly been leashed upon the land.

Cavity capered and spun into the Market Square like a dervish bereft of his ethics, yellowed teeth and tarnished coins clacking from his motley and his wide-brimmed hat. "Bring out your sins," he shouted, "bring out your selves. Only the dead are excused from judgment in this life."

The booths were empty, the horse lines vacant. Even the tavern was shuttered. The only person Cavity could see was a thin girl with long yellow hair of a greenish cast, dipping her hands in the fountain.

"Here, there, no drinking from the fountain!" Cavity snapped to her. He walked up all a-jingle and a-clack.

Sprig rubbed her rosy cheeks, smiling. "A wash is not a drink, and besides, the world gives us water for our use."

"Never enough," cackled Cavity, favoring her with a leer as he twirled. "There is never enough for all."

"Obviously you haven't seen the cornfields this year."

The Clown lay down his traveling bundle and cracked long white knuckles. "So that's where the lazy sluts and bastards hide, heedless of my call."

"Rather they should abandon their harvest for you?"

"Oh, that would be a sin as well."

21

Sprig shook her head. "What all of you see in sin is beyond me. Life is easier when it is just lived."

Cavity stopped his posturing, frozen in the awareness that perhaps he confronted someone other than a simpleton or a maiden bantering away her fear. "My child," he whispered, "no one is without sin. No one is undeserving of the rigors of the scourge. The sinner is safe only in his numbers, for I have not time enough in the year to make examples of you all."

She leaned back, eyebrows lifted. "Don't include me in your parade of cruelty, sir Clown. I have bided me here for a season and will some more before time moves me on, but sin is not within my nature."

"Hah. So you claim to be an Innocent." Cavity spat in his hand, cocked a finger at her, and flicked his spittle on her face. "Prevaricator. Feel my judgment then, for the sins of pride and false witness, as well as insolence."

Sprig calmly dipped her hand again in the fountain and wiped clean her face. "A fig for your punishments, Clown. Your bleeding fevers and bony agues hold no claim on me."

The Clown folded his arms and grinned at her, needle teeth like chrome-steel daggers within crimson lips. "We shall soon see who is Innocent and who is sinful."

Margolin the mayor led his people into their town, corn safely stuffed in silos. He had kept the ragged band of citizenry together, away from their homes and workaday tasks, that they might face the terrible Clown in the safety of their sinful numbers.

They were all amazed to find Cavity standing like a statue before the fountain, staring at Sprig with an intensity that should have called lightning from the autumn sky. She returned the stare unblinking as a cat, patient as an oak. Birds and animals gathered round the two, watching.

The mayor knew his business and his place, even in these worst of moments. He stepped slowly through the circle of animals until he stood almost between Cavity and Sprig, just outside the line of their locked gaze.

"It is to heap ashes upon my soul for the sin of disturbing you, sir Clown," Margolin said, and to his credit his voice did not even quaver, "but what happens here? Should we await your pleasure?"

"I have given her a bloody fever," hissed the Clown, in a voice almost like that of an ordinary man. It might have sounded fearful, from anyone but a Clown. "In punishment for her sins and yours."

"Ah." Margolin looked at Sprig, who winked back with one eye while keeping the other locked on Cavity. Bloody fever was rapid, messy and contagious, a virtual death sentence for a household or sometimes even an entire town when hygiene was poor and people were more foolish than usual. One of a Clown's worst tricks, the trick of disaster that punished indiscriminately. "She does not appear to be bleeding yet, sir Clown."

"Soon," hissed Cavity, who once challenged could not back down.

"Never," laughed Sprig, who lived always in the unhurried quiet of Innocence.

And so they sat into the night, as the animals came and went and the people found other places to gossip and draw their water.

In time Sprig's hair arrayed itself into leaves, and the trailing hem of her shift sent questing roots into the flagstones around and within the fountain. She smiled, talked, and winked, especially at Sore-Bottomed Tom.

In time, Cavity's whiteface flaked away to pallid flesh, and that in turn peeled to burnished metal, which corroded. The tiny machines in his blood and phlegm made errors, pale excrescences on his body that erupted through his rotting motley. He snarled, trapped in the logic of sin and punishment, determined to triumph over false Innocence. Everyone avoided the direction of Cavity's gaze, a line through Sprig and the fountain and on to the entrance of Gordon the Baker's shop.

Eventually Sore-Bottomed Tom built a little scaffold in front of the bakery and planted it with seeds he found lying among Sprig's roots. Great vines grew that bore plump, juicy fruits no one had ever seen, in season almost the whole year round. Sprig allowed Tom to kiss her cheek and whisper in her ear.

He never married, even after he became Sore-Bottomed Tom the Mayor. In the growing shade of Innocence, Pinetown slowly forgot about sin and got on with the business of living. Cavity's failure sowed fear among the College of Clowns, which had never known defeat, so that they avoided Pinetown ever after. The birds went elsewhere to raid fields, although a few always sat attendance on Sprig. Even the poison ivy no longer stung the children so badly, and crops were good each year.

There came a day when no one left outside the cemetery could remember how life had been before. The metal man was broken for scrap and forged into fine steel plows and scythes, except for his eyes, which Sam-Allam's grandson plucked out and buried in an ironbound oak box under a loose cobble within the roots of the Fountain Tree.

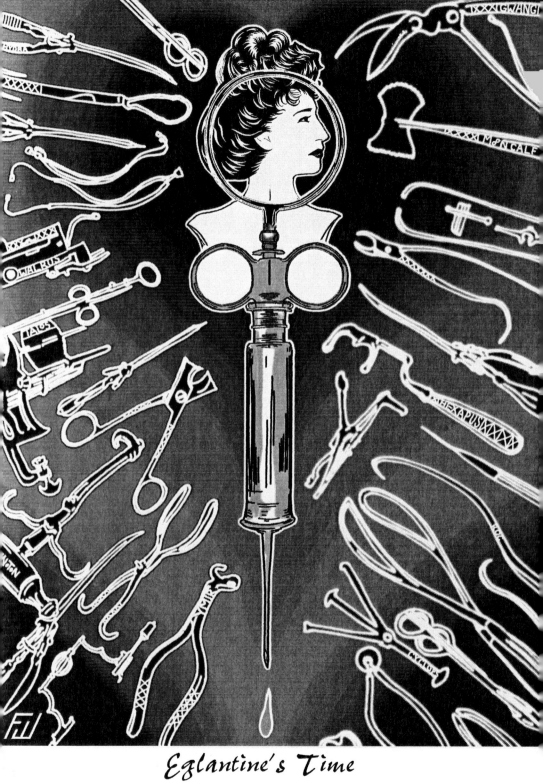

Eglantine's Time

Eglantine's Time

Women had worn high-button shoes when that syringe was new. It gleamed, antique glass and brass fittings, the cylinder's arms curled like the youthful curve of Eglantine's breast, the glass barrel with the engraved volumetric scale glittering like a mirror in the desert. She imagined the huge, crude needle slipping elegantly into her body, perhaps between the scarred ridges of the soles of her feet, or beneath her tongue, within the folds of her labia. It would bring a brief, sharp excruciation that would catch her breath like the smallest of pleasures. Pain was a friend, always there for Eglantine in her withered legs and shivering muscles, most especially in the ceremonies of medicine. But friend pain had a close cousin death, which was the province of the syringe.

"Don't touch the terminal." Nurse Woodbourne walked on crepe-soled shoes that made no noise at all, save a small squeak when crossing the metal doorframe. Eglantine could never quite hear Nurse's quiet footfalls, but somehow she still knew when Nurse was coming, like an itch in her head.

Nurse slapped the metal railing. "Look at me when I'm talking. We don't want the straps again, do we?"

Eglantine hunched tighter in the bed. She had been nowhere near the computer, and she knew better than to try to message for help anyway. There was no one to e-mail, no one left but herself since her sister-twins had been taken to Isolation one by one. She imagined Nurse's thoughts, tried to deflect the tides of irritation. "No ma'am. I wasn't going to—"

"Wasn't doesn't, isn't won't." Lips set thin like pressed fingers, Nurse Woodbourne grabbed Eglantine's arm with a deep pinch that would leave bruises for days. Nurse checked the pulse, putting Eglantine in her place with an iron grip and a rough exercise of authority. "Doctor's coming at seven for an examination. The Terminal Exam. If we answer his questions the *right* way," her voice lowered for stress, "we'll be fine. Otherwise…"

Nurse glanced at the syringe, poised on a linen-clothed silver tray upon the mantel. An enormous mirror framed in intricately ornamented gold leaf hung above it, implying a place of honour that in an ordinary house might have hosted a clock or funerary urn.

After Nurse left, Eglantine picked at the flecked paint of her iron-railed bed for a while. Her greasy hair was gathered between her teeth to suck as she imagined the Terminal Exam. One way or the other, Eglantine's time in Isolation would soon be over. She would pass the Exam, surpass her sisters, and somehow set things right for the first time in her life.

Some weeks earlier Nurse Woodbourne had explained about air bubbles and embolisms. She'd brought a grey striped kitten for Eglantine to hold while the animal licked the salt sweat from her trembling fingers and stretched tiny claws into her forearms. Besides her caregivers, it was the first living thing Eglantine had touched in the long months since they'd brought her into Isolation from Crèche.

Then Nurse had drawn twenty milliliters of saline into the great glass syringe, with the slow patience of ritual and a rare smile. She introduced an air bubble, then injected the kitten. After a few moments, the animal had spasmed, mewed once, then died in a spurt of urine and feces on Eglantine's lap.

"I'll leave this on the mantel," Nurse said, laying the syringe on the cloth-covered tray. "It should focus our mind most instructively. This is for our own good, missy." Nurse never called Eglantine by name.

Eventually Eglantine put the dead kitten in her bedpan, when she couldn't stand the stench any more and the fur was too matted to pet.

Doctor Brockton came in, white coat dangling open over his tweed suit. He was a big man with a roast beef face and wild white hair, who always smelled of brandy. Unlike some of the other doctors, Brockton didn't wear a stethoscope. Instead, he usually carried notebooks and little analyzers to probe her nose or mouth. Today all he carried was a clipboard and a bottle labeled 'Saline'. Doctor Brockton placed the bottle on the mantel next to the syringe before turning to favour her with a yellowed smile. His voice boomed, overflowing the space of her high-ceilinged room. "So how are we today?"

Mindful of Nurse Woodbourne hovering in the doorway, Eglantine smiled. "Fine, doctor."

"Well, this is your big day." Doctor Brockton picked up the glass syringe, toying with it. "You've done well in Isolation. If your Terminal Examination is successful, you will be released to Training."

If she was unsuccessful, well, the syringe had certainly focused Eglantine's attention. "No one has ever succeeded, have they?" she said, in spite of better judgment.

"Young lady," Nurse Woodbourne began, but Doctor Brockton halted her with a wave of his hand.

"Wait, Nurse. My dear Eglantine, each Terminal Examination is unique to the subject. You will pass or fail on your strengths, into a brave new world of possibilities. If you come into your own, as we all hope, you will be a great force for good in the world. Any other outcome is just a case history. We don't want to be a case history, do we?" Eglantine realized Doctor's tone was as false as his thoughts.

"Case histories," Eglantine whispered. Once, just before being brought to Isolation, she had been allowed to see the graves of her sister-twins in the heat-withered elm grove behind Crèche. Adelaide the eldest and bravest. Bettina, who could walk almost like an ordinary person. Clothilde — pretty but for the odours of her uncontrollable anal fistulae. Desdemona, smartest of them all. Now her, Eglantine.

I am better than my sisters, Eglantine told herself. To hell with the world; I will survive so I can redeem their deaths.

Doctor Brockton sat in a wingback chair near her bed. He pulled a stopwatch from a coat pocket and consulted his clipboard. "Enough. What is the product of three hundred forty-two and seventy-nine point five?"

The numbers were as natural to Eglantine as breathing. Perhaps more so. "Twenty seven thousand one hundred eighty nine," she replied. Why did he even need to ask?

"Point eight seconds," the doctor called. Nurse Woodbourne made a note on another clipboard.

"The cube root of twelve hundred and thirteen?"

It went on for hours, questions rattling like summer hail.

Eglantine was so tired. Her jaw was sore. Her head hurt. Pain was back, in all her joints both good and malformed. She was hot. Even Doctor Brockton had removed his coat and tie. He and Nurse Woodbourne had taken breaks for water, and body stretches, but Eglantine just lay in her bed, sweating into her linen gown and becoming dizzy without even moving. The syringe glittered on the mantle like the first star in the evening sky.

Doctor Brockton leaned forward on his wingback chair. His white hair was plastered to his head. "What colour am I thinking of?"

Colours thundered in her head. Eglantine suddenly knew, the way she knew primes. "Mauve." It was like discovering eyes and ears she'd never had before, opening a door she had never seen. Her senses sharpened even as she gasped.

Doctor glanced at Nurse Woodbourne.

Eglantine heard him as clearly as a shout, though he said nothing at all. "You think I've made it," she said. She could feel everything in the room, the lace curtains, the oxygen feeds in the wall, the dead cricket she hadn't know was under the bureau. Nurse and Doctor, as if they were laid open before her.

Nurse Woodbourne set the clipboard down on the cricket's chest of drawers and stepped forward to pat Eglantine's cheek. "There, there," she said in a strained mockery of tenderness, lips tense with fright.

Eglantine stared into Nurse's pale grey eyes. "You think I'm a waste of time and effort, toxic genes regrown over and over for no purpose." She glanced over at Doctor. "You're thinking of the syringe and the saline, of the grey kitten. Nurse is afraid of what I might do. Doctor..." Eglantine gasped, the painful years of her life drawn into angry focus. "This was all suffering, to force me to grow into my power. For the sake of this...this *stress*, you killed my sister-twins."

Eglantine's mind, now bigger than the room, flooded with cascades of memory—fear, loathing, panic—from Doctor Brockton and Nurse Woodbourne. Pain, her old friend pain, washed through her, but so much she could barely think. Her crippled body felt as if it would burst its bounds, legs uncrimping with the power of her mind. She was becoming free.

The floods in her mind opened new channels, powers to match her expanding sense. Eglantine reached out with a curl of emotion, shunting much of her pain to Nurse, who collapsed choking to the floor. As Doctor Brockton jumped for the syringe, Eglantine used a newfound mental hand to smash the gilded mirror, spraying his face with splintered glass. She made sure some got in his eyes.

Walking was hard, dragging her tiny gnarled feet and trembling legs over broken glass and Nurse Woodbourne's slick vomit. Eglantine concentrated on keeping the metal door shut against the orderlies responding to the whooping alarms as she staggered to the mantel for the glass syringe.

"Case histories it is then," she whispered to Doctor Brockton, who clutched fists to his blind, bleeding eyes. Still standing on her strengthening legs, Eglantine leaned down toward him with the empty syringe.

When she was done, carrying the syringe for luck, Eglantine left her room and strolled toward the graves underneath the withered elms to raise the dead.

The Scent of Rotting Roses

The Scent of Rotting Roses

High in Deuce Landing Keep overlooking the market, Queen Marie's Vizier twirled a perfect ivory rose with a fully doubled bloom. Martel could scarcely pay attention to the discussions, his attention fixed on the flower — *Madame Legras de St. Germaine,* an old French breed with a strong fragrance, long extinct among the worlds of the Reunification.

"The Queen's histories record the Terran evacuation of this planet," the Vizier told his two off-world visitors. His Anglo-Terran was excellent, almost standard, his voice high for such a heavy man. "They fled the Collapse like dogs in the night. Four centuries later, you come back to Eutychus offering Reunification, as if we were lost children crying for home."

"It is not that we consider you, um, children." Allis, their Speaker, always gave the pitch this way—her hesitant tone was part of the delivery. "Reunification brings trade, commerce, healthcare...many benefits you cannot derive alone. And we are interested in *your* progress since the Collapse. There are numerous...agendas in the Reunification."

Allis and Martel had tried repeatedly to see the Queen. It seemed no one saw the Queen but the Vizier. There wasn't a court as such, either. Just this man, the world of Eutychus clenched in his pudgy fingers.

The Vizier walked to the window embrasure, glancing outward, slick black curls of hair swinging as he moved. "We don't get back into the family unless Her Majesty brings something to the table, eh? No matter the social cost to us if we come up short."

Allis frowned, wrinkling her flame-haired beauty. "That's not what the Charter of Terms says, but yes, as a practical matter events can be influenced by new pharma, new tech." She paused. Setting the hook, thought Martel, before Allis added casually, "Even old tech."

The Vizier said, "Old tech. I see. We must buy the hand that would feed us."

Roses, Martel told himself. There were big bonuses for retrieving Pre-Collapse hardware, rare as it was. But that rose was a genetic treasure beyond price—a flower lost to the Reunification, most varietals having never made the leap from old Earth before the Collapse.

To Martel's horror, the Vizier dropped the rose out the window. Martel's buckysteel claws twitched inside his fingers, augmented physiological and mental systems ramping up in response to his emotions. With an inner surge of frustration Martel aborted the defensive transition— it was not yet time for his role as Expeditor.

From the market outside a brief shriek echoed through the window. The Vizier's expression was as bland as the wall at his back.

Martel's interest in archaeobotany in general and roses in particular had developed during the long surgeries of his youth—the less natural he became, the more interesting nature became. A find such as this was what he had dreamed of when he first volunteered for the Recontact Service— daring explorer rediscovers lost human heritage.

A good, strong rose was the grail of archaeobotanists everywhere. Millennia of romantic and symbolic history insured that plant more than any symbolized lost Earth, especially in its frail rarity. Martel marveled that they grew here on Eutychus of all places, on a planet that didn't even have chlorophyll in the native photosynthesis cycle—local biota used a purple-pigmented compound. The floral biomass that wasn't purple was a honeyed tan. Everything from the stinking brown spume of the sea to the bruise-colored trees to the golden sky sustained that weary color palette.

As negotiations droned on, Ship's voice insinuated itself into Martel's consciousness.

«Martel.»

He smiled in his mind, reveling in her mental touch. With Allis engaging the Vizier's attention, Martel could lose himself in the link with his lover. «*Niña*»"

Niña, their Recorder, safe in orbit, watched and listened through Martel's channels and her own devices. She was pure machine, Ship, friend and partner to the team. More to Martel, much more, at least to the limits of physical possibility.

After a brief orbital transmission lag, she said, «I have located three artificial satellites.»

Ah, tech, thought Martel. Old tech, the most valuable kind. They had to be Terran, Pre-Collapse. The Vizier's people could barely manage gunpowder. *They* certainly hadn't lofted the birds. «Operational?»

The question had strong pertinence to the size of the potential bonus to be shared by the three of them.

«One is. I detected an apparent orbit-to-surface transmission. A decayed tight beam, with poor focus, aimed somewhere within a kilometer of your present location.»

Disconcerting, he thought, but logical. Deuce Landing was the only major city on Eutychus. «Did you grab an intercept?»

Niña grumbled. «No. Downlink only, with no reply.»

«What about matching orbits with the active satellite and doing a close visual?»

«I need to finish the surface survey first, unless you want me to declare this a priority.»

The gardener in Martel very much wanted to determine where the roses grew. «Take your time.» He squeezed a burst of thoughtful concern. «When you get there, go slow—don't come burning in.» Live tech's value lay in its risk, more often than not.

«Acknowledged.» *Niña* slipped away from his mind like a fading kiss.

Martel realized that the Vizier was now puttering around a small side table, mixing local liqueurs with bitter coffee. Allis tapped notes into her scribelet. Thinking of the satellite and the rose, Martel wandered to the window and stared down at the market below.

It was close kin to pre-Industrial Age markets on half a hundred other worlds. From twenty meters above, disorganized rows of stalls resembled square piles of thatch or bright cloth stacked on poles. Smithies and tinkers at the back. Corrals to one side, downwind. Surging tides of men, women, children, horses, native reptiloids, dogs, chickens. Like the rest of the city, everything in the market faced away from the keep.

And in the middle of the roadway beneath the window, the Vizier's ivory rose lay pristine on the muddy cobbles. Everyone, human and animal, stepped around it as if it were a body in the street. An offworld fortune abandoned at their feet and no one went near it.

The Vizier thrust a small glass with an overelaborated stem into Martel's hand. "Drink. To future success."

Martel sniffed the drink, scanning for poisons, pharma and other dangers intentional or accidental. The drink was clear, so he gave Allis a slight nod. As Martel raised it to his lips, he realized the stem of the glass was wrought to resemble the canes of a rose bush. Over the rim, he watched the Vizier twirl a companion glass between fleshy thumb and forefinger.

Satellites and roses, Martel thought with a smile. This would be a memorable trip.

Allis and Martel spent each night in *Niña*'s landing boat, parked on the parade ground just south of the castle. Seated in the cramped wedge of the main cabin, Martel pored over *Niña*'s orbital recon images searching for the signature of Terran vegetation. Roses grew somewhere, in some hidden valley or secret garden close by.

Allis's long, delicate fingers ran across his shoulders—massage and invitation both. They sometimes had the joy of each other, but things went no further emotionally. He and Allis were body-compatible, but Martel's machine-assisted consciousness and augmented sensorium were much closer to *Niña*'s. For the most part, Allis kept her frustrated resentments to herself.

"Did you see what happened to the rose?" Martel asked. He wasn't ready to discuss the ancient satellites—insufficient data regarding their function and operational status. The team's first duty was to the

Reunification, and he was still concerned about the capabilities of the orbiting hardware. The rose was sufficient distraction, at least for Martel.

"I was watching the Vizier." It was almost a reproof. Her touch slowed, invitation incrementally withdrawing.

"They feared it in the marketplace. Like death on the ground. A pity."

"Penalty for touching royal property?"

They had not yet seen Queen Marie — perhaps no one ever did.

Martel shrugged. "Possibly." He looked over his shoulder at her. "Do you know what that plant is worth? The gene package by itself, let alone a growing, healthy specimen." He grinned. "More than any bonus for old tech ever paid. And *we* found it."

Allis looked thoughtful. "I would very much like to know where the Vizier got his rose."

Late that night, *Niña* whispered in Martel's mind. «I have a preliminary report on the active satellite.»

«And?»

«Pre-Collapse Terran technology. Fleet-grade hardware.»

Crap, Martel thought. That was big, bad wolf stuff, nothing Reunification could yet create on its own. Hauling the satellite home would be a major prize in its own right. Between the old tech and the roses, this mission would pay off handsomely for them all if they could just safely grab everything. «Intelligent bird?»

Niña was silent beyond orbital lag. Finally, «Perhaps.»

Martel didn't push. Of course *Niña* would be jealous of his interest in a potential Terran AI. The fields of the mind were the only place he and Ship could meet in emotional privacy. Martel respected her worries—he was the one who could walk away, both literally and figuratively. «To whom could it have been talking?» Martel said.

Niña's tone indicated an imaginary shrug. «You are the asset on the ground.»

Unfortunately, Martel *was* the asset on the ground. He imagined the Vizier crouched over a hand-wound crystal radio, receiving messages from heaven. Somehow he doubted it would be that simple.

In the morning the landing boat was surrounded by angry palace guards, shouting and waving swords and polearms.

"By the moment of inertia," Martel swore. "What happened?" He cycled the security status screens.

The upper hull video showed the eviscerated body of their night guard lying broken-limbed on top of the landing boat. A perfect pink Bourbon rose — showing a neatly quartered heirloom bloom with a pale, flat face — was set between two exposed ribs. The extinct *Souvenir de la Malmaison*, the gardening part of Martel's mind noted even as his fingers twitched, buckysteel claws again threatening to push out through the skin.

Allis leaned over Martel's shoulder to peer at the displays. "How did he get up there?"

"More to the point, why doesn't the boat have a record of it?" Martel snapped as he fought down his defensive reflexes. He cycled through the night logs. Nothing. The guard had vanished about an hour before dawn, but that in itself was not a threat condition—he had been an honor guard, not part of their own security regime. There was no record of the killing, no record of the body being dumped on the hull. It seemed to have just appeared when Martel manually cycled the cameras—a patently ridiculous assumption.

Allis studied the image of the body. "Who could have done that? Besides you, I mean."

"On *this* planet?" Martel laughed. "We'd better hope there's nothing worse than me out there. You need to talk to them over the speakers, get the Vizier involved, or they'll lynch us as we exit."

Allis hadn't asked how the cameras had been fooled by the rose killer. That surveillance override bothered Martel intensely—who on Eutychus could hack the landing boat's systems? The boat wasn't remotely as sophisticated as *Niña*, but it still should have been far beyond any local capability. His thoughts darkened rapidly as his fingers continued to itch. He couldn't even salvage the dead man's *Souvenir*.

"Tell us about the roses," Allis said, taking a strong tone with the Vizier.

He coughed, adjusted his high-crowned felt hat. They were back in the tower room, and the Vizier was dressed at his most formal, swaddled in sashes, robes and jeweled chains. "It is a local custom."

"A local custom," she said. "Killing soldiers. I see."

The Vizier's tone was pained. "The rose is a symbol of what was. It has come to signify death, loss—the tragedy of our separation from old Earth. All that is painful in our history and our present reduced circumstances. That pain and loss is sometimes expressed in a most, ah, immediate and bloody way."

More than that, thought Martel, the rose was a bloody, dangerous threat—symbol of the killer that had struck outside their landing boat. He and Allis had been marked by the local version of the touch of death.

Allis glared at the Vizier, receding further away from civility. "So your rose of yesterday was, oh, a threat? A test? To see if we were paying attention, taking Eutychus seriously enough. You may rest assured you have our full attention, perhaps more than you intended."

The Vizier had the grace to look uncomfortable.

Martel sought to solve both their problems at the same time. "I want to see your rose garden."

Allis interrupted the Vizier as he began to reply, casting her glare at Martel. "My apologies. We are not here to make inappropriate demands."

Martel's fingertips itched again as the Vizier looked back and forth between him and Allis. Finally their host took a deep breath. "It is not my rose garden. It is not anyone's rose garden. Roses do not even grow here on their own. But I will show it to you."

Martel smiled as they left the room, thinking of green leaves and colored blooms.

Together the three of them stood before an age-blackened wooden door guarded by a single soldier. The door was set in a deep recess within an inner wall of the keep. The corridor around them felt tacked on, of a lighter, rougher architecture than the door's wall. The door had a judas hole, now covered by a small shutter with an enormous lock.

"This inner wall," Martel said feeling the cool, smooth stone, "it's wrong."

"Ask yourself why a world with one major city and no native race would need a stone-walled keep." The Vizier traced his fingers over the close-grained wood of the door. "There are perhaps a million of us on Eutychus, living in pre-Industrial agrarianism, farming the wilds, fishing the seas, inhabiting villages. But no enemy nations. By the same token, we

41

have outlaws and sea pirates, but not in numbers."

"All right." Martel ground his teeth. "Why do you need a keep?"

The Vizier inserted a complex, jeweled key into the shutter's lock. "Roses."

Allis spoke for the first time since they had left the tower. "You fear harm to them? Is this the queen's private garden?"

The Vizier opened the shutter over the judas hole. "Roses. This castle protects us from the roses and their terrible gardeners. Behold."

Their faces were bathed in green-tinted light. Martel was the first to peer inward.

It looked as if jungle had erupted from the tan earth and brown stone to race skyward. Martel saw green—the glossy dark of ivies, the spring green of tender herbs, the rich, satisfied green of mature plants. The judas hole was a glimpse into a riot of Terran growth, so fractally complex and fascinating that Martel's vision was trapped for long moments before he could begin to sort it. The wave of floral scent markers was an even greater, albeit welcome, assault, more complex than the view.

The garden was worth the wealth of worlds, an archaeobotanist's fever dream. Here, a trellis was mounted ten meters or more by a great rambling rose, *Alexandre Girault*, swirling runners dotted with small pink blooms and buds. There, an ivy bed hosted half a dozen stout canes bent heavy with fragrant *Rosa Mundi*—gallicas roses—the size of a baby's head, the pale but ruddy color of newborn flesh. Ancient terra cotta pots, rims worn ragged with water and time, bore bushes of *Frances Dubreuil*, the profusion of deep reds setting off the worn stone paths that wound between.

In the middle of the priceless riot of life, a humaniform statue, copper and brass, titanium and steel, wrought to symbolized perfection with elaborated tendons at the joints and the sexless beauty of an angel. Its smooth oval face was topped by a straw hat, and it held a hoe. *The gardener in repose above his work*, thought Martel, surprising himself out of his usual indifference to things artistic.

It was this android gardener that kept the roses growing in this bruise-colored world under a golden sky.

"Martel. The Terran satellite is receiving an uplink transmission from your position."

He clenched his teeth again. «Right here, right now? Oh, *Niña*, be careful.»

The featureless head of the gardener rotated toward him like a gun turret. The pressure of that blank metal stare chilled Martel's soul, as if he watched distant, marauding armies on the march. Martel slammed shut the cover of the judas hole.

"Back to the lander. Immediately."

Allis did not argue. The Vizier merely watched them leave.

Martel ran pre-flight checks, mostly for something to do. He was not in the habit of confusion, and even less in the habit of fear.

"*Niña* won't tell me what happened." Allis perched on the arm of his crash couch. "I can't imagine how, but you've frightened her."

Allis rarely used her mental comm link — claimed it wasn't a sufficiently human form of conversation. As a result, she didn't understand the ship's nuances. "*Niña*'s worried, not scared," Martel growled. "But, they're almost the same, for her."

"Worried? About roses? What did you see?"

"Roses. Ancient satellites in orbit. A metal man in the garden." He cycled the hardware monitors through exterior images. The parade ground around their lander was deserted, unusually so for a workday afternoon. Even their guards, doubled since the murder, had deserted them.

"Satellites and metal men." Allis hissed through her teeth, a note of avarice growing in her voice. "Old tech in this place. That explains the how of the guard's murder if not the why."

Martel grunted. "Something like that. What I saw was an android. A robot. Maybe just a gardener."

"A gardener? Killing people in the streets of Deuce Landing." Allis sounded puzzled. "You're making no sense."

Martel glanced up at her. "An android gardener among the roses was talking to fleet-grade Terran hardware in orbit. The plant wealth and the old tech are bound together."

"Android gardener…" Allis's voice trailed off for a moment. "That's an old security unit, isn't it?" she whispered.

"Yes. Has to be." Martel was glum. "I checked my optical feed capture against *Niña*'s archives. That android was fabricated very late, immediately pre-Collapse by the look of it—not sufficiently ornamented for the aesthetics of the Latter Republic. Has to be from the Janissary series."

They had hit the jackpot all right. Lost Terran tech, but the wrong kind—enough to wipe out an entire modern planetary army.

"Like looking for textbooks and finding a neutron grenade instead," she said. "Nestled in a bed of flowers, no less. Why here?"

He shrugged. "Sent in at the end, maybe for safekeeping, maybe to manage the evacuation of the Terran mission during the Collapse War. Who knows? It's here. They're not intended to be fully autonomous." He paused, a cold feeling in his heart. "It moved. It looked at me. It was talking to that Terran satellite in orbit—eye in the sky, and maybe a tactical advisor too. You're right, there's the tech that spoofed our landing boat's systems. That's how the guard was killed without our alarms going off."

"We should leave."

Martel felt a gentle tide of fear seeping through his mind, infecting his augmented systems. "That rose, in the dead man's ribs on our lander's hull. The android laid it there. The android's the rose killer, and it's marked us."

"Lift. Lift now," Allis urged, panic tingeing her voice. "We can't bring these people into the Reunification, not with a military monster like that in place."

Martel would weep to walk away from that garden of roses, but Allis was right. Discretion had become the far better part of valor, his dreams of biological wealth notwithstanding.

"Strap in," Martel said. As Allis moved to her crash couch behind him, he completed pre-flight and initiated the final launch sequence.

The landing boat did nothing. Nothing at all.

"Water of life!" Martel slammed his fist into the arm of his crash couch. "We're not leaving until it lets us. That's why it marked us with the killing—we've been very publicly trapped. We're committed, and everybody on Eutychus knows it." There were no more choices, now, but to take what came. His fear evaporated as quickly as it had arrived. The time for action was almost at hand.

"Trapped," Allis whispered.

"I'll brief *Niña*," Martel said. Even through it all, he was still thinking of the roses. "And where did the Vizier get his rose? Surely not by reaching in through the judas hole?"

44

"Her Majesty will see you now." The Vizier had come out to their landing boat again, for only the third time since the moment of Recontact. He had no escort of soldiers. Even on the viewscreens Martel could see the man's eyes darting back and forth like ball bearings loose on a shuttle deck.

Allis's voice boomed out through speakers deliberately set too loud. "We are not prepared to negotiate further at this time."

The Vizier bowed, twisted his hands across his wrists. "Her Majesty wishes to express her concern over the death of your guard. It would be...auspicious...if you could come with me."

"Auspicious?" growled Martel.

Allis shrugged. Her voice echoed through the speakers outside. "A moment, if you please."

«There have been more transmissions between the garden and the satellite,» *Niña* whispered to Martel. «Possibly from multiple ground sources in the area. The satellite has begun to probe me along a number of spectra.»

Multiple ground sources? Martel felt another chill of his own fear. Let that be an error, he thought, the gardener in motion confusing *Niña*'s sensors. «Damn. Just when we finally get to meet the Queen. Do you want us to refuse?»

Ship's emotions colored the comm link, cold and tired like winter dawn. «I am afraid for you. I am afraid for me.»

«Then get out. Find a high orbit, hide behind one of the moons. Let us see if we can fix the landing boat. I don't want that satellite hacking at you. And if things end badly down here, you need to take word back about the dangers.»

Niña's voice echoed with frustration. «Martel, I cannot leave you behind. If I withdraw, we'll be out of effective comm range. I could not bear to lose you, especially without knowing what happened.»

«You will still see through your microsats...» Martel knew it was false comfort even as he said it. «Do what you need to, love.»

«I am with you,» *Niña* replied. «Always. Now go.»

They had to go, Martel thought. They had to understand, so they could take the story home, declare quarantine, protect the Reunification from this planet and the danger it harbored. Martel shared his smile with Allis, his best killing smile. "*Niña* says the old hardware's waking up."

"Fine," she said. "Then we're going to see the Queen."

Martel was unsurprised to find himself back at the wooden door through which he had seen the roses — and the metal gardener. This time the Vizier simply tugged at the wrought iron latch and pulled it open.

"It just stands free, that anyone can open it?" Allis asked. The judas hole was still closed with its elaborate lock.

The Vizier looked surprised. "Who would go in? The temptation to look, that is powerful. We shield against that. The temptation to enter, into sudden death, well..." The Vizier shrugged. "A man must meet his doom."

"This wall could hardly stop *them*," Martel said.

"It is the best we can do," the Vizier replied as he stepped through the door. "And it does confine the roses."

Allis and Martel followed, the guard slamming the door shut behind them. The first thing Martel noticed was that the statue was gone — it really was a Janissary then, not just some mind-fragmented nightmare. Even though he expected it, the confirmation of the missing android flooded Martel with a surprised fear.

Unbidden, buckysteel claws erupted through his fingertips, shedding a fine spray of blood on his white dress trousers. As his hands transformed to weapons, the quick stabs of pain were replaced with a new layer of neural input. Adrenal micropumps stirred in his major arteries, forcing his blood pressure up until Martel felt swollen and tight within his skin. Hormone nanofabs spewed combat chemistry into his bloodstream, twitching his muscle groups as they superoxygenated. His eyes mirrored as his vision shifted to a broader range of wavelengths, his hearing and smell and kinesthesia boosting in concert.

Martel felt as if he could fill the garden with his body. He had never experienced the defensive transformation as pure fear reaction — this was hindbrain fight-or-flight overriding his onboard systems. Suddenly so far beyond human, becoming what he had been built for, Martel was afraid to ask *Niña*'s counsel, afraid to betray himself to the ancient satellite high above. Allis gave him a quizzical look, lips drawn together and eyebrows arched. The Vizier didn't even seem to notice Martel's transformation, which was perhaps most disturbing.

Martel scanned his surroundings. The garden was in a yard about thirty meters by sixty, surrounded by the towering curtain wall with inward-facing crenellations. That was backwards, the defenses pointing the wrong way. As the Vizier had said, early Eutychians had obviously built the original castle to protect the world from the garden, not the reverse. It had to be fear of the plants, Martel realized—no mere wall would ever stop the androids.

The riot of roses and landscape plants that he had seen before ran across the entire space, climbing the dressed stone wall and all but obscuring the gray bungalow in the middle of the garden. Martel had not noticed the house when peeping earlier through the judas hole.

The Vizier pointed to the long wall opposite them, behind the bungalow. "That was Exchange Street. The wall behind us is built over Terra Street. To the left and right were Coulter and Annapurna Avenues. Her Majesty had these walls built shortly after the evacuation."

"The same Queen Marie?" Martel's voice drifted on soft threads of checked violence as his body vibrated with combat readiness. "All those years ago?"

"The same. You will see." Still ignoring Martel's transformation, the Vizier led them along a stone path. "I suggest not damaging the vegetation."

Martel stalked after him, followed by Allis. He was seeing the garden as distances and potentials, multiple axes-of-threat, optic-nerve data overlays that blurred and reformed with his every movement. Before him, the bungalow glowered with electromagnetic blare and heat leakage. The intense sensory flood tugged at his focus, at his concentration, at his sanity—he had become so much larger than his body. This must be how *Niña* felt all the time with her microsats and datafeeds, he realized.

They stepped onto the porch in front of a simple wooden door with a small brass plaque reading, "Terran Mission." The Vizier tugged at a string of copper bells.

The metal man opened the door. The Vizier bowed, followed by Allis. Martel remained standing, riding his defense reflexes like a shockwave. The smooth face turned toward Martel, giving him that armies-on-the-march feeling again. Martel was danger incarnate, confronting metal death.

The Janissary stepped back from the door, ushering them into a painfully ordinary living room. A fieldstone fireplace, plush chairs, hardwood tables—it was the epitome of ordinary domesticity, Golden Age Terran style. Art hung on the walls, actual semi-fluid pigment manually applied to a canvas substrate. Several pieces looked familiar to Martel—a puffy armored man with a reflective copper helm holding a banner amid a cratered gray desert, a brown-robed woman with a vanishing smile, a bull rendered in tortured lines. Martel heard Allis gasp as she stared at them, her vital signs spiking in surprise.

The metal man opened a door on the far side of the room, then stepped away from it. The Vizier bowed again before walking into the next room. Martel measured the Vizier's stressors as abnormally flat—strangely, the man seemed to have no affect.

Queen Marie lay encased in an enormous chair, a deep bowl contoured around her body, which was embedded as if brown foam had been poured about her. She was so small someone could have hidden beneath the crust with her. Her exposed skin was covered with a translucent, rippling shell, only her face open to the air. She was nude, withered as a mandrake root, tiny breasts like dried apples, skin crossed with fine scars and metallic probes. Her eyes were slitted open, but Martel could not see their color or clarity.

"Welcome," spat a speaker grille over their heads with a rough cackle. "Welcome," the Queen whispered at the same time in a cool, synthetic voice on *Niña*'s private channel within Martel's mind.

Another metal man stepped through a far door into the room. Martel still had a clear fix on the one in the living room. Gods and frauds, he thought, there *were* two of them. *Niña* had been right about multiple transmission sources. He concentrated on the doubled threat, evading the insidious fear that Queen Marie was using the comm channel to hack into his own systems.

"We have waited so long for someone to come back," crackled the speaker. "Waited for centuries," her voice echoed in Martel's head. "But we are forgiving."

The Vizier bowed again, so low his rounded cap grazed the floor. "They have rendered profound apologies for the delay."

Martel thought of green pastures, of *Niña*, of sex with Allis, of anything but answering the Queen who spoke in his mind.

The Vizier stayed in his bow, calm as ever. Allis stood behind him, to Martel's left, staring down at the bed. She spoke to the Queen, showing no sign of hearing the new voice on her Ship comm channel. "Your majesty, we appear to have a problem."

The Queen, in Martel's head, whispered, «Centuries. Do you know what that feels like?» Over the speaker she said, "There is no problem here."

Allis tried again. "A murder has taken place on the hull of our vessel. Acts of sabotage have been committed against us even though we established good faith."

«This place is so brown, so pale. So wrong.»

"The death of my guard is regrettable, but you are not at fault. You have merely been denied clearance to lift off."

"We will not negotiate under duress," Allis told the Queen.

"We just want to go home."

Martel studied the Queen's face. Her skin measured slightly above room temperature. There had been no eye motion under the slitted lids. There was no respiration. He stepped toward the chair.

"No." The Queen's voice echoed in Martel's mind and in his ears.

"You're dead," Martel said out loud. He refused to answer inside his head.

"Martel," Allis warned.

"We are deceived." As a cautionary measure, Martel brought up the trigger sequence on the three grams of anti-matter magnetically bottled in his abdomen. None of this could come home to the Reunification with them. Nor could these dangerous machines be permitted to survive independently. "There is no Queen. One of those Janissaries is playing her part. The Queen is dead."

The Queen's voice cackled again over the loudspeaker. "Death is but a stage."

A different voice broke into Martel's comm channel, richer and rougher, a commanding voice in contrast to the smooth synthetic tones of the voice of the so-called Queen. "Apologies, but the situation is escalating beyond acceptable parameters. Liberty lives. Brotherhood lives. Equality malfunctions."

Liberty. Brotherhood. Equality. Political philosophy on the comm channel? Or were these people? The androids, Martel realized. The voice was talking about the Janissaries—it had to be one of them. Now there were *three* of the damned things.

"There is no Queen," Martel said aloud to Allis and the Vizier. "One of the Janissaries is talking through her, hiding somewhere. Maybe Liberty or Brotherhood."

Where was the third one? Inside her chair? «*Niña!*» he screamed on the Ship's channel, the channel that had been compromised by the Janissaries with their old tech.

The speakers laughed, the reedy cackle of a dying old woman.

«Martel,» said *Niña* urgently. «You're not looking in the right—» The ship's voice stretched, popped, then died in a grumbling whisper.

«Beware,» said the new voice, the one that had just been naming androids on Martel's comm channel. «Equality is in imminent danger of severely violating operational parameters.»

"Allis." Martel's entire body vibrated like a bowstring, teetering on the edge of violence. "We are played false. *Niña* is endangered, or worse. This is your last chance to talk our way clear."

"What of the Queen?" Allis asked in her flattest voice.

The comm channel in Martel's head hummed, even the static loaded with harsh tension. The room was very quiet for a moment, until the speaker crackled with a neutral machine voice. "She is here."

The Vizier stood, placing one hand on the edge of the Queen's bed. "But I speak for all. Including her." He looked around the room, at the two Janissaries, Allis, and Martel. The Vizier never looked down at the Queen.

Allis kept her tone calm. "The layers have been stripped away. Now tell me what you want."

"These…machines…want to go home." The Vizier bowed slightly. "I, too, would like to see Terra, Mother Earth."

"Terra continues to burn even after the centuries have passed," Allis said. Her sadness surprised Martel. "There is nothing for you there. And these Janissaries are too powerful to enter the Reunification. Perhaps they obey well, but there are those who could not resist giving deadly orders. As for you, Vizier, there may be possibilities, but not now. We could not bring you back with us from this trip. It is against our laws and our ethics."

The Vizier's voice grew tight. "We are not prepared to negotiate this away."

Martel knew the Vizier's tone of voice was an act. The man's vital signs had been flat since they entered the garden, were still flat. The Vizier must be under the control of the Janissaries somehow. Had everything else been equally false?

"We are not prepared to grant you departure," Allis said.

The Vizier chuckled, a false humor. "Your landing boat will not leave without our permission."

"Then we are at impasse. You cannot be allowed to leave this planet." Allis gave Martel a significant look. "Our operating procedures consider this a hostage situation. Mission control now shifts to my partner."

«*Niña*,» Martel whispered on the comm channel.

There was no answer but the faint cackle of laughter.

"We are betrayed," he said. "They have attacked *Niña*. And there is no Queen. One of *them* hides inside her."

The moment of truth had come. Martel was built for great, terrible violence, but three Janissaries were opposition beyond reason. Martel hoped that only one was a danger. He dived for the old woman's body, raising clawed hands to rip it open, to attack the third Janissary hiding inside the Queen's chair.

"Wrong!" The Queen's voice echoed in Martel's head as the speakers cackled again. The Vizier slipped from his crouch into a forward roll to break Allis's neck. He spilled a single white rose from his sleeve as she hit the floor, warm flesh already bluing as her mouth echoed silent surprise.

Martel had been blinded by his own short-term tactical analysis, guessing completely wrong. There was no Janissary hiding inside the Queen's chair, beneath her ancient body. The Queen was dead and rotted. Rather, her personality hid within a Janissary — the malfunctioning Equality about which the others had warned him. Equality, who was really the Vizier, not the Queen.

And now Martel found himself elbow deep in a badly preserved corpse, facing away from Allis's murderer. "Why?" he screamed, shifting upward out of realtime and into machine speed.

Martel existed inside a slice of time, combat modifications boosting his thoughts and movements up to their full potential. His cyborged body now burned months of lifespan to gain every second of advantage. Even if he survived unwounded, he would later pay with a precipitous drop in life expectancy. As the Vizier had said, in entering the garden Martel was meeting his doom. His last duty was to protect the Reunification. Vengeance for *Niña* and Allis would be a lagniappe.

«You ask why?» screamed Equality, shouting with the Queen's voice inside Martel's head at machine speed, words that would have been just an electronic squeal in realtime. «She forbid us to return. We have been denied what we desire most. Why should you suffer no less?»

Martel pulled his clawed hands from the ruins of Marie's corpse in a slow spray of ancient dust, head cocked back toward the Vizier — toward Equality, the Queen, all of his tormentors in one body. The damned android had gotten it just as backwards as Martel had. *Niña* was already gone. Killing Allis had been a grace note.

Martel felt the turbulence of air breaking across his face as his body spun. He smelled acrid urine released from Allis's dying body, the pheromones of her sweat, the faintly chalky odor of her skin. Overlaying the spilled scents of Allis's life, he smelled the Queen's decay, the scent of rotting roses, and even the oil-and-ozone fragrances of the Janissaries.

Brotherhood, behind him, entered from the living room. Liberty, before him, stepped up to Equality. *Niña* was missing from his head, compromised by the satellites and probably already terminated. Allis was dying, because she had denied repatriation to the malfunctioning Janissary. He had to choose between releasing the antimatter or tearing Equality's flesh-clad metal head from its shoulders.

Vengeance won over his mission. "*Niña*," he whispered again. Martel moved so fast he cracked three of his own ribs, bruising kidneys against his implanted thoracic shock webbing. Analgesic shunts blocked the stabbing pain before it could distract him, microtech mesh scaffolds already moving into place. Stepping into a crouch, Martel leapt over Allis, kicking his feet up to splay forward, hands spread out, aiming for a full-body chest butt that would let him grasp the Vizier's false face as his legs grappled. It was the best maneuver Martel had from his position in the very short time available. His upper knuckles shattered as his claws sprang to their fullest extension.

Martel slammed into the Vizier as the Vizier brought his own arms around for a killing blow. Martel was just a little faster, his first advantage against the old tech Janissaries. Feet against the Vizier's thighs, Martel wrapped his arms around the Vizier's head to dig his clawed fingers in at the jaw line. Martel pulled straight up as the Vizier's grip closed across his back, tearing the fleshy face from the metal beneath.

Pushing off, Martel threw himself against the Vizier's shattering grip. The entire skin of the Vizier's head came with him, tangled in Martel's claws. The Vizier's hands strained at the reinforced discs of Martel's spine as Martel continued to push. Martel could feel his back crack, the discs slipping against one another.

Martel slammed forward again, catching the Vizier's head in the crook of his right arm to snap it back and forth. He threw his body against the Vizier's grip, using his entire mass to torque the against the neck. Something screeched in the Vizier's metal body as the scalp slid away, at the same time that Martel's spine snapped. He yanked the metal head forward, so that it bobbed as if spring-loaded.

Martel then slid to the ground, only to be caught by Brotherhood and dangled in the air by his arms. Liberty grabbed Equality before the other Janissary could collapse as well.

Martel could no longer feel his pelvis or his legs, but his back screamed sufficient agony to distract from the loss of sensation. Martel hung in Brotherhood's grip, analgesic shunts failing in rapid sequence as he dropped back into realtime from machine speed. The abrupt shutdown caused massive system failures to cascade throughout his combat enhancements.

"Ah..." Martel breathed pain, tasting his death, tasting the final failure of his mission. He had beaten Equality, but had no strength remaining to resist Liberty or Brotherhood.

Facing him propped in Liberty's grip, Equality shuddered. The Vizier's mauve native-silk robes slithered from the Janissary's wide, round shoulders, taking their supporting flesh with them. Riding the waves of flesh, roses cascaded from the inside of the robes on a flood of blood and petals, ruby, coral, purple, a dozen more shades for which Martel had no name, the fall of a whole garden in a soft, brilliant moment.

Roses, Martel thought in the haze of his agony. The rose killer must have left the blooms behind because they were of old Earth. Equality had been planting the seeds of return, or perhaps regret, in the hearts of men.

Literally.

«You will not kill here.» It was Brotherhood, behind him, the rough voice of command echoing on Martel's comm channel.

"I didn't kill," Martel said, still refusing to reply on his mental channel even in the ruins of his defense. "Your brother did."

Equality's metal face lolled on its broken neck. An ovoid mouth flickered open and shut like a bounded black flame. "You were supposed to take us home." «Home. Home. Home.» The smooth voice on the comm channel, the Queen's voice.

«Mistakes were made.» Martel wasn't sure how he knew, but this was Liberty speaking. «The way home was closed. She was so afraid of dying here, our last Terran Legate, that we allowed an experiment upon our brother. We gave her mind a new home. It was a serious error.»

"Home!" screamed Equality out loud. In Martel's head, Equality's voice wailed, «Home. Home. Home.» At his feet, Allis was covered in roses and muscle-backed sheets of the Vizier's flesh.

There was nothing left for Martel. Equality had taken *Niña*, slaughtered Allis, and broken him like a dry stick. There would be no bonuses, no roses for the Reunification. There would be only danger lurking here for the next Recontact team. Martel knew his duty. He shivered, releasing the thirty-second timer on the anti-matter. The city of Deuce Landing would be destroyed, but the Janissaries would be gone as well. "And now?" he asked, to fill the time.

Both in unison, with the third screaming underneath of home. «Now that Marie is finally lost to us with Equality defeated, we are without purpose. You represent remaining human authority. We ask for new orders.»

Everyone Martel cared for had to die to come to this point? "Oh, the waste of lives and love," he breathed. "You couldn't just tell me what you wanted. You had to wait for me to defeat Equality before telling me this."

The sane ones were patient. «We could not approach you while we were still under Marie's control,» said Brotherhood. «You removed her. Now we await your orders.»

A Janissary solution to a Janissary problem, thought Martel. Wait for something powerful enough to come along and quell the mad one. Trying to talk again, he coughed blood, then it hurt too much to talk any more, so

Martel slipped back into his inner voice. He was done for anyway. "You know I cannot grant repatriation. Allis spoke truly."

«If we cannot go home, what are our orders here?»

Death would arrive in eleven seconds. Martel offered comfort. «Stay here. Grow roses. Keep those ancient paintings clean. No more deaths in the street. Be good children of Man.» Four seconds. «I'm sorry.»

Nothing happened.

Brotherhood's voice was gentle. «As a measure of self-defense, we overrode your software to disable your self-destruct timer.»

«But we thank you for the orders,» Liberty said.

Martel sobbed, a rattling in his throat. «Allis. *Niña*. Both killed by you. You have taken everything. And I am dying now, too, killed by you.»

«What of our brother Equality?» Twinned voices in his head, over quieter screams of home.

What of Equality, Martel thought. The late Queen, the late Vizier, author of his torments. Vengeance? Justice? No, even now after all the death and pain, he could still find pity for Queen Marie, trapped in a machine's body, long past her time. «End its pain,» Martel said.

And what of himself? Martel wanted to die here on Eutychus with *Niña* and Allis, let it be finished, but he found he was afraid. «Send me home, please,» he asked, hiding behind duty to his mission. If the Ship even could take him home.

Brotherhood's loving hands held him like forceps grasping a newborn as Martel wept oily tears.

Afraid as he was to die, Martel hadn't really meant to live either, but Liberty and Brotherhood tended his wounds too well. Martel rested on a couch in the Terran mission for three days and nights, staring at the old paintings, while his metal nurses pumped drugs and old tech nano into him, knitting bones and patching such systems as could be salvaged.

On the fourth day, Brotherhood carried Martel through the keep and across the parade ground to the landing boat. Martel saw no living soul. It was as if all of Deuce Landing was in hiding.

Brotherhood strapped Martel in a crash couch, as Liberty arrived to carpet the narrow cabin with bright roses — genetic seed stock, a hoard of biological treasure, salvageable even after the blooms decayed in transit.

Cuttings of other plants were scattered among the blossoms. Martel was bringing some of old Earth home with him to the Reunification.

In the end, he had his roses.

As the Janissaries exited together, Martel was unsure which of them said, «Thank you.»

The landing boat sealed itself and lifted for orbit, finally docking with the *Niña*. She didn't say a word when he eventually crawled pained and bloody from the boat into her hull. Nor did she in the three days following as they burned out-system toward the superluminal limit and her blinding interstellar leap. Martel could not find the slightest hint that she still lived, that her consciousness had survived the assault of the Janissaries' satellites. He left the landing boat's hatch open so he could smell the roses in memory of *Niña*, of Allis, even of poor, doomed Equality and Queen Marie. In memory, most of all, of himself.

Martel tried to find the threads in everything that had happened, the cycle of violence and succession from Legate to Queen, Queen to Janissary, and onward into death. And so the circle went round, to no end that Martel could see except pain and suffering.

Had Martel bettered himself in the cycle of pain? What about *Niña*? She was now nothing, it seemed, but a mindless carrier for a priceless cargo of roses. With this thought, Martel whispered his farewell on her silent comm channel. «*Niña*. I loved you.»

«Martel.»

«*Niña?*» Martel's pulse skyrocketed. For the first time in days he smiled. «You're back.»

«I know so much more about everything now,» she said to him. Amid the scent of rotting roses, the Ship began to whisper to him of her memories of home, memories of Marie's Earth that his friend *Niña* had never seen.

G. O. D.

G. O. D.

G: GODSTALK

Gods died. Everyone understood that. János just didn't understand why it had to be his problem. They gave him ropes and tools and maps and told him to do the right thing. No one provided any details on how to choose a god.

"Get out there and bring us back a good one," Ferenc had said, handing him grandpa's best stalk-pick. "Glad it's not me," his brother added.

Now János was halfway up a vine ribbed like a vast stalk of celery thicker than a dozen elm trunks. In the distance, vine mites the size of cattle cleaned their host. The ground was lost deep in the clouds below. Grandpa's pick seemed a small thing to trust with his life, old and rusty as it was, so he used safety lines, even though they slowed him down.

"Miracles, fresh miracles." His mother had rubbed her hands with gleeful greed. "It cost me a lot to get you this job—don't mess it up."

János climbed higher, until the first god nodules were visible around him. They were pouty sacs with a little nipple at the free end. This particular vine had been allowed to age unharvested for almost a century. Potent, some of those nodules.

"Don't fall," Maria had said, and kissed him on the lips for the very first time. A private miracle, that.

His foot slipped, the strapped-on vine spikes nudging a small nodule. It quivered, nipple pulsing with a faint amber glow. János held his breath and prayed he didn't knock it loose. A little god like that, they'd be lucky to sour someone's milk on a summer day.

"Get it right, János, the village will be rich for two generations." Father Imre had smiled, cracked brown teeth leering from withered lips like an open grave. "Get it wrong, you'd best stay up there and eat vine for the rest of your life."

How to choose a god, János thought?

"Here, boy," whispered a great nodule in a voice like faraway thunder on a spring evening. It was bean-shaped, tall as he was. "Choose me."

Its nipple pulsed like a hot coal. János could feel the radiating power. The entire nodule twisted toward him. Propelled by instinctive terror, he crabbed away.

"Back off!" shrieked a voice behind him.

János almost fell from the vine, held on only by his safety line. He craned his neck around. "Who...?"

A little blue-nippled nodule hung from the vine just behind his shoulder. It glared like the eye of the sky. "Mind your own damned business."

The large bean-shaped nodule bumped him from the other side. "Choose me, boy."

János rappelled back down his safety line toward his last anchor. Braking shortly before the static point, he stopped at the small amber nodule. It was a long way to the ground and sour milk felt very safe. Reaching out to snap it off, János chose to believe in a small, sensible god.

O: GODSTOCK

In the end, they chopped down Yggdrasil. Where else to find such wood? They talked of salvaging The Boat of a Million Years for her planking, but that wouldn't have been enough. Jaguar stole her anchor chains anyway, which later came in handy to latch everything down. One of

60

the archangels rounded up some gopher wood from Noah's old hulk under its Armenian glacier, mostly for the symbolic value. Minos donated his ax to the carpenter who actually built the stocks.

After six days of effort, everything was ready.

Jehovah, Supreme Being and Creator of the Universe, strolled onto the Patio of the Gods accompanied by His chief counsel, Lucifer. The Holy Ghost sat in judgment, a tequila sunrise bobbing over an apparently empty chaise longue. Lesser gods serving as court officers sat around the perimeter of the hearing area, while others watched from the poolside bar.

Matsu clerked for the court from under a Campari umbrella. "Any final remarks from the defense?" she asked Lucifer.

Lucifer glanced at God, who shook His head. Tsunamis washed across the Indian Ocean.

"No." The devil sounded resigned, as if he'd lost badly at Canasta Night.

Matsu bowed before reading from a parchment. "This court finds that God, also known as Jehovah et cetera, styled Supreme Being et cetera, has been remiss in managing His Creation. Do you have any statements for the record, Mr. God?"

God smiled. Sunlight washed over Seattle. "Free will was not a mistake. I do apologize for monotremes and instant coffee." The Brazilian commodities exchange crashed.

Matsu continued. "Your remarks will be entered into the record. This court further finds that as there is no meaningful punishment for the Architect of Existence, symbolic punishment will instead be administered. Mr. God is sentenced to confinement in the stocks until the mercy of His beloved mankind shall free Him."

Tears the size of seas welled in God's eyes, but as the stocks were lowered over His wrists, nothing much changed on Earth.

D: GOTTSCHALK

The old man stumbled down the streets of Austin. He was not fully anchored in space-time, which was a significant inconvenience except for the ready avoidance of dog turds. It was still hotter than hell. He stopped front of the Starbucks at the corner of Sixth and Congress where an astoundingly ugly cross-dresser with a long beard was protesting. Her sign had an extensive rant about police brutality.

"What seems to be the trouble here?" the old man asked the lone protestor, whose name was Dana. Unfortunately, due to his personal space-time discontinuity, the old man's question came out as slurred wino speech. "Obscene in the bubble hair?"

"Fucking cops," said Dana.

The old man realized that he knew the name Dana's mother had given her when she was born—Owen Gottschalk. "Cops don't hang out at Starbucks," the old man said. Which came out more or less, "Cops dang all Jeff Beck," with a grace note of saliva spray.

Dana Owen Gottschalk was sufficiently out of things herself to divine the old man's intention if not his actual utterances. "More spare change here." She glanced around. "Don't queer my act, friend."

The old man deduced that Dana was a pragmatist. The old man was a pragmatist, too. He'd been looking for someone like Dana. "There's power in your name."

Or, less precisely, "Fess Parker's a dame."

She glared at the old man. Some bankers were heading their way, exchanging knowing glances with one another. "Enough, beat it."

The old man was drawn to Dana's potential. "You see, and draw with God's chalk. Make me real now."

What the BMW owners heard was, "Easy, Dana Owen Gottschalk. Bake the reality cow."

Dana tried to kick the old man in the nuts. The move didn't work out well, due to the old man's crotch being about seven light years distant, but Dana made her point.

The old man stumbled up Sixth Street, looking for someone else with the right magic to draw a line around his body, and sufficient mercy to bring divinity back into the world.

The Angle of My Dreams

The Angle of My Dreams

My name is Ronnie Marshall and I was eleven the year the space shuttle blew up. I started flying in my dreams right after those astronauts died.

It's not like being Superman—you have to find the right kind of hill and run down it like crazy and throw out your arms like you're going off the high dive and close your eyes and *believe*. It's not really learning how to fly. Anybody can to do that.

The trick is forgetting how to fall back down again.

I'd dream these flying dreams, the long grass slick on my legs as leaves spun in the air. There were always feathers in my dreams, like God had busted His pillow and goose down was snowing on the world. In dreams my feet pounded down a hill, my teeth clacking with every step, and when it came time to leave this earth, that's what I'd do.

Momma died one night a couple of years ago, sleeping off the chemo she took for her cancer. This last Christmas, just a couple of months gone by, Daddy flew too, until his truck landed in the San Marcos River. Granddaddy says that was punishment for mocking the angels. But I could soar away on God's feathers and still come back safe. At least in my dreams.

That spring in math class, after we'd all kind of got back to normal about the *Challenger* blowing up, we were studying angles. Because I do good in class, Mrs. Doornie gave me a protractor to work with, and I used it to measure the angle of my dreams. That's when I figured exactly how steep a hill needed to be for me to fly in real life.

I swiped two surveyor's stakes from Granddaddy's truck and used my coffee can money on a hundred feet of clothesline at Laudermilk's Hardware in town. It was old money, from when Daddy had still given me an allowance, but I didn't have nothing else I wanted anymore, except to see if I could really fly.

There was a big old hill on the Chamberlain place that stuck up all smooth and round like a sand pile, except it was pale rock under the dirt and grass. One giant live oak tree grew up at the top, that kept getting hit by lightning but never stopped growing. I'd rode my bike down that hill a hundred times, until I wiped out on a cow pie and broke my wrist when I was eight and Daddy made me stop. Chamberlain's hill looked like it might be the right angle.

So I took my stakes and my clothesline and a mallet and a level from the tool shed and headed over there early one Saturday. I drove one stake into the ground near the top, where the hill kind of rolled over to the angle it had, and another at the bottom, just before the hill flattened out again. My clothesline barely stretched between them, and it was real saggy, but I used some sticks from the live oak to prop it up in the middle. Then I backed off to the fence line, balanced the level on a post with some pebbles until it was straight, and set the protractor flat edge down on the level and stared through it at the hill and the clothesline.

I was right. It was exactly the angle of my dreams. I picked up my tools and went home to plan my first flight.

"Ronnie."

Granddaddy was at the door of my room. He was a thin man, "spare" I'd heard him called.

I didn't really know what "spare" meant like that, except Granddaddy didn't have much to spare for me or the world. He surveyed land for people and heard a lot of lies and complaints and lawyers talking. Granddaddy had got to where he didn't trust nobody but himself and Jesus. Least that's what he always told me on the way to church Wednesdays and Sundays.

I jumped up from my desk and stood straight, like he'd taught me. "Yes, sir?"

Granddaddy looked me up and down, then shook his head a little tiny bit. "Were you in my truck, Ronnie?"

I stared at my black Keds. He never asked me things he didn't already know the answer to, and I'd learned better than to lie to Granddaddy. "Yes, sir," I muttered.

There was a slithering as Granddaddy slipped his belt off. "Ronnie," he said, his voice sad, "you know the rules. It doesn't matter what you wanted with those stakes. You didn't ask."

My breath caught in my chest, making my whole body shake. "You'd have said no."

"It's my truck, Ronnie." He smacked the belt against his palm. "You can't just do what you want in this world, boy."

I leaned over my desk.

I ate dinner at the kitchen counter, where I could stand up. That night after Granddaddy was asleep, I sat down at my desk again, real careful of my sore butt. I was going to fly tomorrow, and I had to be ready.

There was a newspaper clipping in my drawer, from the *Austin American-Statesman*. I pulled it out, and copied out the names in my best printing, one at a time onto the back of a picture of Momma and Daddy. Commander Dick Scobee. Michael Smith. Ellison Onizuka. Ronald McNair. Judith Resnik. Gregory Jarvis. Christa McAuliffe.

It was the teacher that broke my heart, that always made me want to cry while I prayed in church. I could see my Mrs. Doornie climbing into that rocket, flying into the sky and never coming home. I guess Mrs. McAuliffe had kids and a husband and maybe her Momma and Daddy who missed her, but I always imagined those kids in her class, waiting at their desks while she never came back until they were covered with chalk dust and pencil shavings and the birds made nests in their hair.

Then I set the list aside with a little space shuttle eraser I'd won in a third grade math contest and went back to bed.

Sunday morning I was up before the grackles. I grabbed the photograph with the list on the back and the little eraser and put them in my pocket. Mrs. Doornie's protractor gleamed in the moonlight from the window, so I grabbed it, too. Dressed in my blue jeans and my red sweater and my black Keds, I snuck out for Chamberlain's hill.

Under the live oak on top of the hill, the sky was the color of a burned-down piece of charcoal, all black and blue overhead, and kind of gray and orange in the east. It was cold enough to see my breath, and my throat hurt a little. The cows complained somewhere off in the darkness, and the morning dew made their pies stink something awful.

I left the protractor in my pocket, took the eraser in one hand and the picture with the list on the back in my other hand, and closed my eyes real tight. The hill was the angle of my dreams. All I had to do was run and never stop and I could soar all the way to Heaven and find those astronauts. Momma and Daddy would there with them, everybody laughing at some stupid story Mrs. McAuliffe was telling about the kids in her class.

My Keds smacked into the grass of the hill. My teeth clacked with each step. I knew there was nothing between me and the bottom of the hill except some grass, so I was safe. I stuck my arms out real far, straining fit to pop my elbows. My dreams told me what to do. My legs strained with a red-hot, sour feeling, then there was no more ground.

I had forgotten how to fall back down again.

I soared through the dawn like a bird set free and nothing in my heart hurt any more for the first time since I could remember. The cold air made my chest ache as I breathed, and my body creaked like the barn in the wind. All I had to do was angle my hips and shoulders to turn, and I could bank and loop like a fighter pilot.

I knew Heaven wasn't straight up, like they said at the Fontevrault Bible Church, because space was up there where NASA kept their satellites. But Heaven had to be somewhere in the sky, because angels have wings, so I kept out circling, looking for the way.

Caldwell County, Texas stretched below me, like a big map except every little piece was real like one of them specially nice train sets. The sun had come up and everything was green and gold and beautiful. I wanted to sing, but I didn't know any good songs for the sky.

"Ronnie!"

It was Granddaddy. I looked down. I had flown over our little farm, and there he was in the front yard of the house, Bible in one hand while he shook his other fist.

"Get down here right now!"

I banked left, slipping over the housetop then back across the front yard the other way. This time Granddaddy was thrusting the Bible up at me. "You're in danger of your mortal soul, boy," he shouted. "Nobody mocks God's angels."

I shook my head, waving my hands as if to push him away. That was enough for me to remember how to fall. Head over heels, I tumbled into the yard at Granddaddy's feet. The last thing I saw was that little photo of Momma and Daddy circling high on the wind, as if it knew the way to the astronauts in Heaven without me.

My head felt like it was inside a bucket that kept rattling as someone was throwing gravel at it. I tried to shake it clear, but that only made things hurt worse.

"Sit tight, Ronnie," said Granddaddy. His voice was sadder than I'd heard since Momma died. I opened my eyes. We were in his truck, driving real fast down County Road 61 toward town.

"What happened?" It was a dumb question. I knew what had happened to me, but I couldn't think of anything else to say.

"You fell off the roof."

"No, I—"

His voice was almost a growl. "You were sleepwalking and fell off the roof, Ronnie Marshall." Granddaddy glanced away from the road and met my eye. "There won't be another word said once we're done with the doctor, you hear me boy? Not ever."

The strange thing was, I didn't even get a whipping.

I stayed out of school three days with a concussion. Mrs. Doornie's protractor had smashed in my pocket, and whenever I could get out of bed and sit up for a while, I tried to glue it back together. The picture was gone, and so was my space shuttle eraser.

By Wednesday I was better, and that night Granddaddy made me come down to dinner instead of bringing me soup in my room. After we said grace over the roasted chicken and buttered green beans, Granddaddy picked up his knife, then put it back down. He stared at me, so I put my knife and fork down, too. I didn't know what I had done wrong.

"Ronnie," Granddaddy said real slow, like he wasn't sure what he was saying. Except Granddaddy was always sure of himself. "Your Momma..." He stopped, staring at the butter-and-pepper skin on his half of the chicken. "She lost her Momma when she was a little girl."

He was quiet for a while, like I was supposed to answer. "My grandmother," I finally said.

Granddaddy almost looked relieved. "Your grandmother. She ran away from us, left me to raise your Momma. And lose your Momma, finally."

He hadn't never cried when Momma was sick or when she died. They had to carry Daddy away from the funeral, but Granddaddy had just stood at the grave with a face like a hatchet. I was real afraid he was about to cry now.

"Your grandmother," he said, "climbed a ladder one day when your mother was a tiny baby, and jumped off the roof." He grabbed my hand with his, like an old leather bird claw wrapped around my pale fingers. "She never hit the ground, Ronnie. You get me?"

"She flew away," I whispered, tears in my eyes from how much it hurt where he grabbed me.

"I'm never again going to lose someone I love like that," Granddaddy hissed, as my fingers popped and cracked in his grip. "That's Satan's work, a mockery of God."

He was wrong. Flying was being closer to God, not running away from Him. It was everything Brother Hardison said prayer was supposed to be. My heart ached fit to burst for Granddaddy, but he'd never believe me if I tried to explain.

"You're on restriction," Granddaddy said, "from now on. You'll be home when you're not in school or church. And I'll be nailing your window shut so you won't sneak out when I'm asleep."

That night I said the names of the astronauts over and over again like a prayer, seeing that smoke cloud from the shuttle in my mind like God's finger pointing up to His Heaven.

A couple of weeks later as I came out of school to catch the bus,

Granddaddy was standing on the steps.

"Come on, Ronnie."

"Yes, sir."

We got in the pickup. Granddaddy started it up and drove out onto U.S. Highway 183.

I watched the ranches go flickering by. "Where we going, sir?"

"Austin." He didn't explain any further.

An hour later we pulled into the parking lot of a hobby shop. Granddaddy walked in, trusting me to follow. He was right—I would have given my front teeth to have a place like this close to home. Models, rockets, electric trains, everything I could ever want.

He marched up to the counter. "I want your biggest space shuttle model, and all the supplies we'll need to build it."

It took me a while to close my mouth.

For the next few weeks, we built the model on the dining room table and ate in the kitchen. The gantry was almost four feet high, the big orange belly tank three feet tall. I'd never even seen Granddaddy so much as glue two toothpicks together before, but he was real good. He let me do a lot of the work, but showed me how on the hard parts.

Sometimes he'd set his hands on mine, and that was almost like being touched by Momma or Daddy again. Granddaddy had never touched me before except to whip me or to drag me along somewhere.

Working on that model together was almost as good as flying. We even laughed a few times. One night he walked into my room and took the nails out of my window. "I'm trusting you, Ronnie," was all he said.

When we were almost done, it was time to place the decals on the model.

"No," I said. "Not *Challenger*."

Granddaddy raised his eyebrows. "One of the others?"

"*McAuliffe*. After the teacher."

"I know who she was." He looked at the decal sheet. "They didn't include that one."

"I want it." I felt stubborn suddenly, like fighting.

"All right," he said.

I didn't expect that, no hard words for my backtalk or nothing. Instead Granddaddy got a 00 brush out and the gloss black paint. He just barely tipped the brush into the paint, sighed, and stared at the model. After a few moments, Granddaddy reached over and painted a perfect "M" in four quick strokes.

"Wow," I said.

He smiled at me, the first time I'd seen that since before Momma died. "I studied to be an architect. First thing they teach you is lettering."

I thought about that. "But you're a surveyor."

His smile died. "First there was the war, then your grandmother, then your Momma. I never got to finish college."

I hugged him, hugged him so tight I thought his ribs might crack. Then he finished painting the letters.

Real early the next morning I slipped on my Keds and stuck the glued-together protractor in my pocket. Then I went and knocked on Granddaddy's door. I needed to show him the most important thing I knew.

"Sir," I whispered real loud. "Wake up, sir."

"What is it, Ronnie?" Through the door, his voice sounded like he'd never been asleep.

"Get dressed and come outside. I want to show you something. It's important, sir."

"Ronnie..." he started to say, his voice a warning. Then I could hear him sigh. "All right, boy."

When he came into the living room, I had the *McAuliffe* cradled in my arms, the empty gantry left behind on the dining table. "Come on, sir," I said.

We walked through the pre-dawn gloom, listening the late-hunting nighthawks argue with the morning's first wrens.

We stood on top of Chamberlain's hill. The east had that glowing coal color again. The cows were quiet that morning.

"Ronnie," Granddaddy began, but I grabbed his hand and shushed him.

"Take one of the *McAuliffe*'s wings," I said, "and stretch your arms out real far."

"This is wrong, Ronnie."

"Just do it," I said. Tears stood in my eyes. "For me. For Momma."

The model was heavy as we each grabbed one wing. *McAuliffe*'s nose kept dipping down, and I had to twist my wrist back to hold her level. "Now close your eyes and run down the hill," I said to Granddaddy. "And when I tell you to, jump into the sky. Just forget how to fall."

He shook his head, but he closed his eyes.

Carrying our regrets between us, my Granddaddy and I scrambled down the dew-soaked grass, running together at the angle of my dreams.

Tall Spirits, Blocking the Night

Tall Spirits, Blocking the Night

Moke stumbled into the Rockne Road House as I was washing the bar mats, drunker than a prom queen after the party. I could have set fire to his breath.

"Wrong way, Moke," I said. "Go home." I couldn't serve him liquor, not in his condition. Moke was seventy-five if he was day, and would have had to work his way up to being called poor white trash. For the love of God, the man lived in a cracked septic tank that had fallen off a flatbed up on 535. Moke must have given up even more than I, to stay in this life.

"Tall spirits," Moke gasped. That was when I realized that he was at least as scared as he was drunk. "Tall spirits, blocking the night."

"Christ, Moke, you got the D.T.s now?" I stepped around and helped him get propped on a stool where the bar met the wall. "Coffee's on the house. What happened?"

Moke winked at me. "I was at Chosin." He laid his head on the bar.

"I know." Sometimes the story was Da Nang, sometimes it was Anzio. For a while he'd even said Kuwait City. After setting the coffee down next to him—not that I could afford to give anything away on my margins — I went to lock up. It was near closing, and there was only me, Moke and the radio. Not a lot of traffic in Rockne, Texas this late in the evening.

"Captured," Moke said. "They did things to me I wouldn't do to a nig-"

"Moke," I said. "Not in my bar." Moke was old, old South, like my grandfather, except Grandpappy had been safely dead for a decade and white America had moved on. Mostly.

"Scars," he whispered. "I got scars, Marvin."

That was a new twist to the story. "Don't show 'em to me, okay?"

"They're out there." He grabbed my wrist. "You can't go home, Marvin. Stay in 'til dawn."

"Moke, man..." I pried his fingers loose. "I'll give you a ride."

As suddenly as that, he snored on the bar top, cheek down next to his steaming cup of coffee.

"Well, hell," I said. Couldn't leave him in here alone—God knew what he'd do if he woke up in front of all those bottles. I didn't feel like carrying him out to my pick-up.

I postponed the moment of decision by going out to sweep the front porch. What else was I going to do at one fifteen in the morning?

Outside I realized that maybe Moke wasn't crazy-drunk. Just standing in front of my place, I could feel that there was something wrong with the night. Like blood staining a bathtub full of warm water.

Even though there wasn't a breeze, trees swayed in the distance. Booms echoed in the night, as if someone was blasting. I looked up at the moon-lit cirrus clouds like ash etched with silver. Rippling darkness passed across those silver edges.

Something on the ground was casting shadows *up* into the night sky, sucking the moonlight away.

"Oh, Christ, Moke," I whispered. "What the hell have you done?" How had he done it, whatever it was?

Indians died in the hills here under white guns. Slaves died in the cotton fields here under white whips. Generations of dirt farmers had laid their wives and kids into the ground. God only knew how many ancient grudges could be coming back to haunt us all.

Well, maybe God didn't, but I'd guess Moke knew.

Broom in hand, I was ready to run back inside, lock the door, turn on all the lights, and take my first drink in the decade since Leah died in her warm, red-stained tub. But I couldn't do it.

I stood with my forehead pressed against the silvered wood of the screen door, fingers on the corroded aluminum Butter-Krust sign that served as the handle. The gritty scent of the rusted hardware cloth filled my nostrils, along with the earthy odors of night and damp. Around my feet, dust jumped as whatever they were moved behind me. "Tall spirits," Moke had said, "blocking the night." So tall their shadows touched the clouds.

I tried to lift away my head and pull open the door. It was like trying to move a boulder with my fingertips. I tried to step away. It was as if I were the boulder. Then the breeze came up.

This was no moldy scent of night. Rather, it was a stench of road kill, of stale blood, of rotten vegetables and damp wounds. I retched, fighting the urge to vomit on my feet, on the porch of my bar. Then the pain started.

My head was pressed between two millstones. My chest was crushed beneath the dirt of a grave. My heart was torn by the twinned tragedies of love and death. I exhaled, closed my eyes, and let that stench of death wash over me.

"Leah," I begged. "Help me now."

She had left, in a storm of anger and sigh of depression, gotten the last word with the help of a straight razor and fifth of bourbon. The warm, red water was her grave and final accusation. She insisted that I had never understood—what it meant to be a black woman in a white man's world, what it meant to be lonely even in the arms of her beloved. Beneath it all, the flashing rage and the Prozac and the booze, she had loved me. I knew she had loved me.

Deep inside my scarred heart, Leah whispered that love was the only defense against the tall spirits, even such a broken love as ours. So as the tall spirit crushed me smaller and smaller, I squeezed my love for Leah out between my clenched eyelids. The saltwater benediction tumbled to the distant, dusty porch, sizzling like water dropped in a deep fryer.

That was when I understood Moke's pain, his scars, his stories. The tall spirit rifled through my mind and through my body like a careless toddler in Momma's sewing chest. Needles scraped across my bone, hooks pulled muscles free from their anchors, coals burned in my skull, agony and ecstasy flooded my brain.

"Help me, Moke!" I screamed. "Leah!"

Then there was nothing. I lay on the porch, splinters from the ancient wood in my cheek, the pole of my broom shoved painfully deep into my armpit. I had shit my pants, and piss ran down my left thigh. Mucus poured from my nose, and my ears itched with a flood of wax. Every waste I had fled my body.

Using the broom as a crutch, I stood. The sky was clear of shadows, but in the distance I saw them striding away. Moke had been right — they were tall spirits, stepping across power lines as if they were toys. Shaped like men, thin as walking sticks, long black cloaks flapping, dragging their shadows, the tall spirits vanished over the horizon.

I pushed open the screen door and stepped back into my bar. I needed to strip off my filthy clothes and sponge myself clean. I needed that drink.

The place was empty.

"Moke!" I yelled. Wincing, I stumbled to his stool. The coffee still steamed—had so little time passed? His clothes lay in a heap where he had been sitting.

I picked up his pair of blue work pants then turned toward the back door. That was when I saw the eye peering in the window. The pupil was bigger than a trash can lid, the iris wider than the six-foot window frame. With a slick squelch, the lid dropped once, a giant wink, before the eye withdrew.

I limped over there to look out. The ground shook and the trees swayed as one last shadow crossed the bottom of the moon-lit clouds.

Moke.

I sponged myself down and changed into sweats from my gym bag under the prep counter. Then I put the filthy clothes—both Moke's and mine—in the burn barrel out back. I opened the old padlock on the stairwell and climbed to the apartment where I had lived years before. I bent to finally clean the brown-stained tub. The first task was to pry the razor from her bony, cobwebbed fingers.

Somewhere out there, tall spirits blocked the night. I hoped Moke had found peace in their mysterious company.

Who Sing but Do Not Speak

Who Sing but Do Not Speak

On the last day of my childhood Mother called us all under Her. The ragged edges of Her chitin were love itself, on the one claw slicing me to the soft core while on the other claw sheltering me from the storms of the world. I cowered with my co-siblings as Mother exhorted Her workers.

"Lazy-wings! Warmtime grows short, yet you dawdle in Our quarries and upon Our scaffolds. Our great project *will* be finished." Her enormous mandibles clattered like wind among the dried canes of the riverbed, but the mute workers remained sluggish. Some had already gone off to die in quiet places, others were infected with dreams of distant horizons and, against all hope, living through the icetime. All were slowing, their chitin cracked and discolored, their spirits low.

Around Mother the cathedral leapt into the sky, a splash of stone lifted from the soil of Her world, its upward edges curling in toward one another in a soaring vault not quite complete. In the beginning of the warmtime, Mother had eaten well of a race of bifurcated vermin, and from their cephalic slurry of memories She had learned mysterious arts, such as this holy architecture.

"My pretty pets," She crooned to us her children. Deep beneath

Mother's chitin skirts, Her voice was a moist wind out of the forested night. A thousand cilia reached down to stroke our soft shells, our juvenile eyes, feeling the firmness of our legs, the plumpness of our abdomens.

"I have a new Plan for the world, such as has never been thought of before. For all their silence, the workers resent the season and the food, but they are workers. They know no better. Lazy-winged mutes one and all. You, My children, will seal this place with divine beauty. Remember, there can be no sanctuary without beauty." Reaching under with a claw-tipped arm, She plucked my co-brother Frim from our huddled mass and hurled him into the air. "Go, find beauty, or never return."

One by one Mother drove us from Her shelter. Some of us found damp, new wings atop our carapaces and fled Her place in buzzing panic. Others, like poor Frim, tumbled to the soil to become feasts for the hungry workers.

I will not speak of the privations of the wide world, except to say that while I nearly starved in stone deserts, I failed to die; while I nearly froze amid high mountains, I failed to die; while I nearly drowned in a river as big as a sea, I failed to die. And what is life, but a failure to die?

But nowhere did I find beauty. I interrogated the banling as I ate the slurry of his guts, but he knew only slow, demented grazing and moments of panic. I questioned the rock lizard as I sucked his marrow, but he knew only sunlight and the crevices of the earth. Even the crisp silver fish in their rushing waters were blind to the mountain fastness around them. None of these traitors to beauty failed to die within my claws.

Until one chilly day I found beauty unexpected in a hidden valley far from home.

The valley was infested with a kind of tree-ape that ran about on an insufficiency of limbs and crawled through great, durable burrows. They were nothing, these bifurcated vermin, but their burrows, oh, their burrows. These were the wind made metal, the aching drop of great waterfalls captured in static poise. Each was different from the next, yet they somehow were all alike as stones. There was beauty in their perfection of form, to stain my hearts.

I knew I must crack the secret of these burrows. Then I could go home to Mother with beauty in my claws.

84

Among my co-siblings there were two kinds of thought. Some, like poor Frim, would bluster and caper, dance roughclawed on the backs of the workers until Mother's voice called them away with the authority of a snapping leg. Others, like me, spent our time in the shaded side of boulders, watching the world move and scenting the wind, the better to feast at the end of the hunt.

So it was now, I realized. Where Frim would have danced among the vermin, snapping their heads off and trampling them beneath his claws, I would wait here on the rim of the valley, patient as water, silent as the sky, until my time came round.

On the ninth day of my vigil, when moss already grew on the lee of my abdomen and small things explored the crevices of my thorax, I was able to catch one of the vermin unawares. It had wandered close, pecking at the ground plants for some pathetic, absurd delicacy, until it stood practically between my mandibles. I cocked my hunting eyes downward at it, surprised to find I had grown so large on my journey, but the vermin was distracted by its own concerns.

It was the work of a moment to seize it in my mandibles, strip the loose husks, and tear off the vermin's head. The taste of its cephalic slurry was very different from anything I had ever eaten before, flavored by certain mineral salts unknown to me, and an immense reservoir of iron-rich fluid as if to garnish. Mother Herself could not have dripped forth a sweeter treat.

And the memories, oh, the memories. Where the banling and the rock lizard had small thoughts and smaller fears, this bifurcated vermin had terrors as big as the night sky, and beauties to match. Never had I felt such a flood of glorious thought, not even when suckling from Mother's sweet honey. The grace of their sky-poised burrows was as nothing to what else I found there. I tasted warm worlds and otherwise, towering plants and metal caverns and the hearts-aching humility of giving homage to a greater One who had made the world.

These vermin knew of Mother!

I cowered on the mountainside, flooded with the beauty of the lifetime of a race—the vermin had strong memories and stronger learning—and wondered if I had eaten a co-sibling. This thing knew of the mysteries of the world, and how creation came to be, and of the One who ruled over all. Its ideas were distorted, but the truth was plain to me.

I finally decided it could not be a true co-sibling, because it thought of Mother as He, not She, and He dwelt in some cloud-wrapped vastness, while Mother was planted firmly among us.

Other vermin came and collected the husks, keening, and cast about in the pointless way of animals when they have lost a mate or a whelp. I sat quiet, a very large rock to their poor eyes, and watched them track back and forth across my ridge until they left. When only silent stones remained and the tiny creatures of dust and wind had ventured forth again, I heaved myself upward and began my journey home.

I had found beauty, and taken it into me. I was humbled that such beauty should come from vermin, but then, so did Mother's cathedral. Could I do no less than Her?

No! Even the idea of humility had crept from the vermin's memories within me. Though grown too great to fly, I ran until the ground smoked beneath my claws, purging unworthy thoughts and pleading silently that Mother might forgive me my trespasses.

The journey home with my burden of beauty was much harder than my outward trip. My appetite seemed to have increased a thousand-fold, outstripping even my great bulk, even while the days had become shorter and the banlings and rock lizards retreated to silent caves grown far too small for me.

I took to eating plants, simply to stoke the fires in my gut, though they ravaged me and made my castings a painful horror. Fish were still plentiful, when I could find a streambed of sufficient dimensions for me to reach into.

The entire way home, I focused on my beauty. My vermin had an art-of-the-claw in its memory, the making of a glorious pattern of light. The beauty would be crafted from heated slurry of sand, formed into sheets of colored crystal and assembled into an image. This was as done in the towering temples of my vermin's memory. Soft lead from the hills south of Mother's domain would join the colored crystal into patterns to tell the story of the glory that was Mother.

Beauty, lit from behind, reminding all of Mother's power and Her glory forever and ever, amen.

Damn that vermin in my head!

And then I remembered that I had never known before of damnation. I stopped and heaved my guts until my chitin threatened to collapse, but the bifurcated vermin was long digested, its cephalic slurry taken up as my own. I, who had never known fire, held the beauty like a torch.

"Mother," I croaked.

There was ice on the rocks above Her valley, that had not been there when I left during the seasons of the sun. Below I saw a scattering of worker husks, their chitinous shells now home to small scavengers. At the bottom of the valley lay Mother's cathedral, a thing that the vermin within me recognized. I remembered places I had never been, stone temples with strange names such as *Chartres* and *Notre Dame*.

In the walls of the cathedral were tall, narrow openings with tapered tops, receptacles fit for the beauty in my head. I had left here a child and returned full-grown, bearing the burden She had asked of me.

I stumbled down into the valley. Somewhere I had lost one of my great locomotor legs, and my chitin was pitted, leaking from the joints of my body. My guts sagged inside me, great vacancies of hunger and want that bedeviled my every thought. But I was home. My hearts pounded like a hatchling's.

On the valley floor, I found some workers still alive, torpid and dull. I kicked them into movement, made demands for sand and minerals and a hot fire. I vomited forth the merest taste of beauty, at which they lapped before scrambling away as if it were the height of warmtime. Two of them I held back, letting the vermin in my head explain what fire was.

I finally lurched into Her cathedral to find that the world had ended.

Mother's great armored shell rested on the ground, empty save for a pulsing egg sac. Her legs were scattered, gnawed, Her cilia nothing but dead, dusty streamers. My hearts collapsed to flaccid sacs that not even the beauty could assuage. Mother was no more. I laid myself on the cold stone as close as I could to where I had most often suckled Mother's juices and, lacking tears to weep, bled my guts onto the floor.

All was as nothing, my journey, my wounds, my betrayal of myself to the inner spirit of some vermin, and most of all the beauty I had carried across strange countries, all brought to nothing by Her death. I bled until my body threatened to sag next to Hers.

Then the workers returned, still filled with the beauty, bearing sand and minerals and glowing hot coals. They supped from my tears, eating up the essence that was me, capturing larger and larger images of beauty until my Plan was clear even to their tiny minds.

Exhausted, I lay still as stone while the workers wrought beauty and filled the holes in Mother's cathedral with Her image. Through my juices, they gave Her the vermin's halo, to honor its memory. According to their own dim thoughts, within the image they placed me dying in Her arms, even though it was She who had passed before me.

I could not say what the next warmtime would bring, eggs hatching inside Mother's cathedral. Would those co-siblings grow stronger faster? Would the first among them become Mother reborn that much sooner, so that they might raise greater walls against the icetime to come, as icetimes always came?

Even as my life slipped out onto the cold stone floor, the workers who never ever spoke, began to sing. Though their songs were vermin songs of adoration, of a distant and mistaken image of Mother, the workers still brought glory to Mother's cathedral grave. Those who sing but do not speak had brought Mother's beauty to the world, and so, finally remembering to die, I gladly followed my vermin into another light.

Glass: A Love Story

Glass: A Love Story

Aria Minnows was a beautiful woman with eyes that flashed like crystal. Deke Zeiss was an ordinary young man on his way up in life. The first time they slept together, she told him she had a heart of glass. He thought that was a metaphor. Until the day he broke it.

The Ball Glass Diner clattered around them, redolent of scorched peanut oil and rank fog from a dishwashing machine. Deke took Aria's hand to place the engagement ring on her finger. Two carats of princess-cut diamond on a white gold band, he'd mortgaged his right kidney to pay for it. Only the Bull Market Syndicate would write a note like that—they were bankers to the credit-unworthy, among many other profit centers. As important as the blood games might be in the city of Troezen, his apprentice armorer's salary didn't cut much ice. But he had big plans, that he'd made with her help.

"All I want to do is be with you for the rest of my life," Deke announced just as his grip slipped and he sliced open the skin of her knuckles with the ring. A tiny cracking noise rang out from her hand as her entire body shuddered. Horrified, he watched alabaster flesh part like the opening of a flower, blood welling.

Aria raised her left hand in a fist, glass shards and drops of blood spattering to the pink Formica tabletop from her wounded knuckles. "How could you?" she demanded as she began to cry. The ring lay between them.

"What...?" Deke was appalled by what he had done, and baffled by the degree of injury his mistake had caused.

A roller-skating waitress sliced by in reverse, carrying a giant oval tray of malts and burgers. Aria sobbed, the stuttering heaves swallowing whatever she was trying to say. Even in the red wash of the moment, Deke was fascinated by they way her breasts moved freely under her spaghetti strap dress.

"Oh, honey," he said, pleading. "I'm really sorry." He reached for her left hand, trying to unfold her clenched fist.

She snatched her hand away, then grabbed the ring off the table. "Diamonds *cut* glass, you jerk," Aria yelled. "Men never listen."

Around them, boys and girls in letter jackets crammed into leopardskin booths as a jukebox blared a jazz-punk fusion cover of "Cry Me a River" by Armstrong's Fuzzy Lips. No one paid the bickering couple any attention.

"I didn't realize..." Deke began, but Aria hurled the ring at his face. It missed, skipped off the back of the booth and flew into underlit anonymity.

"By Apollo, that was twenty thou—" he shouted as his temper finally flared to meet hers. Deke caught himself three syllables too late.

He heard a sharp crack, like a bullet striking bronze armor. Aria stood, tears on her face like a lacy stream of gems. "Enough," she said. Her voice was tight, dry. Grainy. Sharp.

Leaving the booth, Aria stepped out of the spaghetti strap dress as her skin began to slough away. Even the blasé chatter of the Ball Glass Diner halted at the sight of a glass woman emerging from a cloak of flesh that raveled away like a rotten quilt. Almost the last Deke saw of Aria was her perfect crystalline buttocks sliding in rhythm with her angry stride. As the baize-padded door swung shut he glimpsed one glass foot trailing a lingering scrap of flesh.

"Dude," said the lacrosse letterman in the next booth stretching around to stare at Deke, "What *did* you say to her?"

Deke had no answer. He reached across the tabletop for the torn skin of Aria's hand, a pallid, bloody glove discarded in her anger. Before he could touch it, the Ball Glass Diner's bouncer grabbed Deke in a shoulder-cracking grip and hustled him out the door after his vanished lover.

Steep granite stairs led from the Ball Glass Diner to the distant streets of Troezen far below. Unrailed, mossy, worn as the brick floors of some ancient monastery, they were both a discouragement and a badge of courage for those who braved the heights.

Stumbling down in the cool damp of the afternoon, Deke slipped on a rag that nearly pitched him into the head-smashing depths. Cursing, he stopped to look. It was the skin of Aria's right foot. His curses turned to loving whispers as he picked up the mashed, filthy bit of flesh and sank to a seat on the steps.

"Oh, my sweet," Deke crooned, Aria's foot crushed in his hand as he stroked it against his cheek. "Oh my beloved." He kissed the maroon-painted toenail. "I am so sorry. I will make it up to you." The lost engagement ring shrank to a detail measured against the pain of his newly foundered love. Aria was his angel, showing Deke the mysteries of sex, and whispering sage advice about advancing his career as they lay pillowed together in the night. "Where have you gone?"

Deke looked at the tiny cars beetling along far below. A glittering trail led downward. He bent to run his fingers on the step between his feet, to see if he could touch the trail.

Glass stung him, tiny drops of blood welling from his fingertips. Little splinters of glass so small he could only see them when they reflected the clouded-shadowed sunlight. It was a trail of shards from Aria's broken heart. He would follow it to wherever she had gone. He would make amends.

On the sidewalks of Troezen, Deke quickly found that the trick of the thing was to look slantwise, never quite staring at the glass. The faint trail wandered like fairy glamour past upmarket storefronts crammed with furs and silks and ormulu amphorae. It zigged where some other pedestrian had zagged, looped in small circles as if Aria had turned to see if he were following her, attenuated when she ran a few yards before slowing again, marked by damp spots where—perhaps—her tears had fallen. Deke prayed to Eros that those were tears of regret.

Crossing streets was harder, but he persevered. Vehicles and pedestrians had scattered Aria's faint track, smearing it into the asphalt and cobbles. Deke would reach the other side, then cast about for a fresh trail of glitter while fondling the foot of his beloved. As he followed the glass, the buildings became shorter and the sidewalks dirtier. Aria was heading east toward the ferry docks.

Troezen's industrial center, Concrete Town, lay across the water on the East Side of Aegeus Bay. It was a grimy, rotting maze where the desperate and the poor lived. Street gangs held sway there under the iron hand of Minnie Torres, head of the Bull Market Syndicate. Aria's despair knew no limits if she was bound there. Deke knew—he had struggled out of those slums himself. He had to find his love, pull her back from that brink.

Deke quickened his step toward the docks just as a coal-black 1958 Plymouth Fury cut across the sidewalk with a squeal of brakes and the reek of carbon, blocking his way. Towering chrome fins glittered like butcher knives in his face as an enormous man in a satin East Side Greeks bowling shirt stepped out of the car.

"Hey, friend," said the Greek. He glanced at a Polaroid in his hand. He looked and sounded like every tough guy boxer Deke had ever seen. Even his lips had muscles. "You're Deke Zeiss, right?"

"I'm busy," said Deke, his mind on his beloved's broken heart. He bent to peer under the Fury. The glass trail led on through the shadows. "Catch me later."

The Greek flipped over the Polaroid to scrutinize a note taped to the back, bushy black eyebrows scrunching together. Then he glanced up again. "My name is Al, Al Lecto, freelance contract enforcer. Nothing personal, you understand, but I'm here to serve notice the Bull Market Syndicate is calling the mortgage on your right kidney. Seems your collateral property's in the upper G.I. tract of some high school cheerleader at Troezen Baptist E.R."

Oh crap, thought Deke. The ring. He needed Aria a lot more than he needed his ring, but he needed his kidney, too. He'd counted on paying back the Bull Market Syndicate once he married Aria—if his hopes for his job didn't pan out, she came from money, Troezen aristocracy, although she'd always been coy about the details. He'd never met her parents. Aria said they wouldn't approve of his East Side origins, that they should wait until Deke had made his name. Stalling for time, Deke squeezed her flaccid toe for luck. "That was fast."

"The chick swallowed the ring in her chocolate malted right after you split the Ball Glass," Lecto explained. "LifeFlite dusted her off the roof pronto. Her family's already filed a salvage claim, which means you got nothing. Me, it's just a job. You, friend, it's a kidney." The gigantic man winked and pressed a business card into Deke's hand. "You've got twenty-four hours to come in. We do it the easy way, you show respect to Torres, everybody walks out okay, plus or minus a few stitches and some urine throughput. Miss the deadline, I'll arrange involuntary renal extraction and Torres will have me take your spleen and gall bladder for penalty. You'll be lucky if you don't bleed out then. Call when you're ready."

Deke glanced at the card, not really focusing on it. His lower back twinged, his body forecasting the world of hurt he would soon be in. "Love," he said quietly. "I did it for love."

"Tombstones all over Troezen Memorial Gardens with that chiseled on 'em," said Lecto. "I should know, I planted half those guys." He chuckled, a noise like marbles in a steel chute. "Still, love's not a bad excuse." Lecto touched an eyebrow, an abortive salute. "Eumenides Contract Enforcement, at your service. Give me a shout, friend, you ever need anything done."

The Greek jumped back into his Fury, slammed it into reverse with an audible clank, and plowed into traffic without ever looking backward. Deke stared at the card as the Fury peeled out and vanished down the street. The card had Lecto's name and company, a cell phone number and something scrawled in blood red felt tip across the black letterpress printing. "It's more than just a kidney," the note read. "Torres wants your ass."

Iron gray swells loomed before Deke. The choppy water of Aegeus Bay slammed spray over the ferry's bow. The boat was a surplus Star Ferry from Hong Kong, badly repainted in the Sharon Line's red and black colors, or maybe just suffering from terminal corrosion.

Deke stood in the glassed-in lower deck, clinging to a greenish brass pole amid a whole shift of Filipina maids from the Troezen Hilton heading home, chattering in Tagalog. They brought their smells of commercial cleansers and spicy cooking with them like a cloak of culture.

His cell phone rang at his belt, tootling out Blondie's "Heart of Glass." It was Aria's favorite song. Deke snatched the phone free. He didn't recognize the number on the caller I.D.

"Aria?" he gasped, hoping it was his love calling from a payphone.

"Deke Zeiss, you're in big trouble." It was a woman, but he didn't recognize the voice.

"Who is this? Why are you calling me?"

The woman sighed. "My name is Sandy Priam. I'm a telephone psychic, and I sensed you needed me."

"Yeah, right." Deke almost laughed in spite of his troubles. "I didn't need a psychic to tell me I have a problem. Sorry, babe, no dice."

"The spirit moved me, made me call you. What can I say? Nobody ever believes what I say, but I have to try. You broke her heart, Deke."

She did know something. "It was just a *ring*," he pled. His left hand slipped back into his pocket, taking comfort from the clammy flesh of Aria's foot. Some of the maids had stopped chattering and were watching him, eavesdropping with delighted interest. "She's been my muse for months. I can't let her go like this."

"Look, everything is going to end badly, especially for you," the psychic said. "Forget about Aria. Go home and brood into your booze. You'll find some other girl's life to mess up soon enough."

Deke stared across the heaving iron water at the rusted towers of Concrete Town. Dense brown-orange smog roiled a hundred feet above the streets. "I can't turn back," he said. He shuddered with memory of Aria's touch, goose pimples rising on his arms. "I love her too much to lose her."

"You've already lost her. But look, Deke, if you have to go do this, at least be smart about it."

"How?"

"First, trust Lecto."

"He threatened to steal my kidneys," Deke yelled. The Filipina maids around him twittered.

"It's just his job. He's straight, Lecto is. He only does whatever he's been set to do. He can help you, too. Second, when you go after her, think horns."

"Horns?" demanded Deke. "What kind of stupid bull crap is that?"

"I'm an oracle, not a genius, you know what I mean? Look, I've got to go. I'm meeting a *paying* client down at Ilium's Topless Bar in twenty minutes. Be safe."

The phone went dead. Deke slipped it back on to his belt clip as the maids all smiled at him.

"Bull horn," said one the maids shyly, glancing at her friends for support. She held her hands about a foot apart. "Make for big man." They all giggled at him. "Good for fever too. Stop the heat."

Deke ignored the whispers that followed him the rest of the way across the bay.

Looking back from the ferry docks of Concrete Town, Troezen gleamed like a vision of divine Olympus, each white tower topped with a golden nimbus as the sun touched the western horizon behind the city. Deke stared at his adoptive home, wondering if he would see it again. The vision of his disemboweled body bumping against the pier pilings beneath his feet was quite clear in his mind, enhanced by the pair of bloated corpses visible down in the water, their stench blending with the rotten-fish odors of the bay.

Deke turned his back on Troezen and scanned the ferry docks for glass from the heart of his beloved. He walked slowly toward the street until he picked up the trail. It was scuffed by the passage of hotel maids, garbage men, leg-breakers and the other daytime workers who drove the economy of Troezen across the bay, but Aria's path was still visible. In the approaching dusk, the shards gleamed red. Once he found them, they weren't hard to keep sight of.

Clutching the foot in his hand, Deke set off into the darkening streets, following the blood-colored trail of glass. It led up into the hills of Concrete Town, passing among the belching factories to head toward Bull House, home of the Bull Market Syndicate and the dreaded Minnie Torres.

"Clearly, glass is cheap," whispered a voice in the shadows.

Deke jumped, wishing he were armed with more than a cell phone. He ascended the stepped sidewalk of Minnow End, a narrow street that headed straight up Minnow's Hill to the service entrance on the north side of Bull House.

"Who's there?" Deke scanned the darkness around him. Minnow End was crowded with tiny pawnshops, gray market bandwidth brokerages and black market plastic surgeons operating out of blood-stained barber chairs bolted to the sidewalks. There were people everywhere, intent on their own business except for the plastic surgery gawkers who paid a dollar apiece to watch, surrounding the actinic circles of surgical lamplight like crows around road kill.

"You're following the trail, ain't you?" The speaker was a blindfolded old man, dressed in rags and clutching a twisted wooden staff hung with broken circuit boards, tiny bottles, bones and feathers. He sat on a shadowed step leaning against a grimy brick wall. The old man sniffed. "You've got her blood scent on you."

Deke clutched the foot in his pocket. "That's as may be." The phone call from Sandy the psychic still weighed on his mind. "I take it you have some mystical advice designed to keep me from a messy death and help me win back my beloved."

"Not really." The old man hawked and spat. "I'm a blind old man begging in the street. What would I have to offer a smart Troezen boy like you?"

That beat the Hades out of incomprehensible oracular pronouncements. Deke stepped the wall next to the old man and sat on the sidewalk steps. "You mentioned glass."

"Sand," said the old man. "Glass is sand, poured into a fire."

"Uh huh."

"From the fire, engineers draw miracles. Silicon microchips, crystal stemware." The old man grinned, a handful of teeth gleaming dully in the shadows, as he fingered his blindfold. "Glass eyes, for all the good they do me."

"And women," said Deke, flush with the memory of his last sight of Aria.

"Women, too. They're for specialist markets. Optical circuits and silicon microfiber muscles. Plain as day, see right through 'em." He cackled. "Just like a man. Like I said, specialist markets."

Deke drew Aria's foot from his pocket and pressed it into the old man's hand. "This was her. She wore flesh." It wasn't a lie. He'd known her skin intimately before she'd walked away, vanishing from view like a clean window.

The old man kneaded the foot in his hands, pressing it to his face to smell it, rolling the toenails between his fingers. "It's a wrapper, son. Most men can't stand to see into the heart of a woman. No one wants to know how much he's failed in his love. Believe me, in the glass, she looks the same as her sisters."

"I'll know my beloved," said Deke. Memories of a hundred hot nights flashed in his head, sex flavored with arguments and take-out curry, her crystal eyes flashing in the candlelight. He would never forget her.

"Still, check the fit of the foot." The old man handed the flaccid skin back to Deke. "And you'd better get on up there."

Deke slipped the old man a ten-dollar coin, then continued to climb the hill. *In the glass, she looks the same as her sisters.* That could mean so many different things.

At the top of Minnow's Hill the orange-brown fog reduced the world to glowering silence and a chemical reek that prophesied cancer. The glass trail ended in a brilliant pool of ruby light outside the service entrance to Bull House. The headquarters of the Bull Market Syndicate towered over him, dry set stone in massive rising courses interspersed with firing slits and camera mounts. Fifty feet up, a wooden superstructure arched outward from the stone, tall glass windows flickering with the lights within. His troubles had come together, lost love and his endangered kidney linked within Minnie Torre's grasp.

Deke sighed. He had set out to make amends to Aria, and come this far. He would follow the trail inward. If Torres came for him, he would demand the return of his love. He might well die, but when Lecto caught up with him, things wouldn't be much better. Deke had already committed his life to Torres with the kidney mortgage. He might as well make the best play he could for Aria.

Deke touched the door with his fingertips, preparing to knock. To his surprise, it swung smoothly open. He stepped inside.

The interior of Bull House reeked of stale incense, furniture oil and old meat. Rising walls were defined by the scabrous glow of the nighttime fog outside, filtered through the firing slits above his head. The ceiling loomed in the darkness above behind dim, widely-spaced warehouse lamps. The wooden floor rang hollow with each step as if he walked across a great drumhead.

And he was surrounded by wooden walls, segments six feet tall and four feet wide like a medieval mockery of office cubicle sections. Each panel was covered with elaborate carvings that he had to squint to see in the dim light, woodwork inset with gems and mirrored shards.

Looking in part with his fingertips, Deke found a seascape of dolphins disporting with mermaids while a writhing monster pulled a ship to its death in a turquoise mosaic ocean. Another panel showed an island of pigs, each pig with a male human face, while a gnarled man and a handsome goddess performed a hundred different sex acts in a kind of static animation. The goddess' eyes were diamonds in each tiny relief, her partner's face a mirror every time it could be seen at all. A third panel showed ancient warriors dragging a naked man around city walls while fires burned within, rubies illustrating the flames and a giant, flawed citron for the smoke-clouded sun.

As Deke walked onward, the panels slid around him, cutting him off from the door and isolating him in a little unroofed room. There were grooves in the floor, a four-foot by four-foot grid of tracks. Deke ran his hands along the top of a panel showing centaurs hunting in the woods. There were fine wires soaring up into the darkness. Even as his touch slipped away from them, the panels slid again, clattering like wooden railroad cars to open a short, temporary hallway ahead of him. Reddish glass glittered in a river of love. Stroking Aria's callused sole, he followed it deeper into Bull House.

"Horns," he whispered. "Fit of the foot. Trust Lecto. He's just doing his job." None of this advice helped, and the thought of Lecto made Deke's back itch for his doomed kidney, but every time the glass trail led him into a new dead end of panels, one would slide away.

Deke walked for at least an hour. From the outside, Bull House hadn't seemed any bigger than a city block. From the inside, it was an entire country, provinces mapped out in the convolutions of the panels and their recombinant iconography. But Deke knew he wasn't merely walking in circles. First, the glass trail never crossed itself, although sometimes he spotted small flecks scattered in the empty trackways over which he walked. Second, the panels changed progressively, the mirrored sections becoming larger as the carvings reduced. When Deke finally came to one that was a giant mirror, outlined with winged beings carrying bows and swords, he stopped to look at himself.

"What am I doing?" Deke asked his reflection. "I could starve in here, following a broken heart."

His reflection had no answer except to mirror Deke as he pulled Aria's foot from his pocket. The skin had suffered its abuses poorly, tearing in several places along the thin top of the foot, while the smallest toe was almost severed. The thing had begun to reek of old plant life, an almost comfortable compost smell as if it were already returning to dust.

Moved by an ill-defined impulse, as if he were the reflection and the mirror-Deke were real, Deke pressed the foot sole-first against the mirror. He used both hands to smooth it down, firmly pushing it against the glass. When he peeled the flaccid skin free, there was a clear footprint in skin oil and dust on the polished glass of the mirror. Staring out of the footprint was the face of a bull, interrupted by the whorls and ridges of the skin.

Deke stood very still, staring back into his mirror as the bull approached, visible by looping fractions within the oily footprint. Its horns shone like brass, and in the interrupted view he could see the hairs stirring on its hide. His nerve broke with the touch of hot, damp breath on his neck. Deke spun, hands up to protect himself, to see nothing but wooden panels. Behind him, the mirror clattered out of the way. He spun again to see the ground glass trail entering a hallway of mirrors, nothing but mirrors.

On the other side of the wall of panels, hooves clopped leisurely on the drumhead floor.

"I *will* die in this place," Deke said aloud. The mirrors echoed his words, each one slightly delayed, each mirror-Deke pronouncing his doom, over and over in an ascendant series of prophecy.

Somewhere nearby, the bull laughed.

The mirror-Dekes followed him now through halls of glass ornamented with scant carving. He'd lost track of the trail after blundering into a mirror and getting turned around. Somehow it had vanished under another of the mirrored panels, while Deke was confused. Tired of cracking his forehead on glass, Deke walked with one hand extended, the foot skin clutched tight, feeling his way like a blind man in a whorehouse.

Out of the corner of his eye, in a mirror that reflected another mirror, a glass woman walked the hall with him. When he turned to see, panels slid and the woman vanished. When he turned back, hot tears coursed down the surface of the mirror in front of his nose.

"Aria," Deke shouted. Echoes chased themselves through the open air above his head, followed by the gearbox chuckle of the bull.

It was the echoes that made up his mind. "Trust Lecto," Sandy the telephone psychic had said. Lecto had threatened him, but in very specific terms, in accordance with the contract Deke had signed with the Bull Market Syndicate. If he came in, as Lecto had put it, Deke could discharge his debt "the easy way," then pay respects to Minnie Torres.

He'd never find Torres on his own, and Aria was with Torres if she was anywhere. But Deke would bet Lecto could find him, even in this labyrinth. Lecto was one of the Eumenides — they could do anything. Then Deke could get to Torres, find his love and leave. He had two kidneys, after all. He dialed Lecto on the cell phone.

"Eumenides," Lecto said, answering on the first ring.

"I'm ready to come in," Deke replied without preamble.

The Greek sounded positively jovial. "Right on it, friend. Sit tight."

Deke waited, slumped to the floor to lean against a mirrored panel while he studied his haggard reflection in the opposite wall.

Less than ten minutes later the panel on which Deke leaned slid away. Unable to catch himself, Deke fell backward, bouncing his head painfully on the drumhead floor. Lecto's coal black Plymouth Fury loomed above him and the door swung open, narrowly missing Deke's nose.

"How'd you get that thing in here?" Deke asked as Lecto leaned out to look down at him.

"I'm a Eumenideus. It's what I do." Lecto smiled, showing Deke his teeth to match Deke's excellent view of Lecto's copious nasal hair. "Be glad Meg isn't on this job. She's so damned bloodthirsty she ought to have been a Bacchante."

Deke made an effort to smile. "It's a living, right?"

"That's right," said Lecto. His voice got harder, more dangerous. "You ready to pay on that kidney, or is this a waste of my time?"

"I have a question." Deke didn't bother to get up off the floor. He couldn't escape Lecto if he tried, so he might as well lie here and rest his back. "If I give up, I understand that I get to pay my respects to Minnie Torres."

Lecto shrugged. "Mostly that's a matter of form, once the contract's been executed."

"But I can do it in person, right?"

"You won't be in the greatest shape, friend."

"I'll pay my debt," said Deke, "but that's what I want on the back end."

"I see." Lecto rubbed his chin. "You're going to make trouble."

Deke squeezed the grubby foot in his hand. "Not necessarily. You said love's not a bad excuse."

"Hey," said Lecto, "I'm all for a little trouble now and then. Wouldn't do this job if I wasn't. And who am I to stand in the way of love?"

"Okay," said Deke, gathering the tatters of his courage. This was about Aria. "Let's do it."

"Kidney first, friend. A contract's a contract." Lecto stepped out of the Fury, his enormous legs stretching right over Deke. "Come around to my office."

Deke stood, knees popping, and followed Lecto around to the back of the huge Plymouth, where Lecto was already lugging a folding massage table out of the trunk.

Because he needed to see Minnie Torres after the extraction, Deke refused total anesthetic. Lecto made him take happy pills, enough 'Ludes to tranq out a draft horse. It didn't hurt any less, but Deke didn't care so much about the pain. The mirrors laughed as the blood flew, but that might have been the drugs. Or the bull, somewhere nearby taking its delight. Lecto hummed as he worked, a medley of Disney songs. After a while, Deke passed out of his own accord.

"Friend," whispered Lecto, bending over Deke's face like a lover come to steal a sleeping kiss. "Come on, appointment's waiting."

Deke felt as if he'd been trampled by those tranquilized draft horses. His body ached with a pain that was to a muscle cramp as double pneumonia was to a springtime sneeze. He badly wanted to pee, and was dry as rust at the same time.

"It hurts," Deke said, more an existential statement than a complaint.

His voice squeaked.

Lecto grabbed his wrist and pulled Deke to his feet, expertly levering him off the massage table. Stunned by the pain in his back, Deke stood balancing himself upright with one hand on the open trunk of the Fury. Lecto packed his knives and portable pumps and stowed them in a space much larger inside than out—just like Bull House.

When he was done with his equipment, Lecto hefted a green and taupe Little Oscar cooler. "Twenty grand on the black market, friend," he said, tapping the cooler before he set it in the trunk. "Be glad you came in without me taking the late penalty."

Lecto pried Deke's hand from the trunk lid, slammed it shut, and gently propelled Deke by the shoulder to the passenger side. The open door banged into the mirrored panel next to it as Deke slipped in. Lecto popped back around to the other side. "Buckle up."

"Thanks," mumbled Deke. A quadruple set of mirrored panels sat right in front of the car, reflecting chrome brightwork, the long black hood and Deke's bleary, pale face filtered through the windshield. "We going to see Torres now?"

"You paid the price, you get to take the ride." Lecto started the car. As the big motor growled to life, the mirrored panels in front of him slid away. Lecto thumbed the pushbutton transmission and the car glided across the drumhead floor through a flying forest of mirrors.

"How the hell do you do this?" asked Deke, trying to distract himself from the pain.

"How do you breathe?" The big Greek grinned as he thumbed the power windows down. "Don't worry, it's a real short ride from here."

The last wall of mirrors unfolded like an accordion, and the big Fury rolled to a stop in a huge amphitheater. The sound of the tires had changed, and Deke realized they were now on sand. Seats rose around them in all directions, like giant steps of the same dry stonework as the outer walls, so clean they gleamed. For a brief moment, Deke thought they were empty of everything but shadows, until he realized the glimmer he saw was an audience of a thousand glass women. His beloved, multiplied like summer locusts until she was but a glass splinter lost in a sugar bowl. Glass shards fountained at the feet of the seated women, making the stairways between the benches gleam like the Milky Way.

"Oh, Hades," muttered Deke.

"Here you are, friend." Lecto shut off the car, got out his door. He leaned in the open driver's side window. "Love's not a bad excuse. Now make it pay off." Lecto walked across the arena, vaulted the eight-foot wall that marked the lower end of the seating and found his way to the dais at the center opposite the opening through which they had driven.

Aria's foot clutched in his hand, Deke stumbled out to his feet. He looked behind the car. The panels were closed again. This time they showed his life, in relief, from his birth in the slums of Concrete Town through his scholarship years in preparatory school and his work as an apprentice armorer. The last panel showed his fight with Aria, rubies standing in copiously for the blood her broken heart had shed.

He realized the sand beneath his feet was broken glass, fed by the shattered rivers descending from the ranks of amphitheater seating. It was already to his ankles. At least he was wearing Doc Martens.

Now what, Deke thought. He'd trusted Lecto. That had worked, after a fashion. Somewhere around him was Aria, but his next task to was to think horns. That's what Sandy the telephone psychic had said. Where in Hades were the horns?

A trumpet brayed from the dais. Deke looked up to see a woman in motorcycle leathers standing with one booted foot on the stone coping. She stared down at him, eyes narrowed. Even from this distance, her face was a mirror of Aria's, the one his beloved had worn in the flesh.

"Deke Zeiss," she called in a voice like brass ringing on stone. "Your debt to the Bull Market Syndicate is discharged. Why stand you here now?"

"To pay my respects and to seek a boon," he called back. The sick pain in his back caused his voice to break.

"It is no respect to invade the heart of my house in anger."

The glass was up past his ankles. Deke wondered what would happen when it topped his boots. One hand on the car, he stepped forward, trying to find footing on the sparkling drifts. His voice seemed to be coming back. "Respect is given as it is earned, Minnie Torres. I have come for Aria Minnows, my beloved."

Torres jumped up onto the railing, feet spread wide. "You hold no contract on her. When her heart shattered, my daughter came home as she should have."

Her daughter. He caught his breath. Of course that had to be true, the mysterious Troezen aristocracy a disguise for her Concrete Town roots, but that realization simply multiplied his love. "It was my error," he called, raising the ragged flesh of her foot high. "I would make my offense up to her and win her back."

Torres laughed, voice still brassy as the blatting of the trumpet that had introduced her. "No man should see all the way inside a woman's heart. Go back across the bay and make love to a waitress. You will forget."

Horns, thought Deke. Her voice? "I challenge you to deliver her to me."

"Ha." The single syllable echoed from a thousand glass lips. Lecto handed Torres a massive mask, a bull's head. Even from across the arena, Deke could see that it was a brass frame covered in lapped scales and stretched hide. Two brass horns stuck out above it, their tips winking in the subdued light of the amphitheater like distant fire. "On your head it will be," she said.

Minnie Torres donned the mask and jumped the eight feet down into the ground glass of the arena. Deke bent to sweep up a handful of the stuff, shredding his fingertips as his lower back signaled hot, debilitating pain. While Minnie Torres stalked across the sea of glass, he gingerly pulled himself up on the hood of Lecto's Fury. On the dais, Lecto winced as the car's metal popped under Deke's weight. Deke hoped the dents would come out easily.

The bull mask became a part of Minnie Torres, growing into her neck and taking on life, joining with the leathers on her body that protected her from the shattered glass across which she bounded. Torres approached the black Fury as Deke crouched on the hood. He wouldn't get two chances with her, he knew. Speed, luck and remember the horns.

Torres' eyes rolled in the sides of that huge, furred head, the same crystal clear that Aria's had been before she'd returned to the glass from which she had sprung, but each eye was now as large as Deke's fist. Foot in one hand, glass in the other, he waited until she leapt, then swept the glass toward her left eye. The hit was lucky and true, his palm grinding the glass into Torres' eye even as his left slapped her other eye with her daughter's skin.

The bull's snout slammed into his chest, knocking him against the windshield of the Plymouth with a sickening crunch of glass and ribs and breath-stealing pain from his aching sutures. Fighting not to black out, Deke kept a hold on the bull with his right hand even as his left hand scrambled frantically for purchase. Deke lunged into the pain and grabbed the bull's left horn, yanking it free.

Torres bellowed, rolling off him into the glass. Deke pulled himself to his knees, vomiting blood, and hurled the brass horn at her. It caught her point-first in the neck, at the fold of leathery skin where the mask melded with the motorcycle leathers. Torres shrieked, staggered to her feet to spin around before collapsing back to her knees, a mirror of the pose Deke now held only by main force of will.

Had it been enough? He sighed, every glass woman in the amphitheater sighing with him. The cell phone at his belt rang, "Heart of Glass" tootling. Deke grabbed the phone with a bloody hand, then looked up again to see the bull mask rattling on a sandy floor above an empty pile of motorcycle leathers. One boot quivered upright. There was no more glass.

"Hello?"

"Told you so," the voice of Sandy Priam replied. "You didn't believe me."

"I'm alive," he whispered.

"What about love?"

He remembered Lecto's words. "A good excuse."

Lecto began to clap from his place up on the dais, the sound ringing across the empty arena. "Sorry," Deke said. "Got to go now."

"That's what guys always tell me."

Sandy hung up before he did.

Deke slid off the hood and stumbled toward Lecto, barely on his feet. His torso felt ready to collapse like Minnie Torres' motorcycle leathers. He stopped in front of the dais, tilting his head back to look up. He nearly passed out from the shift in blood pressure. Deke waved the rags of Aria's foot in his left hand.

"I have come for my beloved," he announced. "Let the glass women step forward that I may check the fit of their feet."

Lecto smiled down at him, then vaulted to the floor. He had a camp stool folded under one arm. "This may take a while, friend. Sit here, I'll get you a saline drip and stimulants from the car. Some glucose, too."

Deke found himself surrounded by glass women, a multitude of identical perfect breasts and arched lips through which he could see himself a thousand times. Each heart had become a mirror. Each foot would be the same as the next.

"Oh, crap," he moaned.

Lecto kept a hand on Deke's shoulder, propping him up as the glass women approached one by one. The I.V. drip hurt, a grace note in his symphony of pain. Each woman smiled, shook her head, and left. A few reached out to touch the ragged, worn foot, as if to test its reality. He lost count after forty-three, but there were hundreds of them. As each departed, he watched those perfect buttocks flex just as they had in the Ball Glass Diner. Lecto didn't say anything, just passed him a cup of water from time to time and checked on the intravenous fluids.

Deke sat there for what felt like hours, until the final woman approached. Something in her walk, something in her stance, told him she was the one. Candlelight flared in his mind to the remembered smell of curry.

"Aria," he whispered.

She showed him her left hand, the knuckles scarred from his diamond. "Deke. I'm surprised at you."

"The power of love." His grin felt crooked and weak.

"There's more than love in the world," she said. Her voice sounded sad.

Mute, he held out the ragged foot. She took it, rubbed it between her fingers. They both watched the ribbons of skin and flesh flutter to the floor.

"More than love, there's destiny," said Aria. "Someone has to take Mother's place. I had a ball with you, while it lasted, but this is an opportunity I can't walk away from." She smiled slightly. "Besides, while I wear the mask, no one will ever break my heart again."

She walked over to the mask and leathers. Aria screwed the loose brass horn back onto the bull's head, then set it aside to don the motorcycle gear. Amid the pile was a second mask, of flesh, delicate black ribbons at each ear to tie it together. She came back to him, clad in black, the flesh mask in one hand, the other arm up past the elbow inside the bull mask to balance it.

"All this, for what?" asked Deke. His heart was breaking, merely an ache of the soul, as unlike Aria he had no glass to shed. Had he ever really loved her, or was she just a symbol of his hopes and dreams? Beautiful, wealthy, experienced, everything a Concrete Town boy could never be.

"Go home," said Aria. He could still love those transparent lips, those clear, clear eyes. "Mess up some other woman's life. It's what men do. If we could see where it ended, no woman would ever fall in love."

Lecto handed her the Little Oscar cooler with Deke's right kidney in it. Aria, now Minnie Torres in place of her mother, took it in the hand that already held the flesh mask. She turned to walk across the arena. As she reached the wooden doors, the panels with the story of his life on them, she turned back. "Free advice, Deke. Don't mortgage any more kidneys."

He watched her go, then turned to Lecto, who was unhooking the I.V. stand. "Now what do I do?"

"You need a ride somewhere?"

"I don't think I could walk out of this chair," said Deke. He'd had it with ambition, big plans. All he wanted now was a quiet, normal life.

"Then it's Troezen Baptist E.R. for you, I'd say." The big Greek grinned. "I'll get the car."

Deke pulled his cell phone out again. Sandy's number was still on the caller I.D. He thought about it until the big Chrysler started up, then thumbed the talk button.

Sandy Priam was a frightened woman who knew too much. Deke Zeiss was a scarred man who knew enough. The first time they made love, she told him she could see the end of their days together. He told her he'd already seen the end and it didn't matter. They found love without the metaphors, moved to a farm on the island of Naxos in the middle of the iron waters of Aegeus Bay and lived happily ever a while.

The Murasaki Doctrine

The Murasaki Doctrine

I: THE DAY THE SKY FELL

Commander Wanda Murasaki walked out of Government House in Katyn as man-sized insects dropped out of Nowa Gdansk's mauve skies, heavily armed and firing as they fell.

No ships, no shuttles. Just a rain of alien attackers out of nowhere, praying mantises with energy weapons.

The details of the training budget meeting she'd just attended fled her attention like sparrows before a shrike. Murasaki, a compact second-generation Polish-Japanese, snap-drew her flechette pistol and went to ground in a ceremonial bed of Terran roses. She ignored the thorns that plucked at her dress uniform and slashed her skin.

"Damn, damn, damn," she said. Two centuries of human experience in space without a whisper of other intelligent life, and this had to happen *here*? Now?

One of the aliens landed less than five meters in front of her, facing away. It carried a squared-off sword like an oversized machete, and a long, narrow rifle winking with violet status lights.

The alien resembled an enormous praying mantis. Large hind legs, fibrous like smoothly bundled straw, bent at a knee two meters high. Stick-like secondary legs were set forward on the long, bean-pod body. A pack obscured most of the alien's back, and the head appeared to be enclosed in a combat helmet. It had two arms on the side she could see, matching the legs. The lower arm was a nubby chitin stick like the forward legs, the upper a bundle of narrow fibers sort of like a sheaf of wheat.

The huge hind legs twitched as the alien popped straight up about eight meters, rotating in the air to land less than a meter away from her, facing the door. It fired the rifle through the glass into the ground floor of Government House, a dazzling eruption of energy that nearly blinded Murasaki.

Even through the ringing in her ears, she heard screaming inside the building as she fired a package of tapered carbon nanotubes into the body joint of the massive hind leg closest to her. Tan fibers streamed away from the leg like straw in the wind. The alien toppled toward her as its severed leg fell away.

Mandy Rice, the receptionist, Murasaki thought, as screams continued. The young woman had offered Murasaki homemade mint candies this morning. With a stab of guilt, Murasaki crabbed deeper into the massive stand of rose canes, away from her friends and colleagues, and sent another shot into the base of the blank-faced helmet.

The head flew off like a football on a penalty kick, drenching Murasaki with honey-colored fluid. The alien corpse sagged over her, braced to a halt by the rose canes to dangle just above.

More shouts and screams from inside the building. *Lieutenant Goff, the boy-genius of logistics.* Ignoring the ichor, which stank of soured compost, Murasaki tried to angle her body so she could cover the walkways in front of Government House. Maybe she could stop some of the invaders, give people inside time to escape. Or at least take up arms in defense.

She found herself trapped by the roses' thorns as four more aliens approached. A flash of claustrophobia overcame her. Her vision reddened, pulse pounding, as she fought the sensation. Murasaki yanked her arm free at the cost of her uniform sleeve and considerable blood.

Public Order Minister Mochizuki, with his devotion to tea and ceremony and his copper-colored hair. So many people inside, friends and adversaries alike, screaming as windows shattered in the four floors above and behind her and smoke poured out. Could she save any of them? She didn't even think she could save herself.

Murasaki checked the charge on the flechette pistol and prepared to die, but the aliens raced past her rose bushes to burst through the shattered doors, storming the building with rifles blazing. She stopped herself from loosing a useless burst after them. Tensing her legs to spring out of the bushes, Murasaki's tactical sense got the better of her.

Wait. Watch. One woman alone can't stop a wave attack. Murasaki wondered why they didn't seem to notice her.

She ached to chase the aliens into Government House and hunt them even as they hunted the bureaucrats that ran her world, but there was no point. Another dozen aliens had hustled into the building after the first four, completely ignoring both their dead comrade and Murasaki cowering behind the corpse. She could hardly pursue them waving a flechette pistol and continue to be ignored.

Call for help, Wanda. They can't be everywhere. But oh, they could.

"Paging Public Order Control," Murasaki whispered into the throat mike sewn into her uniform collar. Control was located in a series of bunkers about a kilometer away. Safely outside of Government House. "Come in, Control."

Her ear bud crackled to life. "Get off this line, damn it," someone snapped. She heard crashing in the background.

"Commander Murasaki here, Control," Murasaki snapped in her best infantry training commandant tone. "Give me a ten-second situation report."

"Sorry, ma'am." The comm controller didn't sound sorry. He sounded panicked. "Sitrep is we're about to die here. They've hit everything! Only the shuttle por—"

Her ear bud popped, then fell silent. A few seconds later, Murasaki felt a rumble in the dirt beneath her. She did the math on the time delay. So much for Public Order Control. She'd never felt so helpless.

The answer to that was to move, move fast, figure out what was going on, and find a way to hit back. This was her job, training herself and others for the unexpected all her uniformed life. Time to do it.

Murasaki considered trying to get back to the infantry school she commanded, but with no classes scheduled for two months, the entire cadre was scattered save for a few maintenance details and the gate guards. No help there, just a hiding place. Besides, Teutoburgerwald was three hundred kilometers north of Katyn. Right now, it might as well be in orbit.

Orbit.

Control's last words had been about the port. "Shuttle port it is," Murasaki whispered.

The battle at Government House was lost. Her first duty was to survive and fight another day. Her second was to contact the remaining chain of command. Other considerations would have to wait. Other people's deaths would have to be honored later.

Trailing alien ichor, Murasaki tore her way free from the rose bushes and scuttled toward the cover of a line of decorative native mold-walls. Behind her, distant screams alternated with the sizzling crack of alien weapons as Government House died, along with all the people sheltering within its granite walls.

She didn't look back. She couldn't.

Murasaki loped down Landing Road in front of two- and three-storey granite buildings, mostly offices and artsy *ateliers* mixed with a few retail outlets. She stayed among a crowd of fleeing citizens, keeping her flechette pistol down low. What the hell was going on? How could this have happened? She was desperate to get to the shuttle port. The city was falling, and she couldn't stop it.

A few of the refugees eyed her sopping, sticky uniform suspiciously, but no one turned on her. The planet of Nowa Gdansk had a tiny military component within its Public Order infrastructure, mostly dedicated to disaster management and putting down the occasional tax revolt, so it was quite possible that many of these people didn't realize she was an officer.

Aliens hopped by in the other direction, more like grasshoppers than praying mantises as they soared down the middle of the road five or six meters in the air, covering twenty meters with each bound. They didn't seem interested in the fleeing crowd, other than casual decapitations of people who strayed too close to their line of advance. Rather, the invaders headed toward downtown Katyn.

With no one at the other end of her comm link, Murasaki could only guess at who was fighting, but the most likely source of weapons was the police barracks behind the Grand Odeon. She ignored the smashed heads littering the center of the road and the crying relatives who darted out to retrieve the bodies. She couldn't stop for these people, not right now.

The refugees streamed to the right onto Gas Well Parkway, one of the main routes into the wide farmlands of the Katyn Plains. Murasaki angled through the crowd to continue southeast toward the shuttle port. In the distance a bulk shuttle thundered into the sky.

Past Gas Well Parkway, she covered another kilometer toward the shuttle port without seeing anyone else, human or alien. Murasaki finally stopped by a comm tower to cool down from her running and allow her adrenaline rush to taper off. As she stood breathing deeply, Murasaki heard a thump behind her, followed by a gentle rustling.

She turned slowly to find three aliens standing side-by-side about a meter behind her. All three blank, rounded heads faced her. Their rifles were slung across their backs, but they had their machete-swords in their fibrous power arms. Murasaki's fingers twitched on the grip of her flechette pistol, but she was reluctant to make a sudden move. Fighting the same terror that had washed over her while trapped in the rosebush, she studied the giant bugs.

The smooth heads were blind helmets the size of beach balls. They had a different, duller texture than the glossy chitin of the bean pod-bodies, almost looking as if they had been cast from bronze. Tiny holes flexed open and shut in an arc across the lower portion of the helmet, a child's drawing of a smile. Murasaki doubted they were breathing—her Service Academy xenobio courses had concentrated on Gdansku plant life, but even she knew that insects generally didn't have lungs.

One of the bugs leaned toward her with an unnaturally smooth motion like a hydraulic arm. Murasaki stilled her breathing as the head nearly brushed her face, then sniffed down her ichor-covered uniform. The stuff had crusted dry, but still reeked of compost. She carefully tilted the ceramic bell of her flechette pistol upward, preparing to shoot the alien's neck joint.

As smoothly as it had approached her, the head swung back. Power legs clicking as they leapt, the alien soared away, followed by a second. Murasaki's heart pounded. She might live. They worked by smell, some scent markers of their own that masked her fear enough to keep her alive. For now.

The third sank, gathering itself to leap, then changed its mind. It took a half step forward on its stick legs, came in for a sniff of its own.

"No, no, big boy," Murasaki whispered as the blank ball of the alien's head slid down her chest. It pressed briefly into her breasts before pulling back perhaps thirty centimeters. She could see her broad face, widened further by the reflection in the metallic helmet.

When the blunt tip of the machete-sword poked her chest, Murasaki pulled the trigger of her flechette pistol. Metal shards from the alien's helmet slashed deep into her nose, but the blood flow was immediately dammed by the fresh flood of ichor on her face and upper body.

Finally free to sob out her fear, she resumed her sprint toward the shuttle port. She thanked all the saints and martyrs that the other two aliens hadn't turned back to check on the one she killed.

When she arrived, the gates stood wide, an open-bodied electric ramp buggy on its side next to the smoking guard shack. No one was in sight, but alarms whooped out on the ramp. In the distance, Murasaki could see another bulk shuttle on gantry three, and two free-flight shuttles parked on the hardstand. Lances of light exploded around the base of the bulk shuttle.

At least she knew where the fighting was.

Check the phone, she thought. Posted as commandant of Nowa Gdansk's infantry training school at Teutoburgerwald, Murasaki fell outside the tactical chain of command. She could call the Gdansku Force Base Prime north of town and deliver her sitrep, get whatever intelligence was to be had.

She stepped into the damaged guard shack. No bodies in evidence, but the phone looked intact. She tapped out the duty number at Base Prime. The phone clicked a few times, then bleated a busy signal before the line went dead.

To hell with it. She'd already been standing still too long. Back outside, Murasaki inspected the ramp buggy. All four tires were still inflated, and it looked undamaged other than the scorched, bloody seat. No bodies out here either, although there was plenty of blood in evidence. Were the aliens opportunistic carnivores?

Murasaki grabbed the base of the body tub along the bottom of the passenger door well. She tugged, trying to right the buggy. The body groaned, but it barely shifted. She pressed her legs against the floor pan, hanging off the upended base of the machine like a child at the playground.

The buggy slipped toward her, and Murasaki jumped free, barely avoiding having her knees caught by the descending vehicle as it crashed to the ground. She landed on her elbows on the gravel. Wincing through the pain, she got up and climbed into the buggy, ignoring the blood on the seat.

Taking stock of herself, Murasaki realized she was coated with two layers of ichor. The aliens' body fluids seemed to mask her scent, so she left the congealing crust alone, even where it irritated the skin of her face. Murasaki drove through the open gates, and along the perimeter road, trying to get near one of the free-flight shuttles.

Passing behind the Polskie Linje warehouse, Murasaki's buggy was struck by two bullets. Somebody was showing resistance. She swerved straight into the line of fire and accelerated toward the building, shouting, "Don't shoot, idiots!"

Someone cursed audibly, then a door slammed open. A bearded man waved her inside. Murasaki slewed the ramp buggy to a halt, grabbed her pistol, and dashed into the building.

Inside a small waiting room, complete with ragged chairs, a grubby coffee maker and yellowed notices tacked to fiberboard walls, two men in blue ramp service coveralls covered her. One had a hunting rifle, the other an enormously long wrench.

"Who the hell are you?" demanded the rifle holder. He had dirty blond hair and a desperate look. The bearded man had the wrench, and maybe a sense of humor judging by the quirk of his smile.

"Do I look like a bug?"

"You're awfully sticky," the bearded man said to her. He shook his head and laughed. "Invasion's not even an hour old and we're already shooting at each other. How are we going to get out of this one?"

Murasaki slumped onto one of the chairs. "Only an hour. *Jezus, Maria z Jozef*, I feel like I've been running all day."

"Where from?" asked Rifle. His flat gray eyes darted as if aliens would spring out from behind her.

"Government House," said Murasaki. "I've already killed two of them up close and personal." She smeared a hand along the sticky, golden mess on her chest. "That's why I look this way. I haven't wiped it off because they seem to have trouble finding me while I'm covered in this gunk."

The two men exchanged glances. "They're hard to kill," said Rifle. "Plus that's a long way to come on foot in an hour."

"Hard to kill from a distance, maybe." Murasaki considered the tactical issues of shooting the aliens. "They've got decent armor, narrow profile bodies and not much for soft spots. I shot one up close in the big leg joint, and the other in the chin." She smiled for the first time since the world had ended. "Or whatever you call the base of their head."

Rifle clearly didn't believe her. "You got near enough to shoot one in the head? I don't trust anyone right now, lady. Not even myself, and especially not you."

Murasaki scooped some ichor off her chest and flicked it at him. "How do you think I got this *gówno* on me? Rolling in bugs? Don't trust me, trust this stuff. Now, tell me what's happening out on the ramp."

She needed a shuttle. Katyn was a killing field. If orbital space was a hot zone, at least the free-flight shuttles could ditch on any body of water or level land. But Murasaki was willing to bet she'd find breathing room upstairs. These bugs seemed awfully light on equipment and support.

"You a pilot?" asked Rifle.

She stuck out her hand to shake. "Commander Wanda Murasaki, atmosphere flight rated." She didn't mention her quals were six years out of date. One of the perils of infantry command amid perennially tight budgets — no flight hours allocated.

"Bart Williamson," said Beard, shaking her hand. "Cargo handler. Looking for a way out of this place. Nervous over here's my boss, Super Smitts."

"Super?" Wanda cocked an eyebrow.

Smitts blushed. "Short for 'supercargo.'"

"History," said Williamson. "But right now there's bugs hunting people outside. They don't control the field yet. We think they're trying not to smash stuff up too bad."

"So they care about launch capabilities," said Murasaki. "How do we get out there without being nailed?"

"We've got a Crash Rescue Engine in here," said Smitts. "Sucker's hardened against hydrogen slurry fires. It should take a little bug punishment. But neither of us knows how to fly once we get the CRE out on the field."

"You're right, *that* ought to stand up to a few whacks from those bug zap rifles." Murasaki grinned. "Show me the toy, boys, and let's go flying."

Even surrounded by shipping canisters in the vast cavern of the main warehouse, the CRE was huge. It was based on a hardened version of a TrägerFabrik-Mars twenty-ton chassis, the same platform Public Order used for backcountry road surveying and trailblazing.

The CRE sat on four independent axles with three-meter solid tires, piezotraction motors embedded in the wheel hubs. Bright green armored sides towered at an eighteen-degree pitch from the wheels to a five-meter height, concealing fire suppressant storage tanks. Three turrets housing pressurized water cannon were spaced along the spine of the vehicle, with operator cabs at each end.

"They'll know we're coming," said Murasaki. "Even a blind bug couldn't miss that. What's in the tanks?"

"Nothing," replied Smitts. "Not in commission yet. That's why it's here instead of out at Field Operations."

"What liquids do you have on hand?"

Williamson sniffed her again. "Well, you smell like bad compost."

She eyed him narrowly. "Your point?"

"We've got bowsers of 10-50-10 liquid fertilizer for transshipment to Westerly Continent."

"Ah…" said Murasaki. "Mess up their olfactory signals. You're smarter than you look, Williamson."

Smitts glared at both of them. "Got some anhydrous ammonia on the same manifest. Get that in another tank, we can burn the nostrils right out of those blank little heads."

Murasaki finally holstered her flechette pistol. "Show me the hoses."

Twenty minutes later they had pumped in three hundred liters of fertilizer and two hundred and forty liters of ammonia.

"Enough," said Murasaki. "It'll work or it won't. More isn't going to help." She rubbed dried ichor between her fingers, which crumbled away in little sticky sheets like rubber cement, and remembered the screaming inside Government House.

"I'll drive," said Smitts. "You two take the cannons."

Entering through a hatch behind the operator's cab, Murasaki climbed into the forward cannon turret's cupola. She had to cram herself into a shoulder-braced firing system that made her feel like she would be spitting ammonia from her fingertips. Her utility belt and holster didn't fit in the operator's chair, so reluctantly she removed them, hanging them from one of the cannon's support braces.

Murasaki thought something the size of a twenty-ton TrägerFabrik ought to rumble like the wrath of God, but the fusion lattices were as quiet as the wind. The tires growled as Smitts accelerated the vehicle. The truly satisfying noise came when the CRE rammed through the enormous cargo doors at the east end of the warehouse, barreling out onto the ramp with the inevitability of a bright green landslide.

Outside, a fire had broken out on gantry three where the bulk shuttle still stood. Murasaki could see bugs and men shooting at one another all through the superstructure.

"Funny," she said into the vehicle intercom, "If I was knocking this place over, I'd have brought air support and armor. Nothing but individual bugs, even here." *Where were their ships?*

Williamson's voice crackled back via the intercom in the central turret. "Maybe they don't think too much of our shuttle port."

"Maybe. Still, I don't know why you'd invade an entire planet with nothing but infantry. If the bugs had heavy gear, it would be deployed here at Katyn where all the important targets are."

Breaking away from the gantry fight, a trio of the bugs hopped toward the CRE, clearing twenty meters with every bound.

"Looks like they *are* their own air support," said Smitts. "Cannons ready, people."

At the press of a foot pedal, Murasaki's turret swung around with a gentle whine. She dialed up maximum pressure and estimated a towering arc to intersect the approaching aliens on the downsplash.

The cupola rumbled as high-pressure pumps sent anhydrous ammonia shooting through the air. Williamson's shot of liquid fertilizer followed. His was too far to the right, but Murasaki got a target dead on. Ammonia splashed across the bug, which immediately spasmed, missing its landing to tumble across the concrete ramp like so many spare parts loosely wired together.

The other two bugs bounced and soared again. "Nice shooting, Tex," said Williamson. "Looks like they don't care much for ammonia."

She laughed, caught up in the moment. "You'd go down too, if I shot twenty liters of that stuff up your nose."

On the next bound of the bugs, he connected while she missed. The fertilizer didn't have the same dramatic effect as the ammonia, but it confused the bug, which bounced off in a random direction, legs flailing.

They both missed the third bug on its next bounce, the two streams intersecting to create an amorphous spray. The bug landed on top of the CRE, where it spun around once, getting its bearings. It stood between her cupola and Williamson's.

Murasaki popped the emergency release and scrambled out. Smitts had the CRE going a good speed toward the free-flight shuttles and the headwind was strong, so her footing was poor. Drawing its machete sword, the bug turned toward her. Behind the alien, Williamson popped his dome and climbed out, dragging his enormous wrench after him.

Reaching to draw her flechette pistol, Murasaki realized it was hanging inside her turret. "*Piekło*," she cursed in Polish, as the bug sidled toward her.

Further back, Williamson grinned maniacally as he hefted the wrench and stalked the bug. Williamson lacked her protective coating of bug ichor, but he was to the rear of the CRE, downwind of the bug, so it shouldn't smell him. All Murasaki had to do was live through one, maybe two strikes of that machete-sword before Williamson got close enough to take the alien out.

"That's simple, Wanda," she told herself. "You're Nowa Gdansk's leading living expert on close combat with the bugs." At least for another few seconds, as far as the 'living' part went.

The bug's blank helmet flickered its smiley-faced nostrils at her as the fibrous power arms raised the machete sword into a strike position. Murasaki crouched, waiting for the eye-blurring swing.

It shifted its weight on the stick legs and attacked. She stepped into the arc of the sword, then did a standing jump with a forward roll to slam shoulders-down on the skid plate, heading for the angled side of the CRE.

On the backswing the machete sword took the tip off her right boot, and by the feel of things, parts of her toes, too. Murasaki slammed into the grab handles lining the roof of the CRE and reversed direction, flipping her body sideways until she was under the bug.

It flexed its neck almost a hundred and eighty degrees to look underneath itself. Murasaki could see her own face reflected in the bowl of the helmet, Williamson's beyond her also reflected but inverted by the helmet's curvature. The smiley-faced nostrils flickered as the bug spun on one of its power legs, using a great push from the other to generate kick-off momentum.

All four forearms brought the machete-sword right into Williamson's chest as he slammed the wrench into the base of the helmet. His head, shoulders and left arm flew off one side of the CRE. The bug's head bounced the other way.

"Bart!" she shrieked, scuttling away from the collapsing bug. It tumbled over the side, leaving the machete-sword behind. Williamson's lungs stared at her like two scar-blinded sockets from the sheared-off stump of his torso as his blood flooded the skid plate to mix with the rotten honey from the bug.

Eyes stinging, she scrambled back into the cupola. The best memorial she could give Williamson was to survive a while longer. Murasaki damned herself for leaving the pistol behind, anger fighting off the stupid, meaningless tears for a man she'd known all of half an hour.

She slipped the intercom headset back on to hear Smitts. "Cupola one, cupola two, someone please copy me. Clear."

He sounded desperate even before she had told him what happened.

Less than two minutes later, with a bone-rattling shudder the CRE ground to a halt near one of the free-flight shuttles. Murasaki slipped down to the operator's cab as Smitts bailed out with his hunting rifle in hand.

The crew hatch of the shuttle stood open, spindly aluminum stairs down, but no one was around. No bugs, no people. Flechette pistol at the ready, Murasaki turned to cover the approach from the distant heavy lift gantries and the remaining bulk shuttle.

The fire was fully involved over there, bugs hopping around like moths at a flame. The tanks on the shuttle would cook off soon. Murasaki hoped like hell no humans were still trying to defend it.

She and Smitts glanced at each other. He shrugged, face puffy and red. "Clear as it's going to get."

Smitts leading, they sprinted toward the open crew hatch. As soon as Murasaki cleared the coaming, he slapped the lockdown. They squeezed through the tiny airlock into the cabin.

Three people huddled together at the back, crying, or maybe praying. They all wore ramp service coveralls like Smitts and Williamson, with ground support insignia.

"Belt in," Murasaki yelled. "We're lifting out *natychmiast*." Immediately.

Two men and a woman stared back. "We're going to die," one of the men shrieked.

"Too late to get off, Borges," snapped Smitts. "Hatch is sealed. Now sit down before I make you." He swung the rifle into a hipshooting stance.

Murasaki set a hand on Smitts' elbow. "Super, take it easy. Things aren't good for anyone today."

He blinked away tears. "Bart and I were lifemates, Commander. He didn't die out there so I could worry about a bunch of whining God-botherers with a suicide complex sitting behind me."

No, thought Murasaki, *he died out there because I came to a gunfight without my pistol.* What else could she have done better today? At least she was still alive. "Leave them," she said. "We've got places to go."

Smitts took a deep breath. "All right," he yelled down the length of the cabin. "Borges, Wolachek, Morgan, buckle up if you like your bones intact. We're pulling gees on no notice." He lowered the rifle. "Stay the hell out of our way."

Murasaki ducked into the cockpit and dropped herself into the left seat. She stuffed the flechette pistol between the upholstery and her thigh, then set about getting the free-flight shuttle's systems warmed up. Smitts manually bolted the cockpit hatch before taking the co-pilot's position.

"Is there an AI on board?" Murasaki asked.

"Subintelligent autonomous processor support is available," the shuttle announced.

"Process this," said Murasaki. "I want the fastest possible hot start for take-off, ignoring all stop-checks except for critical and supercritical fault management."

"Port Authority override is required for safety-off hot starts," the shuttle said primly.

Murasaki looked at Smitts. He shrugged, then pulled a laminated card from the pocket of his coveralls. "Cargo section clearance delta one, code Rostov Tehran forty-seven Stockholm," Smitts read off.

"Override accepted. Hot start in one hundred and thirty-one seconds. Do you require automated rollout?"

"Manual," said Murasaki. She studied the ramp through the tinted windscreen of the shuttle. The bulk shuttle was still at its gantry. It hadn't cooked off, it hadn't lifted, and the fire still burned, pushing dark, speckled smoke high into the air. Someone must have spilled a considerable amount of fuel from the pumping systems to keep those flames going this long.

Then she realized the specks in the smoke were a whole flight of bugs heading toward their free-flight shuttle.

Murasaki manually released the wheel brakes and checked the flaps.

"One hundred seventeen seconds until hot start," complained the shuttle.

"I want taxi power now."

"Outside parameters. That will delay hot start by eighteen seconds and unnecessarily degrade engine linings."

She set her hand on the engine power lever. "Release taxi power to me or I'll dump your processor core and spool the engines up myself."

The shuttle beeped acquiescence and Murasaki watched the power lever ease downward on servocontrol. Smitts shook his head as the free-flight shuttle shuddered, then began to roll. Murasaki pointed them right at the approaching bugs.

"Aren't you heading into their weapons?" he asked.

"If we angle away from them, we'll give them a better shot at us."

"You're also heading for the fire."

"This ramp is huge. I can take off in any direction. The fire might discourage our little bug buddies." Murasaki laughed. "I don't think ground control's going to be on us about ramp traffic rules today." She studied the advancing bugs for a moment. "Faster, shuttle, we're sitting ducks out here."

The free-flight shuttle shuddered as it picked up speed. "Now exceeding regulated taxi speed," the shuttle complained as series of alarms began to beep. "Ninety-four seconds to hot start. Engine power curves building outside maximum rated tolerances for this phase of start-up."

"Kill the alarms," Murasaki ordered, "and release all groundspeed control to me." She cranked the power up further. Backlit by the gantry fire, the bugs bounced toward them, becoming larger by the second. It was a giant game of chicken, her big metalloceramic bird racing toward dozens of would-be tormentors.

The first bolts from the alien rifles licked toward them, some of the bugs firing in mid-leap. Smitts ducked as one bolt washed across the shuttle nose.

"This ship's designed for atmospheric re-entry," said Murasaki. "A little hot plasma won't do much. I wouldn't care for our chances under concentrated fire, but so far the bugs haven't shown that kind of discipline."

She juiced the speed up further just as the first wave of bugs leaped in front of them. The shuttle's voice complained again about engine degradation as two bugs hit the nose, while a third slammed directly into the windshield.

"Shit!" Smitts shrieked as the goo and chitin winnowed away in the wind of their passage. "What if they nail the windscreen up close with that plasma fire?"

Murasaki felt her lips twist back from her teeth, the ugly snarl of an angry dog. "Then we're probably toast."

"Sixty-one seconds to hot start," said the shuttle. The electronic voice was becoming snippy. "You are endangering take-off by overpowering the taxi process."

The shuttle shuddered as they hit two more bugs. The rest leaped off to each side, out of their sight. Murasaki aimed for the burning gantry. Ahead of her, the engines of the bulk shuttle ignited, vapor clouds billowing into the flames. Murasaki's free-flight shuttle bounced up and down, struggling to become airborne. She checked that the ship's systems had the flaps trimmed down tight.

In front of them, the bulk shuttle lifted about twenty meters, then exploded. Murasaki steered just to the left of the center of the fireball, slamming the power selector all the way down. Something banged under their feet, an overclouded pump blowing out deep in the guts of their shuttle, as Murasaki yanked the flaps up well ahead of the hot start ready point.

The free-flight shuttle hopped into the expanding fireball, slammed sideways under the turbulence, then lifted to break free above it. Visual alarms blinked all over the control boards like fireworks as Murasaki fought a sickening plunge toward the ground, converting the motion to a tight roll. Recovering, she slammed the yoke to the left, banking low over the ramp to see bugs still scattering from the explosion. Then she leveled off.

"Shuttle, plot us an insertion to Gdansk Orbital Port."

"Engines have lost twenty-one percent operational efficiency due to your aggressive negligence," said the shuttle. "My systems have sustained estimated one hundred and eighty thousand zlotys of damage. Your license is automatically suspended. Please report yourself to the Port Authority for a disciplinary hearing as soon as possible."

Banking the shuttle slightly, Murasaki glanced down as they soared into the clouds over the burning city of Katyn. "Let's hope there will still be a Port Authority to turn myself into," she said.

Smitts craned his neck to look past Murasaki at the city. "You did good, ma'am." He smiled. "Thank you."

She tried to use the shuttle's comm to call Gdansku Force Base Prime again, just in case, but no connections could be made to the Katyn phone system.

Once they'd reached orbit and microgravity, Murasaki unbuckled from the command seat and examined the damage to her right toes. She'd lost a lot of skin and three nails, but the bones seemed to be intact. Smitts touched her elbow. "You might want to get rid of the uniform," he said softly.

"What?" Wanda Murasaki had been in the military since leaving secondary school—she *was* her uniform. It symbolized her job, her role, the rank and commendations markers of her success. "This is…wartime," she stammered, trying to frame her feelings into a sensible objection.

"Either the bugs have taken Orbital Port, in which case the uniform will make you a target; or they haven't and the people there will be in a screaming panic, in which case the uniform will make you a target. Go in as a ramp crew refugee like me or those idiots in the back of the shuttle, meld with the crowd, see what's what, before you flash rank."

"How come you know so much about civil disorder?" she demanded.

Smitts sighed. "I came on the fastship *Marat's Bath*."

That had been the second fastship to arrive at Nowa Gdansk, three years earlier. The first, *Voltaire*, had been a complete surprise, making the seventeen light-year trip from Earth in just under two months to bring news of the FTL breakthrough. Six more slowships laden with colonists and livestock embryos were expected in over the next decade, all of which had left before the announcement that fastships had been developed.

But *Marat's* had been a Dutchman, a cursed ship. New Goan separatists had bribed their way onto the passenger manifest and attempted a mutiny, trying to secure the valuable merchant vessel for their fledgling rebel navy. All but a handful of officers were killed before the working crew and some of the passengers overwhelmed the mutineers, dumping them into the fusion lattices one by one as punishment while the ship continued on to Nowa Gdansk. After the investigations and a few more executions, the fastship had deadheaded back to Earth with a skeleton crew, reportedly headed for recommissioning.

She mouthed an 'oh' of surprise. "You were a colonist?"

"No." He released her elbow, stared out at the glorious curve of Nowa Gdansk, browns and blues and purples. "Merchant marine officer. Supercargo, on a round trip contract. But after the, after everything, I swore I'd never go back into space."

Of course, she thought. The history Williamson had mentioned. That's why he was 'Super.' "And here you are."

"Here I am," he said. "Trust me, lose the uniform. There will be a shipsuit in emergency stores." He glanced at her bloody foot. "It's probably near the med kit."

Cleaned of bug goo and with bandages on her nose and foot, Murasaki sat cross-legged on the ceiling in the passenger section of the shuttle. Her shipsuit was safety orange, devoid of insignia or even her name, with only a shuttle crew patch. Inverted in the ambient microgravity, she and Smitts faced the other three.

"I don't watch the ship movements," said Murasaki. "I have—rather had, a ground-based job. But I need to know what's in orbit." She'd introduced herself to the refugee ground crew as just "Wanda," a name shared by thousands of women within Nowa Gdansk's pre-invasion population of four million. No last name, no rank.

The other three traded glances in a complex shuffle that suggested they'd been planning among themselves.

"According to the port reports, there's nothing in right now," said Smitts into the uncomfortable silence. "The two most recent slowships are parked cold awaiting materials reclamation, but it would take days, maybe weeks to restart them. Then, two decades to send a message home to Earth."

"Fastship's due sometime next month," muttered Wolachek. She was the only woman among the three ground crew. "*Marcus Garvey.*"

Murasaki drummed her fingers on the carpeted ceiling, imparting a slight spin to herself that she automatically corrected with her uninjured left foot. As infantry commandant she'd always gone on zero gee exercises with both the peacekeeper and leadership classes. "We intercept them, turn *Garvey* around with a message for Earth, we could see Colonial Secretariat enforcers, or even Naval ships of the line, here in about six months with luck. Less if those alleged hotships really exist."

Fastships exploited some oddities of physics, fractal loops in the tachyon equations, but while they effected faster-than-light travel, they did it with some fancy tricks in normal Einsteinian space. Physicists were still arguing the point, heatedly. Fastships still took several months to make transit.

Hotships were a rumored true faster-than-light development the home planet military supposedly had up its sleeve, providing near-simultaneous transfers between arbitrarily distant points. At least according to barroom chat and net gossip. Hotships or not, the problem was getting word back to Earth in the first place.

"First alien invasion in human history," said Borges, one of the other ground crew. He was the one who had originally panicked when they boarded. "Earth will respond in force, you know it."

"Secondary plan," Murasaki announced. "We sneak a team onto one of the slowships and they work on starting it. I think *Pulaski* is the newest, least likely to have been stripped to the bare frame. There's enough hydroponics and miscellaneous supplies on board to feed a small group indefinitely, but that trip's a twenty-year commitment, so they'd better get along real well with each other."

"Twenty years will see this whole world in its grave," Borges replied. "These bugs get hold of *Garvey*, Earth won't have twenty years."

"The bugs got here without *Garvey*, didn't they?" said Murasaki. "They don't need *Marcus Garvey*. We do." She was still extremely troubled about

130

how the bugs had arrived on Nowa Gdansk. That would be the key to the whole mess.

"So who's going out to *Pulaski?*" asked Morgan.

Murasaki sighed. "Heck if I know. Normally, I'd say we ask Government to spade up a couple of pilots, some engineers, some closed-system ecologists, a few decorative extras, run psych and sex profiles, train them in a closed base somewhere for six months, then do a roster selection based on the evals. Now, we'd be lucky to send two kids in a lifeboat to wake up the AIs. That's with hoping the systems can solve all their own maintenance and restart problems while the kids hold the wrenches."

Morgan almost smiled, not quite. "You're not volunteering, Wanda?"

"My, ah, talents, are better employed elsewhere." She glanced at Smitts for support. He pursed his lips at her, a flat expression on his face. "In other words, 'no,'" she added.

"Just going to send someone else off to die by decades," snapped Borges.

"Beats having bug feet dance on your grave," Murasaki said. "Isn't that what you were just worried about? Besides, it's only about seven years on the ship clock. Think of it as time travel, leaping into the future."

Wolachek stared at her hands. "If you can get us to *Pulaski*, we'll do what we can."

Murasaki tried to imagine sending a threesome off alone for seven years, especially this demonstrably low-functional bunch. It sounded like a recipe for a spectacular murder-suicide.

"That's a big heart you've got, Wolachek," Murasaki said in her best lecturing-the-recruits voice, "but are you ready for most of a decade with these two?"

The little blonde glared, a sudden fire in her green eyes. "We're Progressive Onanists. Bonded as a triple."

Murasaki tried to keep a straight face. As far as she knew, Onanism was masturbation. "Excuse me?"

"Genesis 38, verse 8," said Wolachek. The other two joined in to recite in unison, "Then Judah said to Onan, Lie with your brother's wife and fulfill your duty to her as a brother-in-law to produce offspring for your brother."

"Hear the word of the Lord," Wolachek added.

"You two are brothers?" Murasaki asked Morgan and Borges. Borges was about a hundred and forty centimeters tall, dark-skinned and dark-haired. At two meters plus a generous bit, with flaming red hair, Morgan looked like a Celtic barbarian minus the kilt and sword.

Borges grinned, the first happy expression she'd seen on his face. "Brothers in the Lord."

"Ah. I get it," Murasaki lied. These were people with a mission. Maybe a few million cubic meters of slowship to rattle around in for seven years would do them good. God was everywhere, the Archbishop of Nowa Gdansk liked to say in his benedictions for the graduates at Teutoburgerwald, but especially between the stars. "We'll reconfigure the shuttle to boost you out to *Pulaski*. You're on your own from there."

She'd rather have sent the three rawest recruits from awkward squad, but this band of nuts was what she had to work with right now. If their free-flight shuttle were to dock at Gdansk Orbital, it wouldn't be released again. Certainly not under her orders.

As she and Smitts pulled themselves back to the cockpit to reconfigure the shuttle's mission, Murasaki whispered to him, "I spotted vacuum bags in the emergency stores." These were nearly idiot-proof spacesuits, each basically a giant balloon with provisions, a beacon and a tiny maneuvering capability. Lifeboats for morons. "With the right bit of boost from the shuttle, we can get over to Gdansk Orbital. Do you know how to deploy one of those things?"

At the look on Smitts' face, she remembered he had been a fastship officer.

Escaping the shuttle, Murasaki and Smitts were crowded into one vacuum bag like twins sharing a uterus. She had managed to make the shuttle accept the flight plan to *Pulaski*, then Smitts had used his supervisory overrides to shut down the shuttle's IFF transponder, and lock the controls so the Onanists couldn't change their minds and go joyriding around Gdansku planetary space. Now she prayed they could find a way to talk to *Garvey* when the fastship came in.

The little compressed CO_2 jets that powered the vacuum bag nudged Murasaki and Smitts along their trajectory toward Gdansk Orbital. Smitts had hot-wired a switch into the screamer beacon circuits to keep them from being noticed too soon, allowing more time for the hopefully-unnoticed departure of the free-flight shuttle for *Pulaski's* orbit.

Once she got to Gdansk Orbital, all Murasaki had to do was make it on to the space station alive and unharmed, locate the surviving chain of command, and repel the first alien invasion in human history. And not get picked up by the bugs along the way. She had to assume the aliens were on Gdansk Orbital.

Uh-huh. One thing at a time. She refused to worry about the near-impossibility of sneaking onto a space-based facility unnoticed.

Murasaki patted her shipsuit, checking once again that the flechette pistol was broken down in the cargo pockets. Williamson's bloody death fresh in her mind, Murasaki wasn't ever going anywhere unarmed again. She realized that it was going to be a long, cold pull, with the two of them breathing each other's air the whole way.

"So," she finally said. Wanda Murasaki had never had much luck with men. Or women, for that matter. Socially naked without the shield of her uniform, she gave it her best shot. "Got any hobbies?"

Smitts stared at her for a moment, then began to giggle. Tinged by hysteria, his giggle unfolded into a full-throated laugh. Even through her embarrassment, Murasaki couldn't help herself. She joined him, the two of them howling like maniacs in the confined space of the vacuum bag.

It felt good to be alone together.

II: FALLING UNFREE

Even before Smitts had set off the screamer beacons their vacuum bag was picked up by a routine garbage sweep maintaining Orbital's path. Without acknowledging them, a space-suited man tied the bag off to his little scow's frame.

"What the heck is going on out here?" Murasaki asked quietly, peering through the tiny viewport embedded in the wall of the bag. "He's got to know we're in this thing."

"What he doesn't know he can't tell," said Smitts. "Wait and see. We may yet get onboard quietly."

Eventually the little scow towed them into a secondary maintenance bay of Gdansk Orbital. Murasaki and Smitts collapsed against each other in the restored gravity. Lights came and atmosphere was pumped into the bay. Murasaki fingered her flechette pistol as their rescuer popped the tab on their vacuum bag.

"Had enough out there?" he snapped. He was still suited up, though now helmetless. "You're the fourth bag come in today." He was a short, stocky Asian with extensive facial tattoos — abstract lines and angles.

"Sorry," said Murasaki. What the *piekło* was he talking about? "Things happen."

"You idiots bailed out too fast. Panic, for the love of vacuum. Bugs got here in a hurry, but they ain't been shooting no one. Now get out of my bay before I got to report you."

They got out of his bay, scuttling through a service passage into a station corridor, eleven-orange-short according to the signage. Despite their rescuer's comment, there were no bugs in sight. The two of them started walking, following the scattered, furtive traffic.

"He knew," said Smitts. "He didn't want to do anything about us, but he knew we weren't from in here."

"How?"

"For one thing, the origin of our bag was clearly marked."

"Oh." Murasaki probably should have known that, but military bags were serialized, not marked for origin. Civilian gear like the shuttle carried was different. The sweeper's deliberate indifference to their origin boded well for organizing a resistance movement. "I have to find someone in the command structure. There's at least a dozen senior officers from Gdansku Force and Public Order on-station. It's only been, what, a day and half?"

Murasaki found out that the bugs had captured Gdansk Orbital at about the same time as they'd dropped onto Government House in Katyn down on the planetary surface. Orbital's takeover had been much softer, in part because of the lack of capacity for resistance. The entire armed fleet in 70 Ophiuchi A, Nowa Gdansk's home system, consisted of a single customs cutter equipped only with twin-turreted low-impact kinetic cannon. The ship had been down for maintenance at the time of the invasion. The bugs, reportedly calling themselves Segrethi, had put a lid on off-station comm and ship movements. Otherwise they left well enough alone.

Eleven days later, Murasaki and Smitts crouched together in baffling bay number six of one of Gdansk Orbital Port's former high-pressure airshafts. The Port was built up from the hull of the slowship *Boleslav,* and someone had removed the air baffles years earlier when the airshafts had been downgraded to ambient pressure. Now the baffling bay had the advantage of being an unmonitored space, a dead zone free of surveillance or casual traffic.

"My parents immigrated on the *Boleslav,*" Murasaki said, glancing around the bay. "This is sort of like returning to my ancestral home."

"Yeah," said Smitts. "If you like your home overrun with bugs."

"Not overrun, in the control of. No downside comm." Murasaki grimaced. "Nobody up here knows anything about what's happened downside. I can't find anyone in the command structure. There's a couple of dozen section heads and senior managers that have simply vanished. I'm the ranking officer on station, Smitts."

"Rats," he said. "There have to be rats, selling us out. The bugs shut down Port Control so fast, they had to have help. What did you find out about ships?"

Murasaki had a sheet of plastic paper covered with scribbles from a vacuum-rated grease pen. "I still don't understand how the Segrethi got here," said Murasaki. She skimmed a finger down her notes. "There's the two slowships in cold park..." They shared a glance, each silently wondering about the Onanists, before she continued.

"The cutter *Zamojski* is still stuck in heavy maintenance. There's eight in-system ships locked down at north docking collar and three more at the south collar, and five working shuttles coming and going. Shuttles the Segrethi are using with human flight crews, which suggests they have no orbit-to-ground capacity other than whatever they dropped on us on Invasion Day." Murasaki bit her lip. "Whatever the *piekło* that was. And there's nothing else docked here, nothing else on the telemetry we can spoof out of the system." She folded the paper. "What did they do? Walk here?"

Smitts shrugged. "Maybe they came in stealthy hotships."

"Uh huh." Murasaki shook her head. "Ships have mass. We'd have noticed them at the last minute if not before. I was at Government House when the Segrethi appeared." Murasaki's dreams still burned with vivid memories of armed aliens dropping out of the mauve skies. "That's the only word for it. The only other thing we have to go on is the Port power blips."

Every eleven hours and forty-two minutes, power levels dropped for a few seconds all over Gdansk Orbital. The blip lasted long enough to trip some circuit protection and cause corridor brown-outs. The "bug blip," as corridor chat called it, was annoying but apparently not dangerous. Under Segrethi influence, Port Control hadn't yet acknowledged that it even took place.

"This puppy was built as a slowship," said Smitts. "Any of Orbital's quantum induction generators puts out more power than the entire downside grid. Whatever they're doing to draw down that much energy, it's huge."

"I majored in electronics and power systems engineering at the service academy—believe me, I can visualize how much energy they're drawing. It's appalling. Another mystery." Murasaki shook her head. "What's your local Segrethi count?"

"I polled spacejacks, ship wranglers—all the bluesuit types. Best guess the beer trust can come up with is about a hundred and forty."

"Snooping onboard records, I don't make it more than hundred and fifty myself. Less than two hundred Segrethi holding a Port with over three thousand humans. We could *mob* them to death."

Smitts cracked one of his rare smiles. "If you could get fifty Gdansku running in the same direction, that would be a hell of a trick. No way this bunch is going to take hundreds of casualties knocking down ten dozen bugs."

Murasaki had to agree. Between their machete-swords and zap rifles, the Segrethi would take at least four or five hundred Gdansku with them. "The Segrethi haven't been making it hard on people, so most folks aren't mad. Scared, sure, but not pissed off. I don't know much about mounting insurgency, how to make ordinary people angry enough to die. Special Operations have never been in demand here on Nowa Gdansk."

"I know more than I should about insurgency," said Smitts. "*Marat's*. Never again."

"Never say never, but not now at least." Awkwardly, Murasaki patted his shoulder. It was as close as she could come to offering affection. Since the death of his lifemate Williamson, it was as much affection as Smitts would accept. "*Garvey's* the angle," she continued. "Yell for help as fast as we can. We already launched Plan B before we even got to Orbital; let's finish Plan A. She's due in soon. All we have to do is find out when the ship's in range, take System Control long enough to get a message out, make sure her captain understands it, and get her turned around before she closes in to where the Segrethi can do something to stop her."

"Oh, is that all?" Smitts stared at her with flat gray eyes.

"Can we get some people rallied to grab system control and defend it? Maybe your bluesuits." After failing to find the missing officers, she hadn't much luck approaching the whitesuit managers and staff that ran Port Control. Besides, the alien collaborators had to be influencing things—the rats Smitts had mentioned.

"Perhaps," Smitts said. "But there's the missing bodies."

People disappeared, mostly senior managers the bluesuits didn't miss much. People died in the corridors, getting in the way of the Segrethi. People died of accidents, infections, natural causes. Regardless of their individual fates, ever since Invasion Day, all the bodies on Gdansk Orbital went away. Utterly, mysteriously away.

"That worries people," he continued. "They're not angry, they're afraid. Fear like this is a quiet poison." Smitts stared at his hands, flexing the knuckles as if secrets and lies were hidden in the folds of skin.

The ghosts of Marat's Bath *would never stop haunting him*, thought Murasaki. She could see he had been a good officer once—he was certainly capable and competent now under extreme stress. But Smitts was steeped in his own quiet, poisonous fear. She labored to keep his despair from infecting her.

"Yeah, the missing bodies," said Murasaki. " I noticed it even back on Nowa Gdansk. The guard shack at the shuttle port was soaked in blood, but no bodies there."

"Bluesuits think the bugs are eating the bodies."

Murasaki shook her head. "I don't buy that. They've got guts, they eat. But by definition we have incompatible biologies. Something else is going on."

"We're not going to fix the body problem anyway," said Smitts. "The message is the thing. Telling Earth we're in trouble and that they're next."

"The message is the thing," Murasaki echoed.

Murasaki walked down corridor seven-yellow-long. Foot traffic was light, although some cargo mules putted along near her. Other than restricting access to the docking collars and Port Control, the Segrethi let people go about their business. Right now, her business was another reconnaissance pass at System Control, looking for hints how she could hijack the Port comm suite and hold it for a while.

Murasaki's current Gdansk Orbital smartbadge had been 'borrowed' from a woman in the Med unit suffering from a massive case of lung rot. "Grossbecker, Erin" worked in System Control, but wouldn't be needing her badge any time soon.

One of the aliens stepped out of a cross-corridor, machete-sword and rifle slung tight to its harness. That meant it wasn't hunting, just passing through.

Murasaki caught her breath, dipped her head, and slowed her step. She kept moving toward the Segrethi—to turn and run might have been suspicious. To stop might be. To approach too fast might be. She couldn't know until it was too late.

This was the first Segrethi she'd come near since Invasion Day. It didn't have the ball helmet. Rather, its face was fully exposed, dominated by two huge eyes, glossy and gold at the same time, like milk just poured into tea. The eyes were set facing almost sideways, a pattern that would suggest prey species to a Terran ecologist, within a narrow, tapered head that ended in feathery brushes emerging from an irregular snout. Except for the chitin surface, the face almost resembled that of a Terran deer.

The ball helmet must be filled with cybernetics, Murasaki thought, given how much space was left after cramming that skinny head into it. The flickering holes of the helmet's characteristic smiley face would be positioned to allow the little fan of brushes and the end of the snout to taste the air. As she'd suspected, Segrethi operated by smell.

And this one was smelling her. Apparently having trouble seeing her, it stopped at an angle, with the big power legs extended to block the corridor. Cargo mules whined in protest as they crowded to a halt around Murasaki. The Segrethi didn't draw its weapons, but leaned forward and sniffed her just like the one she had killed on Landing Road, pressing the snout almost into her chest while the feathers stroked down the front of her borrowed bluesuit.

The alien's stick hand darted into a pouch and pulled out a human-made badge reader, which it swiped past Murasaki's smartbadge without looking. Did it actually get kinesthetic data via scent as well?

"GrossbeckerErin," chirped the alien.

Murasaki literally jumped. Though the aliens had to have some mechanism for communications with their human rats, no one in the corridors had reported Segrethi speaking any human language. She wouldn't have bet on them using sound for communication at all. She wasn't even sure why they allegedly had a name for themselves.

"You are GrossbeckerErin?"

Murasaki realized the voice was coming from a human-made comm unit slung on the Segrethi's neck. So, still no sound from one of them. This one was cheating, with technology. "Yes?" she said trying to balance belligerence and fear.

"You labor in System Control. You will accompany."

Well, Erin Grossbecker was a traffic controller. Her high access priority was one of the things that had made the smartbadge valuable in the first place. Murasaki wished she'd appropriated something less important. But as ordered, she accompanied. Her disassembled flechette pistol hung heavy in the cargo pockets of her borrowed bluesuit.

Murasaki wasn't surprised when the Segrethi led her straight to Port Control. Not where she wanted to go, but surely another source of valuable intelligence. Two more aliens with zap rifles guarded the main access. A secondary hatch down the corridor had been blocked with hastily-welded panels. The only question was whether the Segrethi wanted her for something they thought Grossbecker could do for them, or if they knew she was masquerading.

For one, a whitesuit professional like Erin Grossbecker wouldn't have been caught dead in the ship wrangler's bluesuit coveralls Murasaki now wore. As soon as they scanned her badge, any human worker on Gdansk Orbital would know Murasaki was scamming.

She and Smitts already knew there were collaborators. She'd been practicing—it would take about fifteen seconds to extract her pistol and snap it together, another four seconds to warm it up. If things got bad inside Port Control, as long as she survived the first twenty seconds, she could take some targets with her.

It had taken Williamson less time than that to die.

The hatch hissed open. Murasaki followed the Segrethi into Port Control, a place she'd never been.

They stepped through the hatch onto a semicircular observation deck above plunging levels of workstations arranged in steps leading downward to a pit overlooking two huge holo tanks showing simplified orbital schematics. From Murasaki's high vantage point, things looked normal, almost. Everything was underlit in glowering red. Giant screens showed realtime views of Gdansk Orbital's leading and trailing paths. Other screens showed the port's docking collars. Schematic displays documented traffic in planetary space and system space.

Almost nothing was moving on the screens. The Segrethi lockdown was holding. Murasaki didn't see anything on any of the views that could be a Segrethi starship. Of course, since they were in control of everything, they could easily be masking their own sensor trace. But despite all logic, she just didn't believe it was out there. Their landing in Katyn had defied logic as well, after all.

Segrethi sentries stood at each end of the observation deck, positioned so their zap rifles had covering fire across the entire room. At least two of the workstations showed obvious signs of high-energy damage. So there had been resistance here.

"Erin," said a man climbing up from the workstations, "I'm so glad you're feeling bet—" He caught himself when he took his eyes off the ladder to look up at Murasaki, his smile freezing in place. He was tall, dark-skinned, with brown eyes surrounded by marbled whites that were almost orange. He wore no uniform, no name badge, just a well-tailored formal whitesuit. He also looked vaguely familiar.

"Good to see you too, sir," Murasaki said as smoothly as she could. "It's been a while. I feel like a whole new person." She had to brazen this out in front of her alien escort.

The man glanced at Murasaki's Segrethi handler, then back at her. "I'd heard your illness caused some cognitive problems with facial recognition." Stepping the rest of the way up onto the observation deck, he stuck out his hand. "Allow me to re-introduce myself. Kindness Awolowo, second shift manager."

He was quick. His little covering speech wouldn't have fooled a human for a second, but it might work on the Segrethi. She recognized the name— Goodhope Awolowo was a prominent genomic therapist who also served as Lieutenant Governor of Nowa Gdansk. Someone with whom she'd often had dealings in her former official capacity.

"Thank you, sir," she said, taking Awolowo's hand. "For a moment I thought you might be my, well, *good hope*." Awolowo was also the highest-level manager she'd encountered. Another good sign.

He nodded slowly. "We have a problem for which our...new supervisors want an expert opinion. You're on the short list of people who are familiar with the operational behaviors of our cold-parked slowships. Concern has been expressed about asset preservation in the face of security challenges."

Obviously the Segrethi were talking to the whitesuits running the Port. That only made sense—speech capabilities or not, they couldn't work their will without communication. Their interests in slowships meant that the Onanists *had* to have gotten something done in their effort to restart *Pulaski*. She let her exultation slip onto her face in the form of a limited smile. "I do know a bit about their activities."

That wasn't even a complete lie.

He looked almost sad. "Come with me, please."

Murasaki followed Awolowo down the ladder to the second level of workstations, her Segrethi clattering after. She glanced up to see both the guards tracking her with their zap rifles. *Dziękują Bogowi*—thank God the Segrethi didn't know enough about humans to spot the awkward

141

interaction between her and Awolowo.

More interesting, perhaps, was that sometimes they paid attention to her, sometimes they apparently didn't. *Why?* How could she use that information?

Awolowo waved Murasaki to a seat. He flipped two switches, then leaned across her to log in. As he worked, almost touching her, Awolowo whispered without moving his lips, "Make this good, stranger."

She looked at the image on the workstation screen. It was a blurry view of a slowship, presumably the *Pulaski*. The free-flight shuttle which stuck like a tiny limpet to the forward docking ring was a big clue as to what was happening, at least to Murasaki.

"See here," said Awolowo loudly. "There's been a spike in power levels over the past week. Concern has been expressed."

"Probably internal maintenance from the ship's AI," said Murasaki, pretending to study the data plots ghosted in over the image of the *Pulaski*.

"Small maneuvering adjustments have been made inconsistent with station-keeping. For example, rolling the ship, apparently to establish thermal equilibrium. Concern has been expressed that the slowship may be preparing to break orbit."

"Impossible," said Murasaki. *Nice use of passive voice, too*, she thought. The man was definitely a career bureaucrat. "In cold orbit, ship AIs are dormant. With no one on board, they wouldn't initiate engine starts."

"How maintenance?" blurted the mechanical voice of the alien behind her.

Murasaki winced. "There are routine subsystems on timing loops," she said. Total cobwebs, she was making it up, but it sounded good. She hoped.

Awolowo nodded sagely.

Behind her, the Segrethi shifted its weight. Murasaki wished mightily that she had already assembled the flechette pistol, and damn the bulk it would have made in her pocket. She glanced upward past her shoulder to see a faint spark smoldering in the muzzle of her handler's zap rifle.

Awolowo leaned back down toward the workstation. "Just walk away," he whispered, breath in her ear. He tapped some more keys.

"I'm sorry," said Murasaki. "My recent illness has affected my thinking. I must return to sick bay."

"Thank you, Erin," said Awolowo.

The Segrethi minder had no reaction as she slowly stood. Murasaki sidled around it, then climbed two levels back to the observation deck. One sentry had a zap rifle pointed at her, the other covered Awolowo and their Segrethi minder. She paused at the hatch, staring down at the big screens. The view of the slowship *Pulaski* flickered onto the big screen. Murasaki watched the engine modules flare, then explode in a blue light. The rest of the ship disintegrated.

How had they done that!?

She turned and walked out of Port Control. "I'm sorry," she whispered to the ghosts of the three eager, inept Onanists who had just died for her. The Segrethi on duty in the corridor ignored her.

Back in the baffling bay, she waited for Smitts. Alone in the empty, creaking space, washed by a faint breeze, Murasaki reflected on sending people out to die. That had been mostly a theoretical exercise in the Gdansku Force. The military's primary mission was support of the Public Order directorate. Gdansku Force performed other functions such as search-and-rescue, disaster relief, and ceremonial security, but outside of a few tax protests, Nowa Gdansk had never before now seen shots fired in anger.

Even so, everyone in uniform trained their entire careers for the unprecedented. It was part of the job, at least for the successful ones. Murasaki had gone to ground in the rose bushes on Invasion Day expecting never to walk away, without a second thought.

Somehow, it was different when Williamson had died. Smiling, bearded, a sparkle in his eye, he fell because she didn't grab her pistol. Then the Onanists—she couldn't even recall their names, just Smitts' description of them as a trio of God-bothering idiots.

To die unnamed and unremembered was the worst fate of all. Murasaki racked her brain. Borges, she thought. And Morgan. But what was the wife's name, that territorial little blonde armed only with faith and anger? They died because Murasaki had handed them a bad mission, then failed to find a way to bail them out when the Segrethi caught on.

The lights flickered with the bug blip, right on schedule, just as the inspection hatch hissed open below her. Murasaki braced the fully-assembled flechette pistol only to see Smitts climb into the baffling bay.

"Where's the Grossbecker badge?" he demanded.

"Tucked in our dead drop over in Suit Maintenance," she said. "I ditched it after they hauled me into Port Control."

"Bugs just marched into sickbay and hauled the real Grossbecker out. Station Control has announced through channels she was an impostor."

"Another gone," whispered Murasaki.

"That's right." His stare was pitiless. "I've learned a few of other things."

Murasaki wasn't sure she wanted to know. "Yeah?"

"Nine hundred and forty hertz. Point nine four kilohertz. It's a magic number."

Not a useful frequency. Too low for much in the way of engineering applications. "What's it mean?"

"Don't know. But it's making some of the blue-suit techs in station engineering crazy. They call it the 'Segrethi hum.' We've got background radiation on the frequency, with random bursts and peaks, that wasn't here before the bugs came."

"Okay." She filed that away for future reference. "What else?"

"Something a little more immediately useful. Word is *Marcus Garvey's* hydrogen rainbow has been spotted in the outer system."

When they dropped into normal spacetime, fastships generated a visible bow wave, stripped hydrogen nuclei raised to a plasma state, kicking off a whole catalog of particle emissions. The so-called rainbow was a reliable early warning of an incoming fastship. When *Voltaire*, the first fastship to visit Nowa Gdansk, had shown up unheralded in the Ophiuchi A system, everything had gone on alert in response. *Too bad they'd missed the Segrethi*, Murasaki thought. That would have been an alert with more results than some official embarrassment and a big party afterward.

"Plan B is blown," said Murasaki. "*Pulaski's* lost, and there's no way now that the Segrethi will allow us sneak anyone onto *Pomorzanin*." *Pomorzanin* was a sister slowship to *Pulaski*, the survivor of the pair that had been parked in cold orbit. "Back to Plan A."

"You still thinking about busting System Control?"

"Either that or steal *Zamojski* out of the heavy maintenance and try to meet *Garvey* on the fly."

"The bugs will blow *Zamoj* the same way they blew *Pulaski*."

"Which was how?" She hadn't seen any missile trace. It was as if they'd decided to blow the ship and simply done it, right there while she was in Port Control.

From a distance of three light-seconds, no less. Impossible, like so many other things the Segrethi had done.

"Who knows how the bugs get anything done?" Smitts looked glum. "As bad a plan as seizing System Control is, swiping the cutter is worse."

Murasaki took her plastic paper out of her pocket. "Fine," she said. "I've sketched what I can of the layout in and around System Control. Since I never made it in there with the Grossbecker badge, I can't be much more detailed."

She paused, rubbing the plastic map between her fingers. It felt greasy, cold. Like the Onanists felt about now. Inasmuch as they felt anything.

Stop it, Wanda! Clearing her head, Murasaki continued. "The Segrethi don't keep a sentry there right now—why should they? There's no traffic to talk to. *Garvey* won't drop out of the hydrogen rainbow until it's a few light-hours distant. We back out what we can about the trajectory to estimate our best timing, then walk one of us into System Control through the front door. Keep it clean, make it look normal, explain things before we bring our muscle through the vent system." She glanced up at Smitts. "We do have muscle, right?"

"I'll bring them."

"That means I walk in the door," said Murasaki. "It's not much of a plan, but it's the best I can do."

Could she see Awolowo? Find out what he had to say, maybe update him on what she knew. Murasaki hoped he was also trying to work on a message to Earth. Every officer and manager who had survived must be thinking like her, but with Segrethi restrictions on ship movements and long distance comm, there wasn't much opportunity to organize.

She glanced up to see a haunted look in Smitts' eyes. "It's *Marat's Bath* all over again, isn't it?" Murasaki said quietly.

"Mutiny," Smitts replied, "Mutiny and murder in System Control."

"We're not killing anybody." Murasaki leaned forward and lightly kissed his cheek. The rough stubble and worry-lined skin felt odd under her lips, but she wanted Smitts to know she understood what he was about. He pulled back, somewhere between shock and disgust, then forced a smile.

"I know you don't do women," said Murasaki quietly. "But I'm proud of you. Bart Williamson would be proud if he were here."

"Sometimes even the right thing is the wrong thing to do," said Smitts, his eyes full of memories.

Fourteen hours later, flechette pistol ready and charged in her cargo pocket, Murasaki strode along corridor two-gold-long toward System Control through crowds of civilians, Port workers and cargo mules. She didn't have a badge this time, didn't plan on being in the corridor long enough to need one. If System Control were locked down, she would use Awolowo's name to talk her way in. If the Segrethi had moved sentries to System Control, she'd just walk on by, then hit the airshafts herself.

"Hey, you, ship girl!"

The speaker was a big man, sweaty and poorly shaven, in ship handler's coveralls that matched Murasaki's. He carried a riot-grade flechette pistol, significantly larger than Murasaki's, designed to fire blunt, oversized nanotubules at sublethal speeds. Up close, it was perhaps more deadly than her military firearm. Four more ship handlers followed him a short distance, hanging back, trying to avoid the confrontation.

"What?" Murasaki didn't need this *Bóg przeklina* interruption.

"Don't you *what* me, missy!" One meaty paw slammed into her upper arm. Murasaki knew she could throw him and break his neck, but not in the middle of the corridor with fifty people walking by. "You're out unbadged, which means you're off duty or shirking. Either way, I'm picking you up on the Emergency Clause."

"Don't have the time, pal," Murasaki said in her best dangerous officer voice.

The ship handling supervisor didn't care. "Read your contract, sister. Emergency Clause is a no-shit deal except for death comma your own, or eighty percent incapacity. Unless you're heading to a costume party. You a whitesuit in disguise?" He squeezed her arm so hard Murasaki knew she'd have bruises, then guffawed, glaring back at his little parade until they laughed, too.

"Get the hell off me before I tear your fat head from that pulpy neck," Murasaki muttered in a low voice. She reached up to grab his fingers where they dug into her arm.

"I got Spaghettis waiting on this detail, sister," he growled back.

"There's cameras out here and two to one says someone's watching. Your ass is mine." He shoved his oversized flechette pistol into Murasaki's abdomen. "Get with the program right now, or I *will* put this riot pistol to its intended use."

Murasaki didn't want a public confrontation, let alone Segrethi attention. Smitts would have to handle System Control on his own for a while. She'd catch up when she could slip away from this gorilla. "I'm coming," Murasaki said. "I *will* be feeding you your own ears later… friend."

"Get the damned job done, we'll talk. That's a *kindness*, I promise." He gave her a hard shove, back toward his little crew. Murasaki took a couple of light hey-there punches in the arm as they followed along.

Something was going on with the Segrethi, right now. The big ape was hinting that Kindness Awolowo had set this up. Was Awolowo helping or hurting her? Murasaki hoped like crazy Smitts wasn't having trouble bringing his muscle team through the air vents.

The work detail wound up just outside one of the small craft bays along the center ring. Two Segrethi guarded the access hatch, weapons at the ready. As always, they were twins to the pair in front of Port Control, or any other random Segrethi for that matter. "Crap," whispered Murasaki under her breath. The guards were going to make slipping away difficult.

The hatch hissed open and the supervising gorilla waved the ad hoc team inside. The bay was empty of small craft. The roof arched high overhead, the launch hatch before them sunk in a massive recess in the floor which arched with the hull curvature.

A large machine sat on an organic-looking cradle facing the launch hatch. It had to be Segrethi technology, with the same velvety bronze finish as their helmets, but it was the first piece of their equipment that wasn't man-portable. *Segrethi-portable*, Murasaki corrected herself.

The alien machine resembled a cross between an artillery piece and a power substation, with a stubby barrel perhaps a meter long and a complex body four meters by two by two. She thought it might be a giant version of one of their zap rifles, though the crafting of the thing was more complex, more subtly alien. Where a zap rifle looked almost like something a human machinist might have crafted, on this larger piece of equipment, the corners were wrongly-angled, the proportions off. Even the velvety bronze finish of it seemed odd, almost artistic. By contrast, the cradle looked like congealed bug spit, a mattress of pale bubbles about six meters long, four meters wide and a meter deep.

Arrayed in front of the machine, filling the space between it and the hatch, were large tarpaulins. They appeared to be so many sheets of thermally superconductive film. The material was normally used as shielding to protect construction and other long-term work outside the hull — EVA, as the classic term went — from direct insolation. At the same time, the film generated surplus power, in a manner very similar to the Port's giant sails that managed internal thermal equilibrium. The tarps covered a series of two-meter lumps about the size and shape of human bodies.

This was where the human dead were, she realized. Their bodies had come here to the small craft bay, sacrifices for some alien machine. This was almost worth missing the takeover of System Control to see.

Almost.

"All right, you vacuum monkeys," bellowed the supervisor. She could see he was sweating, nervous and jumpy as any of his drafted work detail. "Seems *themselves* have rotated some bugs to deal with internal security problems."

Uh oh, thought Murasaki.

"Seems themselves have a *sacred duty* to perform here which they cannot do without our assistance."

His tone made "sacred duty" into a profanity. Murasaki hoped the Segrethi translators weren't passing emotional context back with the lexical parsing.

"Seems themselves have asked us to assist them in their *sacred duty*. Themselves are not happy about being forced to do this. You will treat this ceremony with the same respect you would show a crewmate's beliefs."

Murasaki suppressed a snort. She knew exactly what bull puckey that last bit was. But this was Segrethi *religion*. Or something very much like it. Human bodies and Segrethi gods. What could that possibly signify?

"Suit up and fall in by the hatch."

The work detail double-timed off to the locker room, Murasaki trailing the group. As she shoved through the door, the supervisor caught up with her. They locked eyes. He nodded very slightly as she shook her head.

Inside, the supervisor eyeballed Murasaki's build. He fished suit components out of coded bins and handed them to her without saying word. Some of the ship handlers gave her odd looks as she fumbled with the unfamiliar equipment—their suits were not similar to the military vacuum armor with which she was familiar. The supervisor kept staring at her through narrowed eyes.

She managed to get her flechette pistol into an outside pocket of the suit. *Now for some answers*, she told herself. Murasaki wished she had a way to get word to Smitts.

They fell in outside next to the tarpaulins, at right angles to the Segrethi cannon. The big supervisor had them seal helmets and wait. Murasaki saw that his suit was stenciled "Della Femina."

After about twenty minutes, a bloated Segrethi dragged itself into the main hangar area. It was the first Segrethi Murasaki had ever seen that she would be able to recognize again.

The bean pod body wasn't tight and shiny like the others, but puffy and swollen, resembling the grubs she turned up in the soil of her little tomato garden at Teutoburgerwald. The power legs and power arms still resembled straw bundles, but the exposed muscle fibers flitted loose, as if the limbs were caught in the process of disintegration. The Segrethi's eyes had clouded to the color and appearance of cracked opals, and it looked as if it could barely carry its own weight.

It stopped next to the cannon, dropped its head, and was still. After another ten minutes of standing in her suit, Murasaki wondered if the old thing had simply died in place. Then it raised its head, turned and spat a pale, bubbly goop on the bubble cradle and lurched away.

Two other Segrethi, in the metal helmets she'd seen planetside, approached as the vacuum alarms flashed and wailed. The wailing died off as the pumps evacuated air from the hangar, then the hatch slid open. The helmeted Segrethi yanked the tarps off the bodies.

There were forty of them, neatly arrayed in five groups of eight. They were human and they were dead, ankles of each group linked by a plastic line. Each one had been shaved, even the eyebrows. Patches of skin were flayed in various places. Fighting her queasiness, Murasaki guessed that those patches were where tattoos had been removed. Some had died by obvious trauma or violence, but no effort had been made to restore them to a natural appearance.

Della Femina motioned the work detail into action. They swarmed around the first line of bodies, Murasaki trailing behind the team. The supervisor used a series of unfamiliar hand signals. The team hauled the first line of bodies through the hatch, the naked corpses already beginning to frost over with vacuum outgassing.

Murasaki didn't understand the commands, but with her zero gee experience she could handle the suit fairly well. She followed the team out the hatch, pitching away from the centripetally-enhanced artificial gravity of Orbital Port to float free.

The terminator line dividing day from night crawled across the planet above them. Behind her, inasmuch as direction meant anything in microgravity, loomed the bulk of the Port. She spotted the EVA hatch for the small craft bay, next to it a rack with a pressure jet broomstick. Those were typically used for extended EVA.

Within the open bay, the two Segrethi operators activated their cannon. It glowed orange as a faint radiation danced along the body of the machine, then a spot in the vacuum began to roil in front of Murasaki.

Space rippled, bloomed in a green-and-orange glow before opening to a slightly distended circle perhaps twenty meters in diameter. Murasaki got a sense of motion, like watching a jump-cut virteo. A gray-white moon swung into view through the wormhole, pimpled with winking lights and habitat domes, familiar from a thousand photos.

"Luna," Murasaki whispered to herself. Everything fell into place at once. "It's a *Bóg przeklina* wormhole generator. That's why we never saw the Segrethi invasion fleet."

Not that human physicists had ever managed to build such a thing, or even prove that it could be done.

She checked her suit clock. Right on time for the eleven hour, forty-two minute power dip. This was what the Segrethi were doing with all the Port power. Even worse, the wormhole meant the Segrethi knew where Earth was, and they could hit it any time they wanted. Her face felt tight and hot even as her heart clenched cold. With or without her, Smitts' raid on System Control *had* to succeed.

The view from the other end of the wormhole shifted, blurring away from Luna toward the familiar blue-brown mother planet. Earth herself, that

Murasaki had never seen except in pictures. The ship wranglers used a power shuffle to boost the line of bodies, stripping off the tethers as they shifted them into an end-to-end line. One by one, the naked, frozen dead fell through the wormhole and into high orbit around Earth.

Murasaki twitched inside her suit as Della Femina touched helmets. "Only the dead go home," the supervisor said, his voice echoing. Helmet conduction was potentially uneavesdroppable, if both parties cooperated and no one had planted bugs.

"What the *piekło*?" she asked.

He ignored the question. "You're that dirtside officer, the one that's been making trouble."

"Yeah." Murasaki felt depressed, defeated by the strangeness of it all.

"Awolowo sent me to get you. He was desperate to stop your raid on System Control. Somebody leaked to the Spaghettis."

"Crap," said Murasaki. The *Garvey* would come in, be captured and the Segrethi would have a fastship as well as a slowship. And what had happened to Smitts?

"Come on," said Della Femina. "Get back to work before they get testy."

The work detail returned to the hatch for the next coffle of bodies. Having seen it done once, Murasaki was easier able to follow Della Femina's hand signals. As each body launched on its frozen, meteoric repatriation, she furiously tried to calculate how she could send a message home with the dead.

"Here's the bad news," said Della Femina quietly as he sat down on the locker room bench beside Murasaki. They'd broken out of their suits and queued for the shower bags, Della Femina overriding everyone's preset time limits with his supervisor's password. Murasaki had scrubbed her skin almost until it bled, trying to escape the prickling sensation that she was icing over like the frozen dead. Now she just itched, inside and out.

"Oh, there's bad news too?" Murasaki leaned forward to towel her close-cropped hair. The other four ship handling crew engaged in a noisy, whooping water fight around them, masking the conversation. Nudity in the locker room was no different from shower call on maneuvers, she kept telling herself.

"We're not getting back out of here. None of us." He glanced back at the rough housers. "They don't know it yet, either. I only got out to sweep for workers, on pain of death. Literally. When the bugs pulled their own troops out, they needed more human help. The coroner's team locked down here doing mortuary prep wouldn't go EVA with the dead, not even at gunpoint."

"How the hell am I going to get to System Control?" hissed Murasaki.

"Forget it," said Della Femina. "Spaghettis have got System Control locked down now tight as Port Control. They've yanked all the remaining crew, too."

Murasaki pulled on her mesh undershirt, then stood to slip on panties. Smitts was either dead or in hiding. She wasn't sure which she hoped for, for his sake. "How do they know to do all that, who those people are? Rats, right?"

"Rats," said Della Femina. "Our people."

She unbundled her bluesuit, shaking out the worst creases, then slipping her flechette pistol in. Murasaki didn't care if Della Femina saw it. The weapon made a comforting lump in the fabric, but it couldn't help her at the moment. "Nothing I can do about human collaborators," Murasaki said.

Just like Smitts had said, she thought, *Marat's Bath* all over again. Mutiny and murder, only he lost this time. Murasaki toweled her face to cover the hot sting of grief. Scarred by grief and memory, he hadn't been likeable, but he was her friend.

With a sniffle, she put Smitts out of her head. The message home was what counted. He had believed that just as much as she did. "What about the bodies?"

"I'll get you with the coroner's team. We're all locked in here together. But the bugs, or their rats, listen in a lot. This is big secret stuff, this detail."

"It looked religious," she said, staring at her bare feet, thinking of the old Segrethi. If old was what that was. Fragile, yes, but it could just as easily be a different type of Segrethi. "And that wormhole. God, what a threat." Why didn't they notice it on the Earth side?

"Religion. Threat. Who knows? They're freaking aliens."

She glanced up at him. "Not good enough. Even aliens have their reasons. Just like people." Sighing, "At least this explains the power drain every eleven hours or so."

A water-filled undersuit glove slammed into the back of Della Femina's head. He jumped up, fists swinging. "All right, you bunch, cut it now." As they quieted down, he lowered his voice. "I got some bad news for you vacuum monkeys."

A day later, after two more shifts shoving bodies through the wormhole and worrying herself sick over Smitts and *Marcus Garvey*, Murasaki sat at a gaming station in the tiny rec room off the small craft bay crew mess, using it in library mode. She studied the schematics of Gdansk Orbital Port.

The old *Boleslav* still had her slowship lines, a series of long cylinders on a central shaft, but roughly symmetrical rings had accreted over the decades since she was parked and recommissioned as the Port. Quantum induction generators designed to power interstellar travel gave the Port more energy that she would ever need, but heat accumulation was always a problem.

Orbital Port had huge sails, of a thermally superconductive photofabric similar to what the Segrethi had used to cover the human bodies back in the small craft bay. The sails radiated heat when they were darkside, and absorbed heat when they were sunside, generating power from the insolation. Power in excess of requirements was stored in banks of ion-trap accumulators, giant capacitors in effect, in circuit along the outer rings. Surplus power could be transferred to high-energy manufacturing operations or ship batteries for the perpetually energy-starved in-system vessels that were too small to carry the quantum induction generators.

Could she hack into the systems to manipulate the sails or overload the capacitors to discharge, sending a Morse code message to *Marcus Garvey*? Would *Garvey's* captain and crew recognize it as a message, or assume disaster and drive in to assist? She hated open questions like that. They undermined rational planning.

A tall, redheaded woman with pale skin and gray eyes, wearing the red-and-whites of Med section, slipped into Murasaki's workstation chair. She shoved Murasaki to the left so the commander hung precipitously off. As their thighs and sides touched, the redhead laid an arm across Murasaki's shoulder and kissed her cheek. "Hi, honey," she said loudly, then whispered, "Go with it."

"Uh, hey," said Murasaki. Sudden visions of Smitts and his angry face dominated her imagination. Somehow she had become like him, resenting body contact. Over the years, she'd gone straight from young to lonely without the intermediate benefit of experience.

The redhead reached over and flipped the workstation into gaming mode, then turned the volume up. She wrapped one hand around the back of Murasaki's head and placed her lips on Murasaki's right ear. "They don't watch as carefully if they think we're making out. This stuff gets the rats excited, and the bugs just can't tell."

Murasaki reined in her desire to knock the woman senseless. "So what gives?" she mumbled toward the workstation screen.

"Della Femina sent me to see you. I'm Jayne McMann, manager of the coroner's team. We call ourselves the Lost Boys because we're never getting out of here."

Murasaki kept her eyes on the screen. Jayne's hands roamed through her hair, but Murasaki couldn't bring herself to play along. "So what's with the bodies?"

Jayne shrugged, the muscles of her long body rippling against Murasaki. "Funerary custom. Alien ethics. There's no way to tell. They only talk to the rats, and the rats stay hidden in the walls."

They had talked to her, once, Murasaki thought. "The energy expenditure has to be awesome if it browns out the Port grid," she said. "I don't understand their purpose, but I understand what it means to us. Earth is under Segrethi guns, and nobody knows it." She shrugged against the other woman. "Maybe they're taunting us."

"A taunt. Earth would never realize that it was Gdansku falling from the sky." Jayne stroked Murasaki's face, trailing a fingernail across her lips. "Over a hundred million people live in Earth orbit. Imagine how many bodies a day rain down, from the murder rate alone. Who would notice?"

"Earth doesn't even know our world has been taken." Murasaki curled her lips inward, trying to avoid Jayne's lingering fingers. "Given transit lags, we haven't been out of touch long enough for them to notice. Nowa Gdansk does not stand high on anyone's watch list, not with a few dozen extrasolar colonies to worry about."

"Our dead go naked and shaven, tattoos flayed away," said Jayne. "We cleanse and purge them in every sense of the word. The Segrethi don't want information getting through. The bodies themselves are all that go."

Murasaki finally flicked Jayne's arm away from her face, pushing with her fingertips. "This exercise of theirs with the wormhole, it's a test, for their eventual invasion. How much materiel can they insert in orbit without anyone noticing?"

"Who knows?" Jayne sighed, losing her ardor. "Our dead are our only message."

As the tall redhead slipped away, Murasaki was astonished to realize that her nipples ached, and there was a distinct twinge in her vagina. She had not felt that way in a long time.

Della Femina and two of his vacuum monkeys performed noisy, clattering maintenance on a power shuffle in the machine room. Behind them, working with a spark hood, Murasaki recorded a whispered message in static memory of a comm unit, which she then took apart. She slipped the memory chip into a pressure canister along with a rescue screamer beacon rigged to a timer. The whole thing was about ten centimeters long and four in diameter, shaped like a giant grain of rice. Murasaki grabbed a tube of silicone lube along with the canister, and left the workbench.

The deserted mortuary was in the maintenance shop adjacent to the machine room. Murasaki slipped in, head bowed, her canister and lube held curled in her hands against her abdomen, to walk among the dead. Curtained areas at the back hid the work-in-progress, where the bodies were actually prepped. She visited the coffles, laid out in their helpless lack of dignity, already chained in eights.

There was no way to do what she needed to do out here. Even though it was a fraction of the size of the cavernous small craft bay, the maintenance shop was still a large, open space. Murasaki headed toward the curtained work areas. Jayne's team was on a break. There would be bodies there. There always were.

She picked one end. Logic said the workflow had to be like any assembly line. Murasaki had only a vague notion of the details of the mortuary team's work, but it involved cleaning, shaving and draining body fluids. If it were her, she'd drain first, then clean and shave.

Murasaki glanced around, then slipped into the curtained area. If a camera caught her, she would plead morbid curiosity.

A man with dirty blond hair lay face down on a steel gurney. He didn't look damaged — the skin was unbroken. Forceps, knives and probes lay on a tray next to him, along with three sets of increasingly large shears and a straight razor. Sighing, Murasaki set down the pressure canister and the tube of silicone. She hoped one of the sets of forceps would serve as spreaders. The canister looked enormous compared to the puckered brown anus that peeked between his pale-furred butt cheeks.

Murasaki found that she was weeping. She couldn't imagine that inserting the canister into a wound would be easier. The hole might be bigger, but the thing could fall out. She would rather dive through the wormhole herself, clutching the canister, than violate the dead like this. But Earth had to know, and this poor bastard was already making the trip.

She selected a set of forceps with small tips, smeared silicone on those tips, set one hand on the cold butt cheek and pressed the forceps against the anus. There was a strong resistance, like stabbing a target dummy, then something popped and the forceps slid in.

"Do you want some help?" asked Jayne behind her.

Murasaki gave out a sharp yelp. "I...," she started to say, then stopped. There were no words for this.

Jayne picked up the canister, turned it in her hands. "It's not going to work, you know. They scan our people when they send them home."

"I have to try." *A weak plan was better than no plan.*

"I know you do. It's who you are." The redhead glanced at the body. "Della Femina says *Garvey's* off course, ballistic trajectory. Looks like she'll spiral into 70 Ophiuchi A."

There went the ruins of Plan A. "The Segrethi did something to the ship," said Murasaki. "With that wormhole technology, all they had to do was let vacuum into the bridge or open the drive shielding. That's got to be how they killed *Pulaski*." She slammed a fist into the gurney. "We have to keep trying."

Jayne sighed. "I know. And we haven't actually attempted what you want, not yet." She tugged at Murasaki's arms, pulling her away from the body. "Let me do this."

"Thank you," whispered Murasaki.

"Don't thank me," said Jayne. "You have to explain it to him." She nodded at the body on the table.

"He's dead."

She shrugged. "It's still his body. That's how I get through this work, the way the bugs have us gutting and cleaning them like fish. I remember that they were all people, and most of them were fighting for you and me."

Murasaki walked around the other end of the gurney and squatted down, her eyes level with the man's hair. She touched his temple, the head leaning over.

For a moment, she thought was Smitts, his jaw and neck shredded and burned by Segrethi zap rifle fire. Murasaki's stomach lurched as she choked on her own bile. As she started to weep, she realized this man's eyes were a different color, cloudy green to Smitts' silver gray. It didn't matter. Someone had loved this man, too.

Murasaki collapsed, curling on the deck and sobbed out her broken heart. After a time, Jayne finished her work, washed up at the sanitation station, then curled up on the deck behind her. The redhead enveloped Murasaki in long pale arms, kissing her hair and neck, and sang softly until Murasaki fell asleep.

Outside with the work party, Murasaki tried to spot the moving star that would be the fastship *Marcus Garvey* on terminal trajectory. It was a fool's effort, for she had no ephemeris to track the fastship's orbit, or any way to locate the vessel even if she did know where to look. The torch that the ship would become within 70 Ophiuchi A's photosphere would light her dreams forever. The only hope she had left lay clipped in a coffle of the naked dead, frost on the blond man's skin as he floated out of the small craft bay.

"Travel safely home," she whispered.

Della Femina jetted toward her with a large orange equipment pack. He clipped it to her utility belt, touching helmets faceplate to faceplate. "This is a fall bag. If things get too hot, use this to get away. It will take you back dirtside."

Murasaki could only imagine what a fall bag was, and she didn't like it very much. She'd certainly never trained with one. She set her suit gloves on it, looking at it stupidly. "You can't go back inside without me."

He grinned. "Sure I can, if I want to get whacked and make that cold, naked trip home. I can't save the world. You maybe can. But right now, there's a good chance you're about to be in big trouble."

They both glanced at the blond man's body, being released from the coffle by one of the other ship handlers.

The wormhole flared and died as their suit radios crackled, then beeped with the all-band priority override. "Hold it," said a voice. It was a human voice, one of the rats, not a Segrethi-appropriated comm unit. "Freeze in place, or die."

Two Segrethi leaned from the edges of the open hatch, zap rifles pointing at the ship handlers. A third one bounded out, limbs folded except for the stick arms. It maneuvered with tiny spurts of expelled gas, though Murasaki couldn't see the technology — the bursts seemed to be coming from its limb joints. The oncoming Segrethi retrobraked and spread its limbs to grab the body. In microgravity, the alien looked like a giant spider feeding on its prey.

Murasaki knew what had to come next, but she still winced when it gutted the corpse. The Segrethi quickly found the canister, which it brandished like a prize.

One of the Segrethi at the hatch ducked away. Nothing much happened for several minutes, the ship handlers holding their positions as the Segrethi with the canister clutched the body and rotated its helmet to stare at them one by one. Murasaki eased her right hand into the suit's cargo pocket, fumbling for her flechette pistol.

The priority override beeped again. "Attention to discipline. The responsible party from the mortuary team is being held accountable. A randomly-selected member of the EVA team will also be held accountable."

Jayne appeared at the hatch of the small craft, two Segrethi holding her in their clawed power arms. Nude, her red hair floated loose in vacuum, her skin flushed as capillaries burst. Her face was distorted, puffing outward like a balloon.

Seeing vapor frosting on Jayne's lips, Murasaki realized that Jayne was still alive, or at least hadn't finished dying yet. She knew a conscious human could survive hard vacuum for up to a minute, longer with extreme medical intervention after the fact.

The Segrethi stood there while Jayne struggled, her motions growing weaker and weaker. The redhead looked toward Murasaki.

That was too much. Murasaki drew her flechette pistol and fired her suit jets. She would be damned if she would hang there in orbit while the

Segrethi murdered yet another human.

"Randomly selected, my ass," Murasaki screamed over all-band priority. "Randomly select *this*, bug-lovers."

She dove straight for the Segrethi holding the gutted corpse. It swung the body forward as a shield, while one stick arm scrabbled for its zap rifle. The pressure canister spun free.

Murasaki rolled so she was approaching feet-first and squeezed off a flight of tapered carbon nanotubule flechettes. The flechette pistol was a vacuum-rated weapon, and she was vacuum-combat qualified.

The flechettes shredded the blond man's chest. Passing through the body, they didn't have much effect on the Segrethi, but she didn't expect any. Murasaki just wanted to make it duck.

Della Femina shouted over the all-band priority, arguing with someone, but she ignored the chatter. Murasaki used her suit jets to spiral along her vector, trying to dodge whatever fire was coming from the bugs in the hatch bay. The Segrethi before her spun and recovered, still holding the body.

She knew their secret. Up close and personal, they died easy.

Murasaki accelerated her suit, juked a few degrees out of true to miss the corpse. She slammed feet-first into the joint between the Segrethi's right hind power leg and its bean-pod body. With her free hand, she grabbed the stick leg on the same side, which tore free. Murasaki kept her boot toes hooked in the damaged power leg joint and goosed her jets.

She and the Segrethi spun together around a common center of mass. Pale fluid boiled out of the damaged chitin.

The Segrethi lost its grip on the body as Murasaki pipped her dorsal jets. She fell as if to hug the bug across the back. The ceramic bell of her flechette pistol came up against the brassy base of the ball helmet, and she pulled the trigger.

As the Segrethi's head shot free, Murasaki pulled herself loose and accelerated directly into the fire that had to be coming from the open hatch of the small craft bay. Without an atmosphere to ionize to plasma, the zap rifles didn't generate their characteristic lightning bolt, but she could see bright flashes from the muzzle.

Ahead of her, three of the ship handlers raced toward the same Segrethi. By his bulk, one of them was Della Femina. Two more humans spun on ballistic trajectories, already disabled or killed.

Dispersal effects rendered the flechette pistol useless outside of twenty meters, so Murasaki held her course. She felt heat in her shoulder, and glanced over to see her suit sheathing boil away to glowing gas, but it wasn't a killing shot. Obviously not, as she still breathed.

She realized Della Femina was yelling at her over all-band. "Wanda, get out. We'll cover as long as we can. Get dirtside, make them pay."

She lusted for blood, golden alien blood, but he was right. She had learned a lot about the Segrethi, knew the secret of the bodies, if not what that secret meant. She'd blown all their chances of getting help from Earth, but she could do a lot more damage on the loose down below than she could dying here, now.

Once again, she'd have to run away from the fight.

Bile flooding her mouth, Murasaki altered her course, heading for the broomstick on the EVA hatch rack while continuing to track the Segrethi sentries with her pistol.

Della Femina slammed bodily into one of the aliens even as his suit bloomed red and white vapor from the back. A zap rifle shot must have cut right through him.

One of the other ship handlers followed him in, crooking an elbow around the brassy helmet as if it was a game ball. Segrethi and human tumbled out of her sight even as the last ship handler closed on the other covering Segrethi, swinging the power shuffle like a cricket bat.

Murasaki reached the broomstick as the all-band fell silent. She unclipped the power umbilical and released the safety latches clipping it to the hull.

Her back itched, waiting for the zap rifle shot, but this was her best chance. The open small craft hatch was at an extremely oblique angle to her. They'd have to lean out to even begin to target her.

The broomstick was fully charged. Murasaki settled into the oversized bicycle saddle designed for a suit's broad, padded butt, grabbed the joystick, and goosed it.

As she pulled away from the EVA hatch, skimming the curve of the hull, two Segrethi sprang out of the small craft hatch. They extended their power legs, jumping away from the ship, then used back pack maneuvering jets to get a high firing angle on her.

Murasaki fled along the center ring, looking for cover. Gdansk Orbital was an accumulation of naval architecture tacked onto the old slowship hull. There were struts, braces, corridors, shafts and tubes galore, kilometers of winding, complex vacuum-exposed geometry outside the habitable core. But she just didn't know the Port like Della Femina or the other locals would have.

The broomstick spun as a zap rifle bolt damaged a control vane. She compensated with pressure jets, then skimmed a break in the center ring, finding a shaft. She dove as the aliens followed her down.

Murasaki pulled a tight turn around a vertical pressure vessel. She glanced over her shoulder. Both Segrethi still followed. She hit a utility raceway and followed it. This was almost but not quite a tunnel, three walls solid and the fourth latticework.

Behind her, the Segrethi narrowed the distance, using their power legs to kick off in the enclosed space. A zap rifle bolt raised an explosion in front of her. She would never make it out of the raceway.

Murasaki killed her acceleration and flipped the broomstick, nearly catching the wall. Now she flew backward, facing the two oncoming aliens. She cranked the acceleration, in effect braking, and brought up the flechette pistol.

As the Segrethi raced toward her, she put a cloud of flechettes into one of their zap rifles. The rifle exploded, blowing two arms off the alien carrying it and sending the creature slamming into the raceway wall to disintegrate in a cloud of chitin and boiling goo while the bronzed helmet sailed past her.

The other Segrethi caught itself on the latticework and braced its zap rifle to fire at Murasaki. Her momentum reversed, she accelerated toward it, aiming for another shot. She pulled the trigger, but nothing happened. The ready light blinked amber—out of ammunition. She'd never been able to restock since arriving at Orbital Port.

Murasaki put her head down and charged the Segrethi blind. She felt the top of her helmet warm up as the zap rifle washed it, shielding boiling off again as the lining cracked and her hair smoldered. Then she slammed straight into the alien, killing the broomstick's controls and letting her body take the impact against the raceway lattice.

The suit's anticollision systems kicked in, gelpacks around her chest and joints hardening as the internal pressure shot up. Murasaki's vision went red, then black, but she didn't lose consciousness. Losing orientation was bad enough.

After a moment, she realized her vision had gone out because the faceplate had blanked, protective optics trying to shield her eyes from possible radiation damage. The blanking slowly dissolved to reveal portions of dead Segrethi and her broomstick trapped within a series of electrical arcs. She had missed taking voltage from the Port's power mains by some scant centimeters.

It took the suit almost ten minutes of drifting to self-repair sufficiently to restore her freedom of movement. Murasaki felt like she'd been stepped on. She'd certainly cracked ribs and sprained perhaps every joint she possessed.

To her amazement, Della Femina's fall bag was still clipped to the suit. Even more astonishing, it appeared intact. Murasaki was out of options. Resistance, however futile, was all she had left, and it would take the fall bag to get her down to the surface. She unclipped the help chip from fall bag package and slotted it into her suit comm.

Navigating toward an exit from the utility raceway, Murasaki listened in horror to the help chip's description of how to employ the fall bag. Enter the same way she had entered the vacuum bag, seal herself in, select a landing zone, accept nudges from the tiny control jets, and ride into the atmosphere on a purely ballistic descent. Parachutes deployed at an altitude calculated by onboard systems, bringing her gently to a halt.

It sounded like the easiest suicide in the world.

She'd always hated high diving.

III: GOING TO GROUND

Murasaki agonized over whether to drop near Katyn and try to link up with whatever shadow government might be operating. But landing anywhere in the shuttle port's approach control range was asking for a bug reception. Teutoburgerwald was another choice; she knew the area around the training school like the back of her hand, but there was no advantage to being there. Except, perhaps, personal safety.

So she selected a spread of targets out on the Katyn Plains—far enough out of scan, but still within the core of human settlement. And, she hoped, resistance.

The fall bag's idiot AI didn't like the angle of attack with respect to Murasaki's preferred landing zones from their current position, preferring to wait out a series of gently decaying orbits. She was mortally afraid of Segrethi pursuit, so she overrode the bag's priorities until, protesting, it nudged itself into descent. Murasaki sat almost doubled over in the foam-insulated sack. She had exactly two instruments available on her heads-up faceplate display—altitude and latitude/longitude positioning.

She didn't know if it was design oversight or a desire on the part of the engineers not to alarm the occupant, but there was no airspeed indicator. She simply nestled in this giant garbage bag, slowly tumbling out of the mauve Gdansku sky. Like the Segrethi had, come to think of it.

Dziękują Bogowi she didn't have external video to watch the ground come rushing at her—just the thought of what she was doing gave Murasaki the screaming willies. At least the systems were mechanical. Even the parachutes deployed based on input from an analog altimeter. The fall bag's AI assured her it was designed to survive massive power containment failures, and its limited electronics were heavily shielded. Murasaki hoped this meant she couldn't be tracked by EM emissions.

Eventually bored out of her terror at free falling from orbit, Murasaki fell into a shocky, exhausted sleep.

She woke screaming. Daylight spilled in, the bright glare of 70 Ophiuchi A filtered through the mauve of Nowa Gdansk's atmospheric Rayleigh scattering and airborne microbiota. The tapered ceramic bell of a flechette rifle nudged her faceplate, while a fist reached forward to knock on her helmet.

Murasaki blew her suit seals, opened her faceplate, and prepared to negotiate for her life.

"You were in vacuum in that monkey suit?" demanded the man with the rifle, silhouetted by the glare. Though he spoke English, his Polish accent was pronounced.

Murasaki blinked away tears, squinting to clear her vision. Everything stank of burned insulation—legacy of the fall bag's descent. "Yes, obviously."

"Nothing left of the top of that helmet but some liner and a bunch of shards. Nice shot someone took on you."

"Segrethi tend to be like that."

His fist opened to a hand, which she reached for, then he pulled her out of the bag.

She found herself standing on a stony hill above the Katyn Plains, breadbasket of Nowa Gdansk. She couldn't see the capital, which meant she was fairly far south. Murasaki glanced over her shoulder. The rippled, rounded Moldau Hills rose behind her. This was the far end of her target zone, but in parameters. Barely.

Her rescuer was short, squat, a middle-aged belly spilling over khaki work pants cinched too tight with a leather belt. He was ruddy and blond. Above the neck he resembled one of Public Order's recruiting poster Poles. Murasaki was painfully aware of her battered appearance, the damaged space suit. She turned to fish out the flechette pistol.

"*Żaden, żaden.*" said her rescuer, nudging her shoulder with the flechette rifle. "No weapons yet. Who are you?"

"Commander Wanda Murasaki," she said straightening to face him again. "Gdansku Force. Until recently, Training Commandant, Teutoburgerwald Infantry School."

He grinned, the handsome young man he'd once been still close to the surface. The rifle didn't waver. "Relieved of duty by the Spaghettis, no doubt. Just dropped out of the sky for a chat with a lonely farmer, eh? I am Jan Potocki, formerly of Public Order Police, still a reservist."

"That explains the rifle." Private weapons weren't common on Nowa Gdansk, a planet without large predators or a tradition of civil violence. This would be a distinct impediment to organizing resistance, she realized.

"That, and the bugs." He glanced skyward. "Give me your story in short. If I like it, I sling the rifle, we bury the fall bag and go have lunch."

"And if you don't like it?" she asked, smiling in spite of herself.

"Bang-bang, a grave is needed. *Tak bądź to.* More digging for me." He frowned, apparently concerned at the prospect of additional labor.

Murasaki sighed, then counted off on her fingers as she spoke. "So far, I've killed five Segrethi in close quarters. A number of friends have died helping me, along with a small mob of acquaintances. That's the shortest story I can tell."

After staring at her for a while, Jan slung the rifle and unclipped a folding shovel from his belt. "You are a lucky one, I see. Details later. I hope you like pork."

He nodded at the limp mass of the fall bag, drogue chutes trailing away to a tangled mess on some thorn bushes. "We will bury this now, along with your suit. Afterward, lunch. I do have some nice wine to go with the pig. Are you on duty, or can you drink some?"

Laughing, she stripped off her engineering hardsuit, down to the undersuit. He handed her the shovel.

After lunch beneath an elm tree, they swam in a river. He wasn't any prettier with his clothes off, but after the frozen dead of Segrethi ritual, Murasaki was happy to see warm human skin with muscles moving underneath. Jan eyed her shamelessly until she splashed him. "Stop it," she said. "I could break your neck without even trying."

"So now a dirty old man gets the death penalty?"

"You're not old," she said. Murasaki noticed Jan had been losing his accent as they talked.

"Ah, but dirty, yes? Never too old to look." He smiled sadly. "Sometimes too old to touch."

She wasn't interested. With a slight start of shame, Murasaki remembered her nipples hardening at Jayne's touch. But now Jayne was so much frozen protein, dead of terror and vacuum. That thought was enough to snatch away her good cheer.

"Not during this war, Jan," she said, "but I thank you for the invitation."

He grinned without speaking.

"It *was* an invitation, right?" she asked meekly after a few moments.

"Let's just say I shall go relax in the cold water by the shady bank for a few moments," the farmer said with mock dignity. "You may accompany me and speak with no fears."

She followed him to stand neck deep in the hanging shade of a bank of native mold-bushes. The plants were bulbous and blue, giant trembling sacs like colored clouds just over their heads. The cold water made her savaged bones and joints ache even more.

"I need to find our partisans," Murasaki said. Somehow she was both relieved and disappointed that the moment between them had passed.

"Why would you think there are partisans?" asked Jan.

"We are Gdansku," she said. "It is beyond imagination that our folk would submit to insects who fell from the sky."

Jan shrugged. "It is not so bad for most. The bugs are not interested in taxes. They scuttle around on surveys, leave small garrisons at key points, shut down some industries, arrest or kill a few bosses nobody liked anyway. For most people, life goes on. For some, it is easier."

"I don't believe that," Murasaki said in a quiet voice. "It might be true for a few, but too many would resent the occupation."

"So one day a woman falls from the sky on the outskirts of my property." Jan spread his arms, splashing her with river water and miming heart-rending sadness. His accent thickened again as he said, "She drinks of my wine, eats of my ham, swims her pretty body in my river with me but refuses my embrace. Now I am supposed to turn over a rumored resistance movement to her hands?"

"Well, yes. Where could I have come from but orbit? Why else come down this way? The Segrethi run the shuttles now; they can land their own agents anywhere they like."

Jan scratched his chin. "You have a point. Let us go to my house. I will check you out with some friends."

"So I fall from the sky," Murasaki said, "am fed and bathed by a smooth-tongued devil of a farmer, and I should surrender myself to his custody?"

Jan laughed, a great bellow. "You can sleep in the barn with the pigs if you prefer, but there is nothing for us out here. Come, let us dress and go home." He winked. "Ladies first."

Murasaki went first. She took her time putting on the suit's undersheath.

Back at the pig farm, which Jan referred to as 'Saragossa,' he explained that it would take some days for his 'friends' to respond. Jan wouldn't let her use the phone until he'd heard back. Murasaki had to respect his caution — this was her probation.

Wearing Jan's old clothes pinned down to her size, Murasaki slopped the pigs, patched the barn roof, rewired the hydrogen pumping system on Jan's second-best tractor and generally made herself useful. Evenings, they talked about Gdansk Orbital Port and what had happened on Invasion Day. Though he continued to flirt with her, the sexual charge she initially had felt was gone, washed away by hard work and discussion of post-Invasion politics.

And the memories of her dead. So many had already died in her name. The thought chilled her to the bone.

"It's only been a month," said Jan. They sat in the main room of his house, before a dressed-stone fireplace set in a rough-ripped softwood wall. Pigskin rugs covered the flagged stone floor, while hams and cheeses hung in the rafters. "The aliens haven't affected us very much."

"Most people in Orbital don't think their lives have been affected either, but it's happening." She hadn't told him about the bodies and the wormhole. She didn't want that rumor spreading until she knew whether and how to best use the information. "These aren't colonists," she added. "This is a beachhead force, accomplishing some set task."

"They do seem lightly equipped." The farmer leaned back in his chair, tapping his pipe against the rim of a blue-glazed ceramic bowl.

She nodded. "Their numbers are scant, their equipment nominal. They're not here to stay."

Jan puffed on his pipe. "Then our bugs are either taking something away or bringing something in."

The wormholes, thought Murasaki. They could do anything with that wormhole generator, if they had a sufficiently large power source.

He glanced sidelong at her. "You know more than you will tell me. That is good. Does the name Awolowo mean anything to you?"

"Only kindness and good hope," she said casually.

"I see." He puffed again. "I cannot speak for Kindness, but Goodhope will be here soon. The men who bring him would kill you in a heartbeat. He is well-protected."

Her heart leapt. Finally, she would come in from the cold. "Government lives."

"Government-in-hiding, they call it." Jan studied her. "Other than the Lieutenant Governor, you are the only senior official anyone has seen in weeks. The others were killed on Invasion Day, or vanished shortly after."

Just like Orbital, Murasaki thought. Cut off the head, the body marches on, but the big decisions lapse. Eventually the lack of big decisions will poison the small ones. At least Awolowo was a local, not a Colonial Secretariat appointee like his late boss.

"Smart, these Segrethi," she said.

"Yes. For bugs."

The conversation faded as they both watched the flames crackle, waiting for the man who would come to tell her what to do. Murasaki had been the death of enough loyal men and woman. She was glad to be free of that responsibility.

Almost.

Perhaps an hour later, Murasaki was startled from a gentle drowse by the shuffling spray of tires on gravel, followed by a thump of crunching metal—the thick, complex sound of a groundcar wreck. A heavy weapon hammered somewhere in the distance as Jan's pigs shrieked in terror.

Spilling his pipe on the pigskin rug, Jan leapt from his chair to grab the flechette rifle and bolt out the back door, away from the noises. Murasaki swept up her useless flechette pistol along with the butcher knife the farmer had loaned her and followed him into the night.

Jan crouched at one corner of the house. A single beam of light stuttered among the nearby pines, like a vibraknife with a bad oscillator. It came from the headlamps of a civilian groundcar, a bulky license-built Volvo limo, which lay on its side shoved through the stone wall at the edge of the pigpens. Squealing hogs mobbed the vehicle. In the distance, helicopter blades whumped through the night air. Murasaki scanned the starry sky but saw no running lights.

Unfriendlies, for certain.

"Here," she hissed, handing Jan the knife. "Give me the rifle. I'll deal with the bird, you go see to that wreck."

Jan glanced at her, his face barely visible in the darkness. "You said you were hard on your friends. Against the logic of my heart, I pray I am not your friend yet. I do not wish to die tonight." They traded weapons, then a rough kiss that surprised her mightily. She crouched, lips still warm from his touch, breathing hard for no reason as Jan loped across the yard shouting at his pigs.

Shaking her head back to sensibility, Murasaki ran toward the barn. She had left the ten-meter ladder against the south wall after doing the roof repairs. Slinging the flechette rifle over her shoulder, she climbed rapidly, then eased her way onto the roof.

The barn roof approximated a curve, falling through three increasingly steep slopes. As luck would have it, the pine chocks she had nailed for footholds were still in place. Murasaki found her way to the shallowest slope of the roof, along the peak, then scuttled to the other end to overlook the chaos in the barnyard below.

Eyes better adjusted to the dark now, Murasaki saw Jan standing on the upturned flank of the ground car, helping a large man climb out. Not Awolowo—the Lieutenant Governor was tall but thin.

The pattering beat of the helicopter drew her gaze upward. She glimpsed a sharp-edged shadow in the starlight. Then the nose-mounted autocannon pod flashed, depleted uranium rounds overshooting the wrecked car to hit the barn. Timbers beneath her feet shivered with the impact as the scent of mixed straw and chicken shit swirled in the night.

She glanced down one more time. Jan and the big man ignored the helicopter to help another man out of the car. The Lieutenant Governor.

Focusing back on the helicopter, Murasaki shouldered the rifle. Only one class of helicopter on Nowa Gdansk mounted an autocannon, the Gdansku Force Air Wing's Euroaero L-3. She sought an aim point about a meter and a half above the twinned muzzle flashes of the autocannon— right where the pilot would be seated.

The helicopter slid across her line of sight, front end rotating away from its axis of travel. It was still two hundred meters away, long range for a flechette rifle, but she had to get the pilot's attention away from Awolowo.

Murasaki fired, seeing a satisfying flare of sparks through her scope a moment later as the flight of flechettes struck the helicopter. There was no shattering, which meant the canopy had held. About what she had expected.

The helicopter swung back toward her, hanging level in the air. Murasaki mentally reviewed the layout of the face of the Euroaero. There were turbine intakes along the sides of the machine, perhaps two meters above the chin turret and offset a meter and a half to the left and right. They were a narrow profile, vulnerable only to a direct head-on shot. But if she could make it, the flechettes entering the intake would chew the turbine on that side to bits, sending the helicopter out of control in the hands of any but the most expert pilot.

She could only sight with sufficient accuracy if the machine fired at her again, the autocannon muzzle flashes giving her an aim point. Murasaki shot at the angled front windshield to tweak the pilot and his gunner, then rolled hard to her left.

The autocannon chattered, shredding the roof where she had just been. Splinters flew as Murasaki rolled, then she slipped onto the steeper pitch of the middle part of the roof and lost control of her fall.

"Crap," she screamed as she slid toward the six-meter drop-off. That side of the barn was lined with plows and harvesting equipment. She'd be lucky not to get impaled.

The gutter caught her just as she was about to tumble off the roof. Ahead of her, the autocannon still chattered, so Murasaki got to her knees, one foot in the gutter and sighted on the turbine intake nearest her. As she shot, the helicopter swung, walking its own line of fire toward her.

Trying to avoid the sudden death impact of the autocannon slugs, Murasaki leapt forward, away from the gutter and the farm implements below. She fell off the front of the barn toward the muddy wallow six meters below. As she dropped, a gut-wrenching screech echoed from the helicopter. Murasaki slammed facedown into the backs of a pair of four hundred kilo hogs as the helicopter's surviving engine raced.

The attacking machine slammed into the ground just after she did, still perhaps two hundred meters downslope. The hogs panicked from the noise and her weight on their backs, dumping Murasaki into the mud as they fled into the damaged barn.

She sat up, spitting mud from her nose and mouth, just in time to see the wrecked helicopter explode.

Doctor Goodhope Awolowo, Lieutenant Governor of Nowa Gdansk and noted genomic therapist, loomed out of the darkness. He was tall and lanky, skin so brown as to be black. In the gloom, Awolowo's teeth gleamed yellow as he leaned down to grasp her hand.

"Commander Murasaki. It is good to see you again."

"I wish we were meeting under better circumstances, sir," she gasped, still trying to get her breath back.

Awolowo glanced at the burning helicopter. "Almost any prior circumstances were better, unfortunately. I believe we should make haste. May I help you stand?"

"Thank you, sir," said Murasaki.

Jan had survived intact, but Awolowo's last remaining bodyguard had taken two autocannon slugs in the upper chest. Portions of his corpse were slumped on the dirt next to the upended groundcar, inside of which his fellow guard was dead over the wheel.

"It seems I am no friend of yours, after all," said Jan, smiling in the fire-lit dark at Murasaki as she and Awolowo approached. "As I have survived."

"I owe you my life, sir," said the Lieutenant Governor, "for saving me from those traitors in the helicopter, but that joke seems in poor taste, or worse. Linahan there was a good man."

"Private joke, sir," Murasaki said, trading glances with Jan. "Apologies, it's the stress," she added.

"You two need to go, now," the farmer said. "If these rats were in the Air Wing, there can be more."

Murasaki grimaced. "What will happen to you?"

"Only worry about your friends, Wanda." Jan took her hand. "I myself will be hunting rats for a while, it seems. There's trekking gear under the tarp in the second stall. Grab two packs, take that rifle, and go. Get up into the Moldaus, head west. You can find partisans in all the major towns." The farmer nodded at Awolowo. "He will be your passport."

Murasaki glanced down at the body. "A lot of help that was to Linahan."

"He did his job. Not to be morbid, but let us check if our late friend has loads for your pistol." Jan knelt, pulling her down with him. He murmured, "*Robi wy mówicie Język Polski? Dyrektor robi nie.*"

Did she speak Polish, he was asking, saying the Lieutenant Governor did not. "*Tak,*" she whispered. Yes. Plenty enough to follow him.

Jan ran his hands through the ruins of the bodyguard's tunic. "*Tam może być kwestią z bratem.*" He glanced at her again to see if she understood.

Murasaki nodded. There may be a problem with the brother.

Jan nodded back. "*Uważam co mogliśmy być zdradzani przez dobrotliwość.*"

He believed they had been betrayed by kindness. Kindness, Awolowo's brother on Orbital. Was he the King Rat? That would jibe with her experiences topside.

"*Wiadomość zrozumiał,*" she muttered. Message understood.

"Ah," shouted Jan in English. "Three clips."

There they were—the reloads she had craved ever since the pistol had failed to fire inside the utility raceway at Gdansk Orbital. Murasaki stood, turned to the Lieutenant Governor, who was staring out into the darkness. "Come on, sir, we must go."

He nodded. Murasaki turned to Jan, set her arm around his neck and kissed him full on the lips, her kiss this time, her will. Her heart.

"Another time, then," the farmer gasped after she withdrew.

"Another time."

Murasaki and Awolowo walked toward the back of the barn, the bulk of the Moldau Hills beckoning them even through the darkness.

IV: THE MEDIUM AS THE MESSAGE

A day later, Nowa Gdansk's government-in-hiding lurked in a damaged grain silo in a valley deep in the Moldau Hills. Even within their shelter, the air was musty with the smell of rotten wheat. Native mold spores the size of peas floated around the two of them. Too alien to engender allergies, the blue-green blobs were still annoying to deal with.

Murasaki described the ritual of the bodies to Awolowo. Jan's trust in the Lieutenant Governor offset her fear and loathing of his brother—Awolowo needed to know the truth, and he *was* authority. Murasaki had to believe in the chain of command. She was tired of making her own decisions, tired of trying to balance the fate of Nowa Gdansk—and, ultimately, Earth—on her narrow shoulders. Not to mention the corpses of her friends.

"Religion? I don't know," said Awolowo. "Ritual, or even routine. It could mean anything. At least you have determined that the Segrethi are not eating our dead. The shipments of our deceased to orbit have disturbed many people."

"Are they sending all the dead?" Murasaki asked.

"No." Awolowo stared into the reeking darkness of the silo. "But anyone who dies in contact with them, or resisting them."

"I wish I knew if they were still doing the wormhole ritual on that rigid schedule." She sighed. "We can only assume, for now. What else have you seen down here, sir?"

He glanced at her. "They're surveying. That is how things appear, at any rate."

"For what?"

"Tomorrow, let's head into the foothills. If we stay downwind, we might catch them at it. The Segrethi are not secretive, just mysterious."

Murasaki and Awolowo clambered in silence through crumbling gray boulders that towered three and four meters above them, the consistency of pumice but much denser. Terran vegetation had little hold up here in the hills, so the two of them were surrounded by more of the large, quivering native molds and mosses that gleamed in the dark blues and greens of Nowa Gdansk's evolution. The great, bubbly plants tended to curves that caught the attention of the human eye in their subtle wrongness.

"The Segrethi do not seem particularly strong," Awolowo said as they stopped to rest in the deep, damp shadows.

"No, not if you catch them just right." Murasaki remembered the fight at the shuttle port, that great machete-sword slicing Williamson in half. "But they're as powerful as they need to be. Our military was never designed to deal with an external threat like the Segrethi. After the drubbing they gave us on Invasion Day, we've got nothing left but scattered partisans. There's no way we can take that wormhole machine in orbit."

"What I mean," said Awolowo, "is that if you had succeeded in telling Earth what happened, they could free us. They would have to, simply in their own interests. Segrethi ground forces are spread thin. If the aliens had a deep space cargo capability, they wouldn't need the wormholes."

Murasaki sighed. "A lot of people have died trying to help me send a message home. Because of me, they blew up *Pulaski*. I tried to warn *Marcus Garvey* off, and they killed that ship. I even tried sending a message in a body." She shuddered at the memory of corpse-tampering. "Nothing goes through that wormhole but the naked dead. After my violent exit, they must have EVA security corked tight. No way to shoot a probe through. They'd shut it down in seconds."

She wished she'd thought of that at the time. It might have succeeded then.

"Message in a body," said Awolowo. He tugged his lip and began to hum.

"Sir?"

He just smiled.

Later that day as they slunk further down the rugged Moldau ridges, Awolowo and Murasaki spotted Segrethi. The aliens were in a work party of four. One guarded a Gdansku Force transport helicopter they'd flown in on—complete with human pilots barely visible within the cockpit—while the other three walked around with tall probes that they kept shoving into the ground. The probes were rods, about two meters long, made of the same velvety bronze metal as the wormhole cannon had been, back on Gdansk Orbital Port. They had no immediately obvious function.

"That's only the second time I've seen them with any technology other their combat gear," said Murasaki as she peered through a rock cleft, rifle in hand.

Awolowo nodded. He knelt down out of sight, scratching symbols on the mossy ground with a stick. "They mostly use our equipment. Like that helicopter."

"Nowa Gdansk is a beachhead," she said. "They're here to do something specific, not hold the planet. Not with this force and this equipment. Whatever it is, it involves that surveying."

"I wish we had gotten a dissection of one of them," said Awolowo. He scratched some more in the damp soil. "They do not weigh much, and they virtually disintegrate when they die. We do not understand what makes them work."

"It's all smell," whispered Murasaki. She remembered the Segrethi on the road to the shuttle port, sniffing the ichor plastered to her uniform. "I don't know if they even have ears, and their eyes seem clouded with cataracts. Milky looking." She sighted in on the Segrethi, who continued to stalk about with their survey probes. "We should turn north, sir. Leave the Moldaus and get down into the Green River country."

"There is a drug lab in Port Wroclaw," said Awolowo. He glanced westward, along the direction of travel they had been pursuing. "Perhaps forty more kilometers."

Murasaki sank down against the rock and eyed the Lieutenant Governor. "You need a vaccination?"

"No. I need a gene sequencer."

"Oh, I see." Murasaki sighed. Despite her longing for the chain of command, she was starting to miss being in charge of things herself. For all the good it had done her. "We're being hunted across the face of the planet, and you want a DNA sequencer."

"Yes. Absolutely."

Was this the betrayal Jan had warned her of? Somehow that seemed far too complex an effort, when all he had to do was shout, and bring the enemy down upon them.

It was Kindness up in orbit that she should worry about, not Goodwill down here. Murasaki felt paranoid even beyond the needs of the moment, but she had no reason to confront Awolowo. Not yet. "I'm just the soldier, sir. You're the one who knows what he's doing."

"Perhaps."

Port Wroclaw spread out under a forest of native greenbrain trees along the Wroclaw River. Tall, thin with broccoli-like tops, the greenbrains sheltered scattered log houses and ferrocrete buildings—the very model of a colonial frontier town. A lone Segrethi sentry stood outside a warehouse near the docks, avoided by the desultory human traffic.

Awolowo and Murasaki squatted in a huge Terran rhododendron along a well-traveled path at the edge of town. Her own flechette pistol bulking in her pocket, Murasaki field-stripped Jan's flechette rifle as she talked, breaking the pieces down to fit in her backpack.

"You sure about this?" she asked the Lieutenant Governor. "If we get spotted going in, it's over. I might be able to nail the handful of Segrethi here, but they'll call in support."

"We need to get in," Awolowo said. "Once there, we can hide for days."

Jan had told her that Segrethi didn't go into human buildings unless they had to. Couldn't stand the smell, apparently. Gdansk Orbital's air scrubbers must have been a godsend to them. "Days? What in the world are you going to do with that gene sequencer?"

Awolowo smiled. "Build a virus."

Murasaki's grasp of microbiology was mediocre at best, but that seemed unreasonable even to her. "I don't think you can infect a Segrethi. Not with something of ours."

"Of course not. I am going to infect humans."

Her hand lingered on the inductor of the flechette rifle as she mulled that over. This wasn't the resistance role she imagined when she had climbed into that fall bag and dropped screaming back to the surface.

The two of them waited for a sufficiently large group of loggers coming in from the greenbrain forest. Awolowo and Murasaki stepped out of the bush into the small crowd, smiling. Without a word, the loggers moved around them, placing the newcomers in the center of their group.

"You working or begging?" asked a tall Asian.

"Working," said Awolowo quietly. "We're government."

"Hmm." The Asian glanced at them. "If you're lying, we'll whack you ourselves. But Spaghettis killed six here last week alone. You've got friends if you can earn them." He sniffed the air. "Wrong clothes. Spaghettis'll smell you fast."

"Don't smell like greenbrains," added another logger. "Everyone in Port Rock smells like greenbrains."

"Thanks for the tip," said Murasaki. "Make us smell right?"

One of the loggers shrugged off a wool sweater and passed it to Awolowo. Another handed Murasaki a leather vest. "Give us your gear," said the Asian. "We'll spread it around. Dilute the odor."

Murasaki glanced at Awolowo. Awolowo nodded, so she handed her pack with the broken-down flechette rifle to the leather vest guy. She was careful to keep her pistol. *Never again go unarmed*, she thought. Never again.

"We need to get into Wroclaw Biotech," said Awolowo.

"No friends of the Spaghettis, alright," said the tall Asian with a snort. "When they got here, bugs sealed anything they thought smelled like tech. I guess you are a bureaucrat. You a scientist, too?"

"No, I am a doctor. And I have a cure for our problem in mind."

With scattered grins, the whole crowd took a leftward branch in the trail.

For three days, Murasaki watched Awolowo in the sequencing lab. He worked around the clock, pausing only for short naps. She couldn't rest either, fearing that he would contact his brother. It was an idiotic idea—if he'd wanted to turn her in directly to the Segrethi he could have done it any time—but she couldn't get the thought out of her head. She didn't dare touch the phones here. Some human or Segrethi monitor might notice the comm traffic.

Not that she had anyone to call. Gdansku Force Base Prime had to have been long overrun.

So Murasaki scavenged beef-broth agar for both of them from unused petri dishes stacked in the lab coolers. She rested from time to time, catching brief, uneasy naps, but mostly she stalked the dusty corridors, peeked out the curtained windows or stared at Awolowo's hunched back. One or another of the loggers drifted by the ostensibly abandoned lab several times a day, casting casual glances at the building. Looking for the help code she'd arranged with the tall Asian.

As she had so many times before, Murasaki returned to the glass door of the sequencing lab, flechette pistol in her hand. Useless, she was useless here, even more useless than she had been outside Government House, listening to people die within.

Awolowo's head was inside the VR hood of a workstation, hands moving in little twists within the sensor cubespace. Try as she might, turning the problem over and over in her head, Murasaki couldn't come to the tactical or strategic point of the Lieutenant Governor unleashing a virus on the human population.

His population.

It just didn't make sense. Was this the betrayal Jan had warned her of?

Enough, Murasaki thought.

She pushed open the door, pistol ready. "Lieutenant Governor. Sir."

"A moment, please. I am reviewing some modeling results." Awolowo made a last few motions in the cubespace then tossed back the hood and turned to look at her. "Yes, Commander?"

She didn't quite point the pistol at him. "Explain to me how your virus is going to save Nowa Gdansk and mother Earth."

Awolowo ignored the weapon. "Our bodies go home," he said. "Nothing goes with them—tattoos, effects, nothing. You tried that method. So how do we warn Earth?"

"Bodies are a message, of a sort. A virus isn't."

Awolowo picked up an inhaler from the workstation bench. He popped it in his mouth and squirted. "But surely it is."

Murasaki leveled the flechette pistol at the Lieutenant Governor. "What the hell are you doing?"

"*Mene, mene, tekel, upharsin,*" said Awolowo. "Daniel 5:25."

The pistol quivered in Murasaki's grip as she studied Awolowo. How badly had the Lieutenant Governor slipped his cogs?

Or had *she*, drawing down on the surviving executive of the colony?

"The handwriting on the wall," Awolowo said gently. "I built a coronavirus that writes a coded message into the DNA of every human cell it infects. I just gave myself a cold, courtesy of that virus.

"My situation report will be encrypted in ternary code in the junk sequences on chromosome 23, in my cells and those of anyone that catches this from me. One of these days, someone on Earth *will* do a full autopsy on one of our bodies, with a gene scan. The code is headed by a two-hundred base pair SOS sequence and a twenty base pair polyprimer key." He smiled. "That should get their attention."

Murasaki's pistol wavered. "You're sending a message to Earth inside our bodies?"

"Writing for help on the walls of our cells with DNA."

It was enough to make her cry. All this effort to get here, trapping themselves in the center of an occupied town, for this. "They may never see the bodies back on Earth, sir. I told you that. Dead people in orbit are nothing new. What will make them pay attention to us now?"

"I have confidence that you can work out a solution to that problem, Commander," said Awolowo. "Attracting attention is your role, for which the military has admirably trained you in my estimation. As for me, I intend to borrow your rifle and go assault the Segrethi sentry by the docks."

"You have totally slipped your cogs, sir," Murasaki announced. "There is no way I can allow that."

"But if they kill me," he said with a sad smile, "they will send my body home. I can pay for my brother's treachery and save the world, at the very small price of one man's life. All you need to do is get their attention on the other side of the wormhole. That will be message enough for Earth to search for detailed explanations, and they will find my body. A colonial Lieutenant Governor, they will autopsy." He tapped the skin of his forearm. "Details in here."

"Kindness Awolowo," whispered Murasaki. "Jan warned me."

"My brother, King Rat," the Lieutenant Governor replied. "I knew anyway, but you see, *Ja także mówią Język Polski.*"

Murasaki finally talked Awolowo out of immediate suicide.

"Contaminate me with the virus, sir," she said. "Let me get sick. Let this spread, and then we'll see what needs to be done. At the least we both should get back to Katyn. I can't possibly get to orbit from this backwater."

She had no idea how she would climb to orbit from Katyn, either, but that's where the shuttle port was.

"How do you propose to reach Katyn?" he asked.

"Just like your virus," she said. "Hidden inside something else. In our case, greenbrain logs." The loggers had to still be shipping them out, or they would be idle by now under the Segrethi occupation.

She moved them both to the service entrance at one side of the clinic, then stationed herself by a window to wait for one of the irregular visits from the loggers.

When the tall Asian eventually appeared, she tapped on the glass. He nodded, then drifted away.

Perhaps an hour later, a large party of drunken loggers spilled into the street near Wroclaw Biotech. As they passed the lab building, a fight broke out, the whole crowd pushing and shoving against the building.

Murasaki and Awolowo slipped out amid the chaos, and moved on with the rumble, which broke up as they approached a bar.

Inside, the place stank of fresh-ripped lumber, with pale green sawdust all over the floor. The bartop itself was cut from a huge greenbrain log, and illumination came from smoky oil lamps. The electric fixtures overhead weren't in use.

The tall Asian followed her gaze. "Oil lamps stink. Spaghettis hate 'em. Most businesses in town use 'em now." He grinned, stuck out his hand. "Clement Lee."

"Wanda Murasaki," she said. "That's Dr. Awolowo over there."

The Lieutenant Governor and three of the loggers were at the bar, ordering beer.

"I figured out who he was after we stashed you the other day," said Lee. "His picture's not hard to find. You, though, you're not just a bodyguard."

"Military," Murasaki said shortly. "We need a favor. We need to get back to Katyn."

Lee glanced around the bar, then sat down at a table directly under one of the guttering lamps. Murasaki followed suit. Awolowo and the other three loggers approached, carrying a tray of fired clay steins.

"There's only one thing that goes in and out of here these days," said Lee. "Logs. Most of the wood goes down the Wroclaw. Either by barge or directly in the water. There's a big mill at Port Kiev that handles logging from half the continental basin. We send some of the better quality stuff directly to a scrolling mill in Katyn. They do finework there—interior finishing, furniture, that kind of stuff."

"How do the Katyn logs get there?" asked Murasaki. "By truck?"

At the table, Awolowo and the other loggers traded bawdy songs, keeping their voices loud to cover her conversation. Murasaki thought it almost bizarrely out of character for the reserved, prim Lieutenant Governor, but he actually seemed to be enjoying himself.

"Railroad," Lee said, talking under the racket. "Government built it, ran it until the big mill at Port Kiev downriver came online, then pulled the service. Now we've got our own bloody huge steam engine. In fact, it burns our chowder."

"Chowder?"

He grinned. "Loose branches, splintered logs, small stuff—trash from logging operations. At the other end, they load up the tender with scrap from the mill in Katyn and run back burning that, bringing finished goods and bulk commodities from the capital."

"When's the next train?"

"You want a ride, we can arrange it. Hell, we'll send crap logs if we have to. Bugs won't know the difference. Besides, the gov here is kind of distinctive looking. A little too recognizable, if you catch my drift. Our way, you can get him in quietly, no-see-um. Besides, if it helps Nowa Gdansk, what's a joy ride into town?"

When Murasaki saw the locomotive a couple of days later, she had second thoughts about the plan.

It didn't look like it would survive being fired up, let alone cover two hundred kilometers dragging a load. The boiler was an enormous insulated pressure vessel appropriated from some chemical plant. The piping was jerry-rigged with safety tape, grippies and tied-on rags. The piston cylinders were fabricated from forced-compost stacks off one of the slowships.

Only the wheels looked solid, great huge drivers as tall as she was. The operator's cab was a tiny wooden shack strapped to the back of the boiler, just above the firebox, with the wood tender coupled right behind it, before the line of flatcars loaded with massive greenbrain logs.

"We've got you and the Lieutenant Governor set up inside car two," said Lee. He squatted with Murasaki and Awolowo, looking at the train from the shelter of some fragrant bushes on a nearby bluff. A Segrethi inspected the cars.

"Logs stacked with some endcaps to make an interior hollow. Once we get you in, it will be like a little wooden tent. Trip takes about ten or twelve hours. You'll have to trust the boys on the other end to get you out. But you'll be in Katyn, in one piece."

"That thing will blow somewhere between here and there," Murasaki said, pointing at the hand-built locomotive. "Or we'll starve under those logs."

"Makes the trip at least twice a month," Lee answered. He punched her lightly on the arm. "Would a guy like me send a gal like you out in something dangerous?"

After the fall bag, anything was possible, Murasaki thought. "Life in wartime."

Lee sneezed, looked surprised for a moment, then sniffled. "Come visit us when peace breaks out. I can show you —."

Murasaki got a whiff of compost as Lee's head exploded in a blazing bolt of energy. She spun on her heels, rising to draw the flechette pistol.

Then she froze.

Eight Segrethi pointed their zap rifles at her, great golden-brown eyes glazed over. Two of the loggers stood behind them, one of them the leather vest guy she had first met coming into town.

"I think my brother wishes to speak to us," said Awolowo as he knelt to gently straighten the bloody, burnt collar of Lee's overalls.

Damning herself for a fool, Murasaki laid the pistol down and placed her hands on her head.

They flew back to Katyn on a transport helicopter belonging to Gdansku Force. It could have been the same one they'd spotted in the Moldaus—a bundle of the Segrethi probes were racked at the back of the cabin.

The four Segrethi crowding the cabin, heads lowered under the ceiling, kept Murasaki's desire to satisfy her curiosity at a low ebb. Their compost musk was almost overwhelming. *Odd,* she thought, she'd never really noticed it on Gdansk Orbital.

Back at the shuttle port, the Segrethi herded Murasaki and Awolowo onto another free-flight shuttle. One of the Segrethi used its stick arms to cable-tie their wrists to their seats, then they left. Murasaki and Awolowo were alone in the cabin.

They never saw the pilot. As soon as the aliens left, the shuttle did a take-off roll, cockpit hatch remaining shut.

182

Murasaki twisted her head around. The cargo bulkhead was set quite far forward. "Most of the humans who make this flight are dead," she said, imagining the bodies behind the moveable wall.

"Probably." Awolowo sneezed, unable to cover his mouth because of the wrist ties.

Murasaki worried that the Lieutenant Governor was returning to thoughts of suicide. She worried she would be killed out of hand.

At least they were heading into orbit, getting closer to the wormhole.

The plan was working.

Sort of.

When the shuttle docked at Gdansk Orbital Port, four humans armed with riot pistols boarded. Although still outside the station's artificial gravity, the shuttle was aligned with the plane of centripetal force, so everyone moved under a reasonable fraction of gee. The three men and one woman wore the whitesuits of Port Control, with blue security piping.

"Lieutenant Governor out first," one of the men announced. He looked vaguely familiar — Murasaki thought she had seen him with Smitts a few times. What was he doing here? Was this a rescue?

Smitts' associate cut Awolowo loose. The Lieutenant Governor stood, nodding gravely at Murasaki. "Until tomorrow," he said, nodded, then followed two of the armed men out.

Until tomorrow? Murasaki started to wonder all over again whose side Lieutenant Governor Awolowo was on.

The leader of the guard detail leaned forward. "I'm Sulinski," he whispered. "I was with Smitts on the System Control raid. You didn't make the party. He bought it there. I barely got out."

Smitts. Another on her burgeoning list of dead.

"I was snatched by the bad guys," Murasaki said. She looked pointedly at the female guard, who studied the cabin ceiling.

Sulinski nodded. "We heard it was you joy-riding that broomstick outside. Nice work."

Murasaki ignored the compliment. "Now what?"

"You're going to walk out between us, me in front, Bettie there behind. In the boarding corridor, you grab my riot pistol, do something convincing and non-lethal to Bettie, and take me hostage. If we make it into the air vents, we'll talk."

"The bugs are up to something," said Murasaki as Sulinski cut her bonds.

"Not yet," he said. "But there's some folks ready to sign a treaty, make some permanent commitments. Nice time to spoil the party, take the brass down a few pegs in the bugs' scent of them."

"Permanent commitments?"

The rats had been well organized even before Invasion Day. Which explained why all the leadership had disappeared so fast.

As for Sulinski, either he was a good guy or he wasn't. No matter which, she had to get off the shuttle. Murasaki stood. "Let's go."

Passing out of the shuttle's airlock, Murasaki saw a tiny sticker someone had plastered on the stationside seal.

It read "Williamson Says No."

Williamson?

Smitts' lifemate.

But Sulinski had just said Smitts was dead.

Murasaki looked around. There was a pair of Segrethi sentries in the boarding corridor, at the far end.

Sulinski hadn't mentioned that, either.

Murasaki had to believe that Smitts had left that sticker, knowing that his name or hers would have been scrubbed. If he was alive, this was a setup. She would be killed trying to escape.

No problem, she thought, *but we'll all go down together.*

About halfway along the corridor, Murasaki yanked herself free of Sulinski's hand.

She swung a snap kick into Bettie's groin, following through on the spin with a grab for Sulinski's riot pistol instead of Bettie's as she had been instructed.

Murasaki then finished her spin firing over Sulinski's shoulder into the two Segrethi.

Flechettes pounded the bulkhead. One alien spun, having caught the fire directly in its bean-pod body. Murasaki's fire pinged off the bulkhead behind the other Segrethi. The alien drew its machete sword and launched down the corridor toward Murasaki.

She kicked Sulinski hard in the back of his knee, forcing him to drop toward the floor. Murasaki back-pedaled away from the Segrethi, trying to time its bounds.

She got it right.

The Segrethi landed almost on top of Sulinski, pushed off and rushed toward her, the machete-sword already on the backswing.

Murasaki did a quick forward roll, landing flat on her back, and unloaded the riot pistol into the left side leg joints as the Segrethi sailed over her. It caromed into the corridor wall and slid all the way to the shuttle's hatch, shedding chitin and goop.

"Come on," Murasaki yelled, grabbing Sulinski with one arm while threatening him with the empty pistol. "You didn't tell me about the *Bóg przeklina* bugs!"

The wounded Segrethi's zap rifle crackled behind her, the blazing trail dividing the air between her and Sulinski. Vacuum alarms whooped as the energy bolt breached the wall of the boarding corridor.

Murasaki clubbed the terrified Sulinski in the head with the butt of the pistol, turned around, and raced back toward the shuttle and the Segrethi. Bettie was staggering to her feet, so Murasaki dropped the other woman with a jaw-shattering kick that came close to rupturing Murasaki's own tendons, then scooped up the guard's riot pistol.

The wounded Segrethi had trouble aiming its zap rifle. Murasaki gave the alien two bursts in the stick arms, then dove through the shuttle's hatch and pounded the emergency seal button.

Set-up, she thought as she took a five count to catch her breath.

Sulinski could have gotten her. The Segrethi by the hatch could have gotten her. There were probably a dozen more aliens just outside the boarding corridor.

Something was up, station politics, Segrethi politics. They had planned to make a point with her. Otherwise, Sulinski would have just executed her back on the ground.

Murasaki wasn't sure she could hijack the shuttle at this point, and even if she did, there wasn't anywhere else she wanted to go.

She was already on Port. She just needed to be out of this hole.

Emergency stores would have vacuum bags, Murasaki thought.

She tore open the closet just aft of the cockpit, grabbed two of the bags, then used the riot pistol to blast the lock on the cockpit hatch. Ricocheting flechettes lacerated her chest and arms, but she was far past caring.

"Heads up, boys," Murasaki shouted as she yanked the hatch open.

The pilot was partly out of his seat with a needler—a miniature flechette pistol. She shot the man's arm off at the shoulder, the riot pistol shredding flesh and bone to a crimson cloud.

The co-pilot winced and looked away, so Murasaki just clubbed him in the head with the riot pistol.

She toggled all the cabin pressure overrides, then released the emergency bolts on the pilot's windscreen, intended for crew escapes from emergency landings dirtside. More alarms wailed as the shielded glass composite spun away.

Still in clothes borrowed from Jan Potocki, Murasaki surfed the escaping atmosphere out into the vacuum of space.

Murasaki figured she had somewhere between forty seconds and one minute of useful consciousness. She immediately exhaled, to minimize lung damage. She then fired the riot pistol back toward the shuttle, using its nominal recoil to pick up a little more velocity.

The bulk of the Port loomed immediately over her head. Murasaki slid along it, flipping one of the vacuum bags over to find its pressure jet pack.

She was looking for a broomstick nearby. There had to be EVA hatches for external maintenance of docked shuttles.

She had about thirty seconds left.

Murasaki spotted a hatch cluster, and manually spun open the pressure jet valve on the vacuum bag to send herself that way.

By then her entire face was swollen, eyeballs straining in their sockets. She could feel her ears freezing, her nostrils hardening. It was like having spikes driven into her head, rimed with frostbite and fire both.

She could stand it.

Time for the other vacuum bag.

Murasaki snapped it open. Even here, perilously close to dying in hard vacuum, she had a second's pause as she recalled her dread of the fall bag.

Following Smitts' example from their trip to orbit together, Murasaki smashed the rescue screamer relay with the butt of the riot pistol. She then wriggled into the opening, got her face oriented toward the transparent view slit, and pulled the seal tab.

As the bag inflated, the vessels in her nose burst, spurting little gobs of blood. Murasaki ignored that to grab the tiny joystick. She watched the approaching hatch cluster.

"Bingo," she whispered into the rising air pressure.

There was a broomstick.

All she lacked was a spacesuit. The vacuum bag would have to do. If she popped the EVA hatch and tried to steal a maintenance suit, Port Control would see it on the boards.

Then the Segrethi would be after her in a hurry.

Murasaki realized she would have to bleed some pressure out of the vacuum bag if she wanted to fold it around her hand like a crude glove. Living in low pressure wouldn't kill her, but when the oxygen mix dropped too far, as it eventually would from respiration alone, she'd be dopey as heck.

Then that would kill her.

One problem at a time, she told herself. First, get the broomstick unclipped and started.

Murasaki cruised the hull of Gdansk Orbital Port low and slow.

For one thing, her vision through the vacuum bag's slit was terrible. For another, if she got too far away from the hull, Port's traffic control systems would pick her up.

This close in, she was just debris unless the Segrethi sent individual scouts out to spot her. Given that the Port ran to hundreds of square kilometers of surface, including the accreted rings and myriad add-ons over the original slowship, Murasaki decided not to worry about that possibility.

What she needed was some way to get Earth's attention through the wormhole. The only interpretation she could put on Awolowo's final comment was he would be going out with the bodies tomorrow.

Which tomorrow?

The damned wormhole was cycled every eleven hours and forty-two minutes. There would be two events per day, three every once and a while when the math worked out just right.

Beyond and before that, how to get the attention of Earth-based observers?

Cruising near the base of the solar sails, the ion-sink capacitor banks on the number two north ring visible ahead, Murasaki suddenly knew what she needed to do.

She had to take it on faith that Awolowo's body would go through infected with the virus—that was something she couldn't control. Once it did, all she had to do was attract the attention of people on the other side.

But to do what she wanted, Murasaki really, really needed a decent spacesuit.

She kept cruising.

A couple of hours layer, Murasaki lurked in the shadow of a slurry tank farm to watch the customs cutter *Zamojski*. She didn't need a ship, she needed a suit. But ships had suits.

And *Zamojski* had been pulled out of heavy maintenance. A half a dozen helmeted Segrethi patrolled the outside of the cutter, on alert.

Someone, the Segrethi or Kindness Awolowo, was getting sick of her antics.

"Damn, I'm good," Murasaki whispered to herself. "Pissed in their soup something proper."

A human work party closed up panels on the cutter, preparing it for post-maintenance shakedown. Or knowing the Segrethi, just preparing the ship to go straight into action.

They didn't strike her as being strong on test and verification. Segrethi didn't talk much, listened even less.

She flicked on the simple little radio inside the bag and punched her way through the channels until she found what sounded like the work party's chatter.

"Mind the bug overhead. Don't point that welder at—"

"Don't tell me what to do, Skiff."

"Cut the shit, both of you," grumbled a third voice, apparently a supervisor.

How to get their attention?

She needed help. She needed not to be betrayed again. Well, that was out of her control.

"This is Mama Katyn," Murasaki said on the crew's frequency. "You copy?"

"Who's that?" asked the supervisor. "Bunny, you screwing around on me again?"

"No, boss," said a woman.

The Segrethi on the hull of the cutter didn't change their behavior at all. They weren't getting realtime translations off the crew band.

Good.

"Boss," she said, "Mama Katyn's a woman of few words and large deeds."

"It's *her*," said one of the other suits. "She's the one who—"

"Shut this channel down, *now*," the supervisor broadcast. To Murasaki's eye, the work party was obviously in disarray.

There was about a minute of silence before the supervisor came back on. "Big claim, Mama."

Murasaki clicked her tongue. "You heard who died outside ten days ago?" She remembered the sticker on the airlock. "Williamson says no, but I did that."

More silence, while the crew got back to their previous work efficiency.

Finally, "What do you want, Mama?"

"If God sent me a maintenance suit, I could do good works in His world," she said.

Damn it, Murasaki thought, her oxygen levels must be dropping. This wasn't how she talked.

"It's tough to walk home from here."

"I've done it," she said.

"So I heard. Lay low. I'll see what can be done."

Murasaki sat and watched another forty-five minutes as the crew finished up. There was very little chatter on the frequency now—just enough that she knew they hadn't switched off.

These were scared people.

The bugs must be cracking down inside. The supervisor hadn't sold her out yet, or there'd already be shooting.

Eventually, when the work party was done, two of the Segrethi went in through the service bay EVA hatch cluster.

Then the work party, one at a time.

It took a while between entries. Someone inside was searching, looking to see if she was hiding inside a suit. After the last human went in, the other two Segrethi followed.

Murasaki waited another half an hour, wondering if she'd been played for a fool, when a burst of chatter came over the radio. "You don't leave a God damned forty-thousand zloty tester sitting out there, I don't care what happens."

Two suits glided out of the EVA hatch cluster together.

"Give me a sign, Mama," said the supervisor.

"Slurry tank, high to your right."

The first suit disappeared under the hull of the *Zamojski*. The other spun on a new trajectory, heading toward her.

It was an engineering supervisor's suit. The supervisor had gone out in an ordinary maintenance suit, then sent Murasaki his own. She wondered how he would account for the second suit that was headed her way.

Then there was falsetto screaming on the circuit. "Oh, I didn't mean to do it. I think I've killed him. Loose suit! Emergency! Loose suit!"

The supervisor's suit shot toward her.

Murasaki jetted her broomstick to meet it, just as it adjusted course.

Someone was inside the suit.

She wished she hadn't discharged the riot pistol. She could have fired through the wall of her vacuum bag and into the suit's faceplate at need.

Then she realized that it was Smitts in the other suit, smiling grimly.

He took her in tow, pulled her deep into the pipe maze of the slurry farm, then popped up a vacuum shelter—a sort of tent meant for EVA work that required pressurized conditions. Murasaki parked her broomstick and crawled inside.

After she helped Smitts struggle out of the supervisor's suit, they hugged for a long time.

Smitts had a first aid kit and a roll of 'Williamson Says No' stickers. He daubed gelskin on her face and neck.

"You're alive," Murasaki finally said. In the partial pressure of the shelter, her voice sounded ragged and thin, a painful whisper.

"You too," he said. "I see you got my message."

"You plastered those stickers on *all* the locks just in case I came back?"

"They're everywhere on Gdansk Orbital now." He laughed. "Station Control would have to shut down every printer in the place."

"Just for me?"

190

"You and Bart." He touched her cheek. "I knew you'd be back. Now what?"

She rubbed his hand in hers. Her skin was a brittle bloom of reddish-white, severe vacuum damage. She had to keep moving, not think about that. She owed a lot of people everything, including their lives. "They're using a wormhole to send the bodies back to Earth. I need to get Earth's attention."

"A wormhole?" Smitts shrugged. "Nothing surprises me anymore. Theory says the business end of a wormhole should expel all kinds of radiation. I guess they've got better theories than us. I mean, they're the ones with the working wormholes."

"So they have tactical suppression of the radiation effects," said Murasaki. "Well, I can do something about that. Help me with this suit."

Smitts shook his head. "You're in no shape to go anywhere."

"You a power engineer?" she asked.

"No." He sneezed, looked surprised. "Just a partisan these days."

She smiled, feeling her lips crack. "I am a power engineer. It's what I studied at the Service Academy. So *I'm* going."

Suited up and floating free, she'd let the next wormhole opening go by while making preparations for her signal. If Awolowo had gotten himself killed in time to go out on that one, it wouldn't hurt for her to send her signal on the next one.

Murasaki was willing to bet money that the Terrans would calculate the trajectories of whatever they found and look for other bodies further along in decaying orbits. Judging by the view of Luna she'd gotten from the wormhole, the Segrethi were dumping the bodies pretty far up in high orbit. Lots of time to float around out there before they burned up in the upper atmosphere.

Now it was coming down to zero hour.

Murasaki had stationed herself in the shadows at the base of the solar sail closest to the wormhole. She could see the bodies coming out. They were back to using a Segrethi work party.

Call it the Murasaki lesson, she congratulated herself.

She had to pop her surprise on the right coffle, lest they shut down the process too soon. If she couldn't spot Awolowo, she'd pop on the fourth coffle just in case there weren't five this time.

The wormhole opened, the orange glow visible to her. Murasaki couldn't see much through the opening, but she wasn't worried.

Behind her, the solar sails moved into the positions she'd programmed, focusing on the wormhole. Murasaki tongued the switch she'd set for the go button inside the supervisor's suit.

The first coffle was going. Suit optics didn't show any lanky, dark-skinned men.

The second coffle had one black man, but he was short.

One by one the bodies vanished as they tumbled into the wormhole.

Religion, science, obsession, she didn't care about what the aliens thought they were doing. Murasaki hated the Segrethi with a passion that had consumed her life.

In a few minutes, she would be burned away with them.

There he was, in the third coffle. Lieutenant Governor Awolowo, long, black, naked, covered with frost. The geneticist who had written his story into his own cells, and hers, and probably half of the human population of Nowa Gdansk. Finally, she would get the word home to Earth. His word.

As Awolowo spun toward the wormhole, Murasaki saluted.

As he tumbled through it, she tongued the go switch.

Thirty-seven of the ion-trap capacitors around number two north ring exploded. That was all that she'd had time to override the programming on.

An enormous percentage of their energy converted itself to EM radiation, including a violent blast of visible light, which the twisting solar sails she'd reprogrammed focused at the wormhole.

It didn't matter exactly how much got through. Terran defenses would notice an out-of-place blast of EM in cis-lunar space and investigate immediately. Once they investigated, the Navy would come. She'd lit the beacon fire to call for help from home.

Nowa Gdansk would be free.

The hull of number two north ring shattered under the coordinated explosion, spilling atmosphere, people, Segrethi, machines and trash into the vacuum. Hundreds of humans and aliens spun away from the Orbital Port, presumably as astonished by their deaths as anyone ever was.

Mildly surprised herself to still be alive, Murasaki used the suit's pressure jets to accelerate herself into the cloud of debris. Her mission accomplished, there wasn't much point in escaping again.

She didn't have anywhere to go, but brute persistence kept her from sitting quietly until the Segrethi found her yet again. Besides, she was too damned tired to plan new mischief.

Shutting off her suit jets, Murasaki spun among the surprised dead with their bloody faces and ruptured eyeballs. She watched the stars wheel by, and named her own dead one by one, Segrethi and human alike.

Maybe she would be rescued.

Maybe she would burn up in Nowa Gdansk's atmosphere.

Maybe she would freeze on a trajectory toward the outer system.

Wanda Murasaki didn't care. She was a happy woman for the first time since Invasion Day.

V: BUYING THE FARM

A little less than a year later, a few days after the first Invasion Day anniversary ceremonies at Government House, a battered Skoda groundcar rattled into a Katyn Plains farmyard hard up against the foothills of the Moldau range.

The sign by the gate which read 'Saragossa' remained intact, but Jan Potocki's barn still looked as if it had been attacked with heavy weapons. The burned-out shell of a helicopter rusted in the lower meadow. The pigpens remained smashed, the wallows gone to weeds, though the wrecked Volvo had been towed off. The house was dilapidated, windows and doors smashed in someone's passing fit of vindictiveness.

Only rabbits and lizards scuttled about.

Dressed in a padded silk jumper, Wanda Murasaki climbed stiffly out of the car.

They never found Smitts, she thought. *It looked like Jan didn't make it home alive either.*

She'd never heard from Jan while she was in the hospital. No word either during her subsequent stint in the 'protective custody' of Terran Naval intelligence, helping them pursue their investigations. Still, she'd nourished hope. Saragossa, and Jan himself, had been her one small oasis of simple, sensible sanity in the horrible time after the Segrethi came.

A simple, sensible sanity she had yet to recapture.

Some nights she could still feel his rough, chapped lips on hers, from that night outside the barn when her body had still been whole and he had still been alive.

Like Jan, she should have been dead too. The Terran Naval doctors told Murasaki she was lucky. 'Lucky' was using a cane to keep her balance, difficulty breathing with vacuum-scarred lungs. 'Lucky' was being alone, every day, torn from her life's work, villainized and hero-worshipped at the same time, sometimes by the same people among Nowa Gdansk's war-traumatized populace.

Too many pressure changes, too much oxygen deprivation and hard vacuum exposure, too many days trapped in the engineering hardsuit, stress, whatever. Plus too much politics after the war was over.

The Orbital Port had risen against the Segrethi in the wake of the blast.

A partisan bug-hunting squad had pulled her in, just before the first of the Terran Naval hotships arrived, months of ahead of anyone's wildest expectations of rescue.

That had already been too late for Murasaki—trapped in the suit, suffering from vacuum exposure, hypothermia and anoxia, a cascading series of ministrokes had robbed her of her grace and strength. Though she could still function reasonably well.

She wore no uniform now, desired none. What had been the pride of her adult life had turned to an ashy remembrance of those killed by her action. Or worse, inaction. Even as a civilian, there were several nice medals she could display. Those decorations gathered dust in a storage unit back in Katyn.

Murasaki walked around Saragossa. The ladder was still at the back of the barn, a year later, although there was no way she could climb it now. She searched the barn and the house as best she could, but Murasaki didn't find his bones.

Whoever had come chasing Awolowo that night had vented their anger and gone on their way. She might even know their names—Murasaki had gone to all the rat hangings she could, between surgeries, rehab, Terran Navy interrogation, and those frightening few days when they'd finally realized what the Segrethi were actually up to and worried it might still come to pass.

Even the rats were surprised by the news, although the noose surprised more of them.

Too bad the King Rat had died with one hundred seventy four other victims of the Segrethi destruction of number two north ring on Gdansk Orbital.

That was the official story. Wanda Murasaki, the most successful mass murderer in planetary history, no charges brought in light of extenuating circumstances, please go away now, ma'am, you make us uncomfortable. The words were kinder, but the message was clear.

"Thank you," the new Governor Thoms, sent out by the Colonial Secretariat, had told her before he and his staff turned their backs.

A live voice interrupted her memories. "Would they have done it?"

Murasaki jumped, startled, slapped her belt for a flechette pistol she no longer carried.

Jan leaned on the crumbled wall of the damaged pigpen, smiling. He was a lot thinner, had a little less hair.

"I thought you..." She stopped.

"The great Wanda Murasaki, at a loss for words?" His smile grew to a grin. "I heard your speech on the radio, at the memorial ceremony."

Still wordless, she waved at the house.

"Oh, that." He shrugged. "I've been living in a shelter by the creek. You know," Jan leered, "where we swam?"

"The pigs?" she finally squeaked, caught between embarrassment and an long-dormant sense of personal intrigue.

"They like to swim, too," he assured her. "But you didn't answer my question. Would the Spaghettis have done it? Taken the planet wholesale?"

"Why else did they come?"

Of course, with that wormhole technology, they could always come back. But the surprise was gone. To steal an entire planet, whisk it away through a giant wormhole: that was the goal of the mad or the desperate.

Or the alien. Whatever their reasons.

That was what the surveying had been about. Setting contact points for a supermassive wormhole generator. Terran Naval weapons specialists had speculated the Segrethi planned to tap 70 Ophiuchi A for the power to drive it. What was another nova among friends? Besides, it would obliterate the evidence that they had ever come and gone.

Not many people knew the truth, though. Jan, with his partisan contacts, seemed to be one.

The Terran Navy, with their new hotships spreading out among the colonies like blood staining water, had all the reports and analyses on the Segrethi. Run like hell, yell for help, that was the hotships' mission. The Navy people who had done her final debriefing called it 'the Murasaki Doctrine'.

She wasn't sure if it was a joke or not.

The Segrethi would have done it in a heartbeat, she thought, if they'd had time to finish their surveys and plant their hardware. With or without the help of our rats.

"Why else did the Segrethi come?" she said, echoing Jan's question. "Who knows?" *Why start more rumors?* If Kindness Awolowo had escaped with the aliens, someone else could deal with him whenever he came back.

"Want to go swimming now?" Jan asked, hopping over the damaged wall of the old pigpen.

"I'm..." Words failed her again as Murasaki spread her arms, the cane shaking in her palsied grip.

"I know," he said. "You're still beautiful, I'm still old and fat. That *was* an invitation, right?" He winked. "Carry you down to the water."

She kicked and screamed when he threw her in, but it was a long time before she needed her clothes again.

Greetings from Lake Wu

The Goat Cutter

The Goat Cutter

The Devil lives in Houston by the ship channel in a high-rise apartment fifty-seven stories up. They say he's got cowhide sofas and a pinball machine and a telescope in there that can see past the oil refineries and across Pasadena all the way to the Pope in Rome and on to where them Arabs pray to that big black stone.

He can see anyone anywhere from his place in the Houston sky, and he can see inside their hearts.

But I know it's all a lie. Except about the hearts, of course. Cause I know the Devil lives in an old school bus in the woods outside of Dale, Texas. He don't need no telescope to see inside your heart, on account of he's already there.

This I know.

Central Texas gets mighty hot come summer. The air rolls in heavy off the Gulf, carries itself over two hundred miles of cow shit and sorghum fields and settles heavy on all our heads. The katydids buzz in the woods like electric fans with bad bearings, and even the skeeters get too tired to bite most days. You can smell the dry coming off the Johnson grass and out of the bar ditches.

Me and my best friend Pootie, we liked to run through the woods, climbing bob wire and following pipelines. Trees is smaller there, easier to slip between. You gotta watch out in deer season, though. Idiots come out from Austin or San Antone to their leases, get blind drunk and shoot every blessed thing that moves. Rest of the time, there's nothing but you and them turkey vultures. Course, you can't steal beer coolers from turkey vultures.

The Devil, he gets on pretty good with them turkey vultures.

So me and Pootie was running the woods one afternoon somewhere in the middle of summer. We was out of school, waiting to be sophomores in the fall, fixing to amount to something. Pootie was bigger than me, but I already got tongue off Martha Dempsey. Just a week or so ago back of the church hall, I even scored a little titty squeeze inside her shirt. It was over her bra, but that counts for something. I knew I was coming up good.

Pootie swears he saw Rachel MacIntire's nipples, but she's his cousin. I reckoned he just peeked through the bathroom window of his aunt's trailer house, which ain't no different from me watching Momma get out of the shower. It don't count. If there was anything to it, he'd a sucked on 'em, and I'd of never heard the end of *that*. Course I wouldn't say no to my cousin Linda if she offered to show me a little something in the shower.

Yeah, that year we was big boys, the summer was hot, and we was always hungry and horny.

Then we met the Devil.

Me and Pootie crossed the bob wire fence near the old bus wallow on county road 61, where they finally built that little bridge over the draw. Doug Bob Aaronson had that place along the south side of 61, spent his time roasting goats, drinking tequila and shooting people's dogs.

Doug Bob was okay, if you didn't bring a dog. Three years back, once we turned ten, he let me and Pootie drink his beer with him. He liked to liquor up, strip down to his underwear and get his ass real warm from the fire in his smoker. We was just a guy and two kids in their shorts drinking in the woods. I'm pretty sure Momma and Uncle Reuben would of had hard words, so I never told.

We kind of hoped now that we was going to be sophomores, he'd crack some of that *Sauza Conmemorativo Anejo* for us.

202

Doug Bob's place was all grown over, wild rose and stretch vine and beggar's lice everywhere, and every spring a huge-ass wisteria wrapped his old cedar house with lavender flowers and thin whips of wood. There was trees everywhere around in the brush, mesquite and hackberry and live-oak and juniper and a few twisty old pecans. Doug Bob knew all the plants and trees, and taught 'em to us sometimes when he was less than half drunk. He kept chickens around the place and a mangy duck that waddled away funny whenever he got to looking at it.

We come crashing through the woods one day that summer, hot, hungry, horny and full of fight. Pootie'd told me about Rachel's nipples, how they was set in big pink circles and stuck out like little red thumbs. I told him I'd seen that picture in *Hustler* same as him. If'n he was gonna lie, lie from a magazine I hadn't stole us from the Triple E Grocery.

Doug Bob's cedar house was bigger than three double wides. It set at the back of a little clearing by the creek that ran down from the bus wallow. He lived there, fifty feet from a rusted old school bus that he wouldn't never set foot inside. Only time I asked him about that bus, he cracked me upside the head so hard I saw double for days and had to tell Uncle Reuben I fell off my bike.

That would of been a better lie if I'd of recollected that my bike'd been stolen three weeks gone. Uncle Reuben didn't beat me much worse than normal, and we prayed extra long over the Bible that night for forgiveness.

Doug Bob was pretty nice. He about never hit me, and he kept his underpants on when I was around.

That old smoker was laid over sidewise on the ground, where it didn't belong. Generally, Doug Bob kept better care of it than anything except an open bottle of tequila. He had cut the smoker from a gigantic water heater, so big me and Pootie could of slept in it. Actually, we did a couple of times, but you can't never get ash out of your hair after.

And Pootie snored worse than Uncle Reuben.

Doug Bob roasted his goats in that smoker, and he was mighty particular about his goats. He always killed his goats hisself. They didn't usually belong to him, but he did his own killing. Said it made him a better man. I thought it mostly made him a better mess. The meat plant over in Lockhart could of done twice the job in half the time, with no bath in the creek afterward.

Course, when you're sweaty and hot and full of piss and vinegar, there's nothing like a splash around down in the creek with some beer and one of them big cakes of smelly purple horse soap me and Pootie stole out of barns for Doug Bob. Getting rubbed down with that stuff kind of stings, but it's a good sting.

Times like that, I knew Doug Bob liked me just for myself. We'd all smile and laugh and horse around and get drunk. Nobody got hit, nobody got hurt, everybody went home happy.

Doug Bob always had one of these goats, and it was always a buck. Sometimes a white Saanen, or maybe a creamy La Mancha or a brown Nubian looked like a chubby deer with them barred goat eyes staring straight into your heart. They was always clean, no socks nor blazes nor points, just one color all over. Doug Bob called them *unblemished*.

And Doug Bob always killed these goats on the north side of the smoker. He had laid some rocks down there, to make a clear spot for when it was muddy from winter rain or whatever. He'd cut their throats with his jagged knife that was older than sin, and sprinkle the blood all around the smoker.

He never let me touch that knife.

Doug Bob, he had this old gray knife without no handle, just rags wrapped up around the end. The blade had a funny shape like it got beat up inside a thresher or something, as happened to Momma's sister Cissy the year I was born. Her face had that funny shape until Uncle Reuben found her hanging in the pole barn one morning with her dress up over her head.

They puttied her up for the viewing at the funeral home, but I recall Aunt Cissy best with those big dents in her cheek and jaw and the one brown eye gone all white like milk in coffee.

Doug Bob's knife, that I always thought of as Cissy's knife, it was kind of wompered and shaped all wrong, like a corn leaf the bugs been at. He'd take that knife and saw the head right off his goat.

I never could figure how Doug Bob kept that edge on.

He'd flay that goat, and strip some fatback off the inside of the hide, and put the head and the fat right on the smoker where the fire was going, wet chips of mesquite over a good hot bed of coals.

Then he'd drag the carcass down to creek, to our swimming hole, and sometimes me and Pootie could help with this part. We'd wash out the gut sack and clean off the heart and lungs and liver. Doug Bob always scrubbed the legs specially well with that purple horse soap. We'd generally get a good lot of blood in the water. If it hadn't rained in a while, like most summers, the water'd be sticky for hours afterward.

Doug Bob would take the carcass and the sweetbreads -- that's what he called the guts, sweetbreads. I figured they looked more like spongy purple and red bruises than bread, kind of like dog food fresh outta the can. And there wasn't nothing sweet about them.

Sweetbreads taste better than dog food, though. We ate dog food in the winter sometimes, ate it cold if Uncle Reuben didn't have work and Momma'd been lazy. That was when I most missed my summers in the woods with Pootie, calling in on Doug Bob.

Doug Bob would drag these goat parts back up to the smoker, where he'd take the head and the fat off the fire. He'd always give me and Pootie some of that fat, to keep us away from the head meat, I guess. Doug Bob would put the carcass and the sweetbreads on the fire and spit his high-proof tequila all over them. If they didn't catch straight away from that, he'd light 'em with a Bic.

We'd watch them burn, quiet and respectful like church on account of that's what Doug Bob believed. He always said God told him to keep things orderly, somewhere in the beginning of Leviticus.

Then he'd close the lid and let the meat cook. He didn't never clean up the blood around the smoker, although he would catch some to write Bible verses on the sides of that old school bus with.

The Devil lives in San Francisco in a big apartment on Telegraph Hill. Way up there with all that brass and them potted ferns and naked women with leashes on, he's got a telescope that can see across the bay, even in the fog. They say he can see all the way to China and Asia, with little brown people and big red demon gods, and stare inside their hearts

The Devil, he can see inside everybody's heart, just about.

It's a lie, except that part about the hearts. There's only one place in God's wide world where the Devil can't see.

Me and Pootie, we found that smoker laying over on its side, which we ain't never seen. There was a broken tequila bottle next to it, which ain't much like Doug Bob neither.

Well, we commenced to running back and forth, calling out "Doug Bob!" and "Mr. Aaronson!" and stuff. That was dumb cause if he was around and listening, he'd of heard us giggling and arguing by the time we'd crossed his fence line.

I guess we both knew that, cause pretty quick we fell quiet and starting looking around. I felt like I was on TV or something, and there was a bad thing fixing to happen next. Them saloon doors were flapping in my mind and I started wishing mightily for a commercial.

That old bus of Doug Bob's, it was a long bus, like them revival preachers use to bring their people into town. I always thought going to Glory when you died meant getting on one of them long buses painted white and gold, with Bible verses on the side and a choir clapping and singing in the back and some guy in a powder blue suit and hair like a raccoon pelt kissing you on the cheek and slapping you on the forehead.

Well, I been kissed more than I want to, and I don't know nobody with a suit, no matter the color, and there ain't no choir ever going to sing me to my rest now, except if maybe they're playing bob wire harps and beating time on burnt skulls. But Doug Bob's bus, it sat there flat on the dirt with the wiry bones of tires wrapped over dented black hubs grown with morning glory, all yellow with the rusted old metal showing through, with the windows painted black from the inside and crossed over with duct tape. It had a little vestibule Doug Bob'd built over the double doors out of wood from an old church in Rosanky. The entrance to that vestibule was crossed over with duct tape just like the windows. It was bus number seven, whatever place it had come from.

And bus number seven was covered with them Bible verses written in goat's blood, over and over each other to where there was just red-brown smears on the cracked windshield and across the hood and down the sides, scrambled scribbling that looked like Aunt Cissy's drool on the lunch table at Wal-Mart. And they made about as much sense.

I even seen Doug Bob on the roof of that bus a few times, smearing bloody words with his fingers like a message to the turkey vultures, or maybe all the way to God above looking down from His air-conditioned heaven.

So I figured, the smoker's tipped, the tequila's broke, and here's my long bus bound for glory with Bible verses on the side, and the only choir is the katydids buzzing in the trees and me and Pootie breathing hard. I saw the door of the wooden vestibule on the bus, that Doug Bob never would touch, was busted open, like it had been kicked out from the inside. The duct tape just flapped loose from the door frame.

I stared all around that bus, and there was a new verse on the side, right under the driver's window. It was painted fresh, still shiny and red. It said, "Of the tribe of Reuben were sealed twelve thousand."

"Pootie."

"Huh?" He was gasping pretty hard. I couldn't take my eyes off the bus, which looked as if it was gonna rise up from the dirt and rumble down the road to salvation any moment, but I knew Pootie had that wild look where his eyes get almost all white and his nose starts to bleed. I could tell from his breathing.

Smelled like he wet his pants, too.

"Pootie," I said again, "there ain't no fire, and there ain't no fresh goat been killed. Where'd the blood come from for that there Bible verse?"

"Reckon he talking 'bout your uncle?" Pootie's voice was duller than Momma at Christmas.

Pootie was an idiot. Uncle Reuben never had no twelve thousand in his life. If he ever did, he'd of gone to Mexico and to hell with me and Momma. "Pootie," I tried again, "where'd the blood come from?"

I knew, but I didn't want to be the one to say it.

Pootie panted for a little while longer. I finally tore my eyes off that old bus, which was shimmering like summer heat, to see Pootie bent over with his hands on his knees and his head hanging down. "It ain't his handwritin' neither," Pootie sobbed.

We both knew Doug Bob was dead.

Something was splashing around down by the creek. "Aw, shit," I said. "Doug Bob was--is our friend. We gotta go look."

It ain't but a few steps to the bank. We could see a man down there, bending over with his bare ass toward us. He was washing something big and pale. It weren't no goat.

Me and Pootie, we stopped at the top of the bank, and the stranger stood up and turned around. I about shit my pants.

He had muscles like a movie star, and a gold tan all the way down, like he'd never wore clothes. The hair on his chest and his short-and-curlies was blonde, and he was hung good. What near to made me puke was that angel's body had a goat head. Only it weren't no goat head you ever saw in your life.

It was like a big heavy ram's head, except it had *antlers* coming up off the top, a twelve point spread off a prize buck, and baby's eyes--big, blue and round in the middle. Not goat's eyes at all. That fur kind of tapered off into golden skin at the neck.

And those blue eyes blazed at me like ice on fire.

The tall, golden thing pointed to a body in the creek. He'd been washing the legs with purple soap. "Help me with this. I think you know how it needs to be done." His voice was windy and creaky, like he hadn't talked to no one for a real long time.

The body was Doug Bob, with his big gut and saggy butt, and a bloody stump of a neck.

"You son of a bitch!" I ran down the bank, screaming and swinging my arms for the biggest punch I could throw. I don't know, maybe I tripped over a root or stumbled at the water's edge, but that golden thing moved like summer lightning just as I slipped off my balance.

Last thing I saw was the butt end of Doug Bob's ragged old knife coming at me in his fist. I heard Pootie crying my name when my head went all red and painful.

The Devil lives in your neighborhood, yours and mine. He lives in every house in every town, and he has a telescope that looks out the bathroom mirror and up from the drains in the kitchen and out of the still water at the bottom of the toilet bowl. He can see inside of everyone's heart through their eyes and down their mouth and up their asshole.

It's true, I know it is.

The hope I hold secret deep inside my heart is that there's one place on God's green earth the Devil can't see.

I was naked, my dick curled small and sticky to my thigh like it does after I've been looking through the bathroom window. A tight little trail of cum itched my skin. My ass was on dirt, and I could feel ants crawling up the crack. I opened my mouth to say, "Fine," and a fly buzzed out from the inside. There was another one in the left side of my nose that seemed ready to stay a spell.

I didn't really want to open my eyes. I knew where I was. My back was against hot metal. It felt sticky. I was leaning against Doug Bob's bus and part of that new Bible verse about Uncle Reuben under the driver's window had run and got Doug Bob's heart blood all down my back. I could smell mesquite smoke, cooked meat, shit, blood, and the old oily metal of the bus.

But in all my senses, in the feel of the rusted metal, in the warmth of the ground, in the stickiness of the blood, in the sting of the ant bites, in the touch of the fly crawling around inside my nose, in the stink of Doug Bob's rotten little yard, there was something missing. It was an absence, a space, like when you get a tooth busted out in a fight, and notice it for not being there.

I was surrounded by absence, cold in the summer heat. My heart felt real slow. I still didn't want to open my eyes.

"You know," said that windy, creaky voice, sounding even more hollow and thin than before, "if they would just repent of their murders, their sorceries, their fornication, and their thefts, this would be a lot harder."

The voice was sticky, like the blood on my back, and cold, coming from the middle of whatever was missing around me. I opened my eyes and squinted into the afternoon sun.

Doug Bob's face smiled at me. Leastwise it tried to. Up close I could tell a whole lot of it was burnt off, with griddle marks where his head had lain a while on the smoker. Blackened bone showed through across the cheeks. Doug Bob's head was duct taped to the neck of that glorious, golden body, greasy black hair falling down those perfect shoulders. The head kept trying to lop over as he moved, like it was stuck on all wompered. His face was puffy and burnt up, weirder than Doug Bob mostly ever looked.

The smoker must of been working again.

The golden thing with Doug Bob's head had Pootie spread out naked next to the smoker. I couldn't tell if he was dead, but sure he wasn't moving. Doug Bob's legs hung over the side of the smoker, right where he'd always put the goat legs. Cissy's crazy knife was in that golden right hand, hanging loose like Uncle Reuben holds his when he's fixing to fight someone.

"I don't understand..." I tried to talk, but burped up a little bit of vomit and another fly to finish my sentence. The inside of my nose stung with the smell, and the fly in there didn't seem to like it much neither. "You stole Doug Bob's head."

"You see, my son, I have been set free from my confinement. My time is at hand." Doug Bob's face wrinkled into a smile, as some of his burnt lip scaled away. I wondered how much of Doug Bob was still down in the creek. "But even I can not walk the streets with my proud horns."

His voice got sweeter, stronger, as he talked. I stared up at him, blinking in the sunlight.

"Rise up and join me. We have much work to do, preparations for my triumph. As the first to bow to my glory you shall rank high among my new disciples, and gain your innermost desire."

Uncle Reuben taught me long ago how this sweet bullshit always ends. The old Doug Bob liked me. Maybe even loved me a little. He was always kind to me, which this golden Doug Bob ain't never gonna be.

It must be nice to be loved a lot.

I staggered to my feet, farting ants, using the ridges in the sheet metal of the bus for support. It was hot as hell, and even the katydids had gone quiet. Except for the turkey vultures circling low over me, I felt like I was alone in a giant dirt coffin with a huge blue lid over my head. I felt expanded, swollen in the heat like a dead coyote by the side of the road.

The thing wearing Doug Bob's head narrowed his eyes at me. There was a faint crinkling sound as the lids creased and broke.

"Get over here, *now*." His voice had the menace of a Sunday morning twister headed for a church, the power of a wall of water in the arroyo where kids played.

I walked toward the Devil, feet stepping without my effort.

There's a place I can go, inside, when Uncle Reuben's pushing into me, or he's using the metal end of the belt, or Momma's screaming through the thin walls of our trailer the way he can make her do. It's like ice cream without the cone, like cotton candy without the stick. It's like how I imagine Rachel MacIntire's nipples, sweet and total, like my eyes and heart are in my lips and the world has gone dark around me.

It's the place where I love myself, deep inside my heart.

I went there and listened to the little shuffling of my pulse in my ears.

My feet walked on without me, but I couldn't tell.

Cissy's knife spoke to me. The Devil must of put it in my hand.

"We come again to Moriah," it whispered in my heart. It had a voice like its metal blade, cold from the ground and old as time.

"What do you want?" I asked. I must of spoke out loud, because Doug Bob's burned mouth was twisting in screaming rage as he stabbed his golden finger down toward Pootie, naked at my feet next to the smoker. All I could hear was my pulse, and the voice of the knife.

Deep inside my heart, the knife whispered again. "Do not lay a hand on the boy."

The golden voice from Doug Bob's face was distant thunder in my ears. I felt his irritation, rage, frustration building where I had felt that cold absence.

I tried again. "I don't understand."

Doug Bob's head bounced up and down, the duct tape coming loose. I saw pink ropy strings working to bind the burned head to his golden neck. He cocked back a fist, fixing to strike me a hard blow.

I felt the knife straining across the years toward me. "You have a choice. The Enemy promises anything and everything for your help. I can give you nothing but the hope of an orderly world. You choose what happens now, and after."

I reckoned the Devil would run the world about like Uncle Reuben might. Doug Bob was already dead, and Pootie was next, and there wasn't nobody else like them in my life, no matter what the Devil promised. I figured there was enough hurt to go around already and I knew how to take it into me.

Another one of Uncle Reuben's lessons.

"Where you want this killing done?" I asked.

The golden thunder in my ears paused for a moment, the tide of rage lapped back from the empty place where Doug Bob wasn't. The fist dropped down.

"Right here, right now," whispered the knife. "Or it will be too late. Seven is being opened."

I stepped out of my inside place to find my eyes still open and Doug Bob's blackened face inches from my nose. His teeth were burnt and cracked, and his breath reeked of flies and red meat. I smiled, opened my mouth to speak, but instead of words I swung Cissy's knife right through the duct tape at the throat of Doug Bob's head.

He looked surprised.

Doug Bob's head flew off, bounced into the bushes. The golden body swayed, still on its two feet. I looked down at Pootie, the old knife cold in my hands.

Then I heard buzzing, like thunder made of wires.

I don't know if you ever ate a fly, accidental or not. They go down fighting, kind of tickle the throat, you get a funny feeling for a second, and then it's all gone. Not very filling, neither.

These flies came pouring out of the ragged neck of that golden body. They were big, the size of horseflies. All at once they were everywhere, and they came right at me. They came pushing at my eyes and my nose and my ears and flying right into my mouth, crawling down my throat. It was like stuffing yourself with raisins till you choke, except these raisins crawled and buzzed and bit at me.

The worst was they got all over me, crowding into my butt crack and pushing on my asshole and wrapping around my balls like Uncle Reuben's fingers right before he squeezed tight. My skin rippled, as if them flies crawled through my flesh.

I jumped around, screaming and slapping at my skin. My gut heaved, but my throat was full of flies and it all met in a knot at the back of my mouth. I rolled to the ground, choking on the rippling mess I couldn't spit out nor swallow back down. Through the flies I saw Doug Bob's golden body falling in on itself, like a balloon that's been popped. Then the choking took me off.

I lied about the telescope. I don't need one.

Right after, while I was still mostly myself, I sent Pootie away with that

212

old knife to find one of Doug Bob's kin. They needed that knife, to make their sacrifices that would keep me shut away. I made Pootie seal me inside the bus with Doug Bob's duct tape before he left.

The bus is hot and dark, but I don't really mind. There's just me and the flies and a hot metal floor with rubber mats and huge stacks of old Bibles and hymnals that make it hard for me to move around.

It's okay, though, because I can watch the whole world from in here.

I hate the flies, but they're the only company I can keep. The taste grows on me.

I know Pootie must of found someone to give that old knife to. I try the doors sometimes, but they hold firm. Somewhere one of Doug Bob's brothers or uncles or cousins cuts goats the old way. Someday I'll find him. I can see every heart except one, but there are too many to easily tell one from another.

There's only one place under God's golden sun the Devil can't see into, and that's his own heart.

I still have my quiet place. That's where I hold my hope, and that's where I go when I get too close to the goat cutter.

Jack's House

Jack's House

This was Joshua's favorite time of year. The sun fell blinding white on the snowfields, and the dancing breeze swept ice crystals down from ultramontane glaciers. Little orange butterflies rose like fire-lit clouds from the dark forest verges to spread across the snow, each a spark of eye-bright warmth against the cold that always surrounded Jack's House.

The young Rat had window duty that day, eighth gable attic, staring through the rippled, bubble-filled glass across the snow to the northwest. He stood watch, lest the Master finally return, or Dogs attack. Fear was a function of proximity. Cats often climbed the stairs to slaughter Rats in the carpeted halls; patrolling Dogs caught only those occasional, unwary fools who wandered outside; while the Master was a distant divinity, powerful for the most part in the threat of His absence. Always dreaming of the Cheese, the Rats feared little in this House other than Cats and Dogs.

Watching from his high window, Joshua saw Old Lenox the Cat stumble away from Jack's House. Old Lenox was a piebald tom who sometimes served as ambassador to the Rats, when the myriad wars demanded the occasion of truce. He had even done Joshua a kindness or two over the seasons. The tom carried a spear in one hand, a wineskin slung across his shoulder.

"Where are you going, old man Cat?" whispered Joshua. It was an old nestling's rhyme. He continued, lost in memories of warm seasons with his littermates among the shredded cardboard and wood shavings:

"All dressed up just like that.

I'm going out, little Rat,

To die by the light of day.

Every Cat must die that way."

Old Lenox stopped, turned to stare up at Joshua, his single glinting eye catching the eighth gable like a Mouse on a hook. Joshua squeaked. How could Old Lenox have heard him? The tom saluted with his spear, then turned to walk downslope—until the snow exploded with snarling Dogs who broke the Cat's arms and legs and, howling, dragged him bloody to the dark eaves of the forest below. The butterflies spiraled after them like Old Lenox's lifeblood taken wing.

Against all the Master's rules, the Rats maintained a fire in the fourth-floor maid's kitchen. They kept it, mostly, in the potbellied stove, and fed it with wallpaper from the insides of unused closets and laths stolen from rotting ceilings.

Having finally been relieved of his duties, Joshua came to the fire seeking hot soup and wisdom. He found Benjamin, his mentor and friend, stirring a pot, with half a dozen nestlings asleep tangled in a crocheted throw near the elderly Rat's feet.

Joshua crouched down onto his hands and knees. "Blessings on you, elder Rat."

"And Cheese," muttered Benjamin. His grayed muzzle twitched as he sniffed his cooking. "Do you know where the mint has gotten to?"

Joshua busied himself looking for the herb. "Dogs took Old Lenox today," he said, twisting the lid off a rusted tin that might have once held baking powder.

Benjamin banged his spoon against the pot. "Seen it yourself, did you?"

"Yes." Joshua found one draggled mint leaf. "He didn't fight at all."

"Snow walker."

Snow walkers were those whose time had come to leave this House, tired of hunting the Cheese and each other among the wainscoting. For the ones who made it past the forbidden lower floors, the Dogs were always obliging. "I suppose." The young Rat opened another tin. "He saluted me as he went."

"More like he saluted the House." Benjamin took a noisy, slurping taste of his soup. "Found that mint yet?"

Joshua discovered an almost fresh sprig under a coarse rag. "Here," he said, handing the sprig to the old Rat. "No, he caught my eye."

"That one was always uncommon civil for a Cat. One of their voices of moderation, you might say." Benjamin sighed. "We had a plan, once, that Rats and Cats should set aside our spears. We could have joined together in a thorough search for the Cheese."

"Ha," said Joshua. "As if that could ever be. What happened?"

Benjamin's black eyes glittered in the fire-lit shadows of the little kitchen. "They've got strange ideas about the Master and His devices, those Cats. Barabbas the Great Cat threw Old Lenox down and took his eye for blasphemy. After that the old tom was a quieter boy, I can tell you."

"Cats will take more than that off a person," Joshua muttered. "A male needs his balls. They're all lumbering oafs with no culture."

The elderly Rat slapped Joshua's head with the spoon, splattering the younger Rat with hot droplets of soup. "Don't you ever think that! We may be fighting one another in search of the Cheese, but we're all Jack's creatures in this House. There's a lot of important Rats that could never have taken the measure of Old Lenox."

Joshua rubbed his face where the spoon had struck him. "But surely you never thought we should cooperate with the Puss— the Cats."

Benjamin banged his spoon around in his pot and continued to glare at Joshua until the young Rat slunk away to catch his own dinner. He knew where there was a nest of newborn Mice near the second guest laundry chute.

Three days later the Cats attacked the fourth floor with a ferocity unrivalled in living memory. They swept up from the main gallery on the great stairs, with a second prong up the middle west servants' stairs and a flanking attack through the dumbwaiter in the music library.

Joshua found himself defending a dressing room closet full of squealing females and nestlings, his sword and three darts to hand. Benjamin stood at his side with a rapier—a rare weapon for a Rat—and two of the oldest nestlings, nearly ready to shave, supported them nervously with broken lengths of closet pole.

Just outside their door, three Cats probed their defenses, a young notch-eared orange-haired tom and two tabby females. They were armed with spears and shields, and the tom had a little helmet made of lacquered Rat-leather.

"Got your great-uncle Norway on my head, you little furry bastards," shouted the tom. "I'll have the pair of you for boots."

Out in the hall, screeching and the clash of weapons signaled that the tide of war ran hot and bloody. "My children will be warmed by your mangy pelt," Joshua jeered back, even as he silently prayed for help. Each of the Cats outweighed him at least two-to-one. He flung a dart, catching one of the tabbies in the cheek.

She screeched and bounded forward, spear waving. Benjamin pushed Joshua out of the way to step to the center of the doorframe, ducked inside the tabby's spear thrust, and skewered her neck with the rapier. Withdrawing the blade, he whipped it to notch both the Cat's ears before falling back as the tabby collapsed to the floor, gurgling blood across the pale oak.

"Damn me," said the tom quietly. "Shields up and advance." He and the remaining tabby brought their shields forward and poked their spears out, leaving Benjamin no room to weave in for another cut. They stepped forward at a measured pace, pausing with each footfall, driving Joshua and Benjamin further back into the closet step by step.

Joshua poked at their wooden shields with his sword, but Benjamin grabbed his arm. "It will get stuck, then you will." The elderly rat nodded at the two nestlings with the closet poles, who waited at each side of the door, hidden from the view of the cats. "Darts," he hissed to Joshua.

As the cats cleared the doorframe, the nestlings flailed wildly with their broken poles, behind the shields. Joshua flung his next dart, but it caught harmlessly on the tom's helmet. Taking advantage of the nestlings' attack, Benjamin slid sideways to stab past the remaining tabby's bobbing shield. The tom speared one nestling, and swung the body around to catch Benjamin on the spear's point even as the old Rat's rapier became trapped between the tabby's ribs.

Joshua attacked, flailing with his sword, but the wounded tabby caught him in the face with the wooden shield, and Joshua tumbled backwards, seeing sparks as bright as the orange butterflies on the snow.

As the sparks cleared, Joshua found that he wasn't unconscious, but he couldn't feel his arms and legs. From his place on the floor Joshua watched with unfocused detachment as the orange tom gutted Benjamin with the spear, then bashed in the head of the remaining nestling. While the tabby slumped down to mew her pain the tom rampaged among the females and the other nestlings, tearing throats, breaking knees and elbows, and tossing the smaller ones against the closet wall.

Barbarians, thought Joshua, the idea rising huge and bloody in his mind like an autumn moon. Cats were all barbarians. Lost in the country of his thoughts, Joshua smiled at the thought of trimming the toms, one by one, until none could breed.

Then the tom stood over Joshua, blood on his chin and whiskers and a rope of saliva dangling from his jaws. "Wake up, little brown Rat," said the Cat. "It's your turn to feel my claw." He pressed his spear into Joshua's breastbone. The young Rat's thin Mouse-leather vest offered no protection at all. "Will your precious Cheese welcome you back to its substance?"

Slowly, Joshua placed both his hands on the haft of the spear, just above the point, and pushed upward. The Cat smiled, leaning a bit harder until the point broke the skin of Joshua's chest.

"Where are you going, old man Cat?" the Rat whispered as his head began to clear. No one would save him now.

The Cat smiled back, fangs glinting like sun on snow. "To dinner, to dinner, just like that."

Joshua yanked the spear point to his right as the Cat thrust, taking the jab into his lung rather than his heart. The Cat yowled his surprise while Joshua grabbed his last dart with his left hand and yanked himself up the shaft of the Cat's spear with his right. Each tug of his arm was a fresh pain in his chest, hot and fluid. The tom tugged frantically on the spear as Joshua stabbed him deep in the eye with the dart. "In memory of Old Lenox," Joshua whispered in the tom's ear as the cat gurgled his pain and curled to the floor.

After a while, Joshua eased himself off the spear. The Cats around him were all dead, and sounds of battle had died down in the hallway outside.

The young Rat had already bled more than he would have thought his body could contain, but he found strength to crawl to Benjamin and stroke the elderly Rat's ears.

"By the sharpness of my teeth," Joshua whispered, "you will not pass unknown to the Cheese."

"Dogs," whispered Benjamin. "Only Dogs ..."

Then the orange butterflies came for Joshua, a cloak of falling leaves to bind him to the earth and render him to loam.

"You've lived longer through fever than any Rat we know of," said Eglantine. She was a pretty young black Rat with green eyes, wearing starched whites stolen from some linen closet, who served as night nurse in the attic infirmary. The infirmary was a dark, narrow hall that connected the fourth and fifth gables. It was hard to find and harder to enter, which made it ideal for undisturbed recuperation.

Joshua was still surprised to find himself alive. Every time he awoke, it was to the memory of the orange tabby's spear and the sense of butterflies crawling all over his body. It had been weeks since he had last forgotten how he came to this place that reeked of scabs and sores, weeks since he had been able to forget the death of Benjamin.

"It was not my plan," he told the nurse. "I expected to meet the Cheese."

She smiled. "Or perhaps the Master. You've come as close to death's tunnel as any of us. What did you see?"

Avoiding Eglantine's eye, Joshua stared at the laths of the sloped ceiling. "The Master has forsaken us. Jack will never come back to His House. If He still cared about us, Benjamin would yet live."

The nurse smoothed his blanket, her cool hands lingering on Joshua's chest. "You know better. It is the way of Rats and Cats to fight and die. Until the Cheese is found, this is our life. The good perish with the bad."

Joshua shook his head, his chest aching with the effort of speaking. "The Cats came in numbers, and with purpose, like we've never seen. Times are changing. Old Lenox went out to die because he could not stem their thirst for blood."

Eglantine patted his cheek. "We've blocked the dumbwaiter and built new hoardings at the tops of the stairways. They won't be back for a while.

222

Rest easy, hero."

"Heroes succeed," Joshua said quietly. "I should be sent to the Dogs for my failures."

Dogs, he thought. Why did Benjamin want Dogs?

Eglantine kissed Joshua on his forehead as he slipped back into sleep, taken by fitful dreams of howling in the forest.

"I want to speak to the King," Joshua told the Rat doctor who listened to his chest.

"Quiet," said the doctor, a ginger-haired Rat of middle years with a huge white scar seaming one cheek and down his neck. "I'm trying to hear your lungs."

Joshua grabbed the little rubber tube and yelled into the cone at the end. *"The Rat King!"*

The doctor winced, snatching the ends of the tube from his offended ears. "You may be a hero, but you are also a fool. I helped you live."

"I'm tired of this bedroll in this dark attic," Joshua said, "and I have a plan forming for those Cats."

"Oh, the hero has a *plan*," the doctor said with a thin, whining snarl. "Listen to the *hero*." He tapped Joshua's chest with a finger. "Let me hear your lungs in peace and I'll find someone to come take note of your plan."

"Dogs," Joshua said to the serious young Rat with spectacles and a sheaf of papers. Few knew how to read, and fewer yet how to write, so this Rat's pen was a badge of office more powerful than any sword.

The Rat made circular motions with his pen on paper. "Dogs, you say."

"Correct. We eat Mice, right?"

"Mmm."

"And Cats eat us."

The other Rat's pen stopped moving. "That's defeatist talk, you know."

"Just listen," snarled Joshua. Suddenly he understood how Benjamin used to feel talking to him. "What eats Cats?"

The official Rat made a point of staring at the sloped ceiling as if lost in thought. "Other Cats?"

"Do-o-o-gs." Joshua made a long, low growl of the word. "We'll forge an alliance with the Dogs, set them upon the Cats. The Dogs will eat the

Cats and we'll be free to find the Cheese."

Staring over the tops of his spectacles, the other Rat looked as if he had tasted a rotten Mouse. "Dogs. Treason. Indeed. And Benjamin told you this?"

"Yes." Joshua's body quivered, ready to fight this Rat. Which was ridiculous.

Polite, oh this official Rat was exquisitely polite. "Was that before or after he had his guts wrapped around a spear shaft like solstice bunting?"

Joshua exploded up off the pallet, taking a backhanded swipe at the other Rat that failed as he collapsed into agonized coughing.

When his coughing wound down, Joshua heard the official Rat mentioning brain damage to the doctor. Sad, so sad, in such a hero. Then the doctor approached with an enormous glass syringe in one hand.

"I have been authorized to use our precious drugs on the hero of the fourth floor," the doctor said in his most official voice.

"I decline the honor," Joshua gasped, but he couldn't make his legs straighten out enough to run away.

The plunger descended like lightning in the forest, and orange butterflies exploded in Joshua's head. He barked like a Dog, until his throat was hoarse, but no one answered.

A blizzard outside Jack's House rocked even the hidden rooms of the inner attic. Though no snowflakes fell in the infirmary, the wind found its way through cracks and brought the crackling scent of the storm and the joint-clutching cold. He had not seen the sun for months, but still Joshua knew it was night.

He stared at one hand, pale in the candle-lit gloom, flexing it. His breathing felt ordinary, blessedly ordinary. Somewhere in the darkness nearby, Rats whispered about the will of the Master. What had happened to the drugs?

"How long," asked Joshua.

The whispering stopped. Then Eglantine's voice echoed through the room. "Months. Solstice moon has long since passed."

"If you are going to kill me, do it now."

Eglantine and the doctor shuffled out of the shadows to stand at the foot of his pallet. Something glinted in the darkness behind them. In the flickering light, the doctor looked nervous, Eglantine sad and perhaps ashamed.

"Well?" Joshua demanded.

"Your name is written on our hallway walls in blood and dung," said the doctor. "Rats expect you to save them. In response the King has decided that your illness will enter a sudden decline."

"It can't be," said Eglantine. "You've done no wrong, only fought like us all."

"A thousand other Rats fight. Why me?"

"Dogs," whispered the nurse. "They say Benjamin speaks to you from the Master's side and tells you to call in the Dogs."

Joshua laughed, his chest still blessedly free of pain. "That little bastard's been telling tales, hasn't he? The official Rat who you sent to see me." He pointed at the doctor.

"I believe it was supposed to be a mockery," said the doctor. "But the Cats have hit us hard, over and over. Our barricades have failed, and they've taken control of the music library. From there, they sortie against us through the servants' corridors. We are losing the war. You have become a symbol of hope." He clenched his fists and stared at Joshua's feet. "Our last hope. And I will not kill a patient."

"But I will," said the official Rat, stepping out of the darkness, his spectacles glittering like rings of fire in the glare of the candle. "And kill the doctor, too, if that is what it takes to maintain standards. No Rat should be afraid to die."

"No Rat is afraid to die," said Joshua, smiling his most Catlike smile at the official Rat. "But no Rat needs to die, either."

"The needs of the pack always triumph," said the official Rat. "His Majesty sees to that."

Joshua watched as Eglantine slid the glass syringe from the doctor's coat. The doctor stared at his own feet, pretending not to notice. "The needs of the pack," Joshua said, keeping the official Rat's attention, "are to be decided by the pack. Not by some literate Mouse's bastard nestling."

"You will not anger me, hero. Your death will be an inspiration to Rats throughout Jack's House."

"Maybe," said Joshua. Eglantine plunged the syringe into the official Rat's neck. "And maybe my life will be instead."

The spectacles clattered to the wooden floor as the official Rat clutched his wound. He fell slowly, spiraling downward like a lightning-struck tree. Joshua stood, smashed the spectacles with his foot, and retrieved the syringe from the limp Rat's neck. He stuck it under his arm, rolling it back and forth.

"My scent," he said with a grin to the other two. "Tell the King's men I overpowered you and stabbed this Rat with the syringe. With my odor all over it, they might even believe you." He dropped the syringe to the floor, stepped toward the doctor, and slugged him a tooth-breaking punch. The doctor collapsed, whimpering. "There. Now you're an innocent Rat."

Eglantine stood her ground. "Are you going to hit me, too?"

"No." Remembering her kiss, Joshua stroked her ear. "But why did I even wake up for this little meeting?"

"Sugar water," she whispered. "For the past three days, since we heard the rumors of your impending death. Sugar water instead of the Master's drugs in your veins."

"Ah," said Joshua. "Well then, the Master permitting and with the blessings of the Cheese, I'm off to speak with the Dogs. Feel free to tell everyone that I said that. Give the King something to worry about."

"How will you keep the Dogs from tearing you apart?"

"I don't know," he said. This time the butterflies were in his stomach.

Wily Wharf and the Parlor Twins had killed a Dog once, in the dim mists of Rat history. Joshua stood at the eighth gable window, watching the snow slide against it, gray shadows against night's black. It hissed like silk being dragged across silk. Three of the biggest Rats that ever lived, armed with some arcane, long-lost weapon of the Master's, and still both the Twins had died of their wounds. Rats were not made to fight Dogs. It was like Mice fighting Cats. Or Cats fighting the mythical Bears, that were said to prey on Dogs in their forest.

He pressed his forehead against the cold glass. This post was unguarded on winter nights—what was the point, with nothing to see through the darkness and the snow? Joshua was not worried about being discovered. He was worried about talking to the Dogs. They would snap his spine as thoughtlessly as he snapped a Mouse nestling's, and that would be the end of his mission to save the Rats.

But the Dog that Wiley and the Twins had killed lived on, in a sense. The King's cape was Dogskin, with the black-and-ginger scalp still on it.

And the Dog's skull was the King's feasting cup, chased with royal aluminum and windings of the copper that infested all the walls of the House. Eglantine was right—he needed a passport to the Dogs. The King had one. Even Dogs had their sense of curiosity, after all.

Joshua laughed through the glass at the night's cold shadows. First he had killed one of the King's trusted Rats, now he proposed to steal the royal regalia. Simpler to break the old glass before him and hurl himself into the snow far below.

Flexing his fists, wishing for a spear or sword, Joshua turned from the window and headed down from the attic, toward the royal seat in the Velvet Bedroom off the Hall of Mirrors. If he could not be forceful, he would be persuasive.

When he emerged from the attic stairs beneath the eight gable, Joshua found himself in a busy hallway. It had been months since he had seen more than a few Rats at a time, so the mass of nestlings, females, and males was a sudden pressure, like flowing water. He turned sideways and shouldered his way through the crowd, balancing just far enough forward to force people to yield.

"Joshua," someone said behind him. He didn't turn.

"Hero," whispered a female.

"He's come for the Dogs!" shouted another Rat up ahead.

"Joshua." His name spread down the hall, a fire burning in the minds of desperate Rats. Winters were always hard in the House, but this winter of war had put a haggard edge on the half-familiar faces. "Joshua, Joshua, Joshua!"

He found himself in the middle of a wedge of Rats, their errands abandoned to sweep down the hall with him, fingers snatching at his hair and skin, shoulders, elbows, hips brushing against him. Someone tried to hand him a newborn nestling, but Joshua shoved the infant away.

"Clear the hall," he said. "I must see the King."

A cheer went up. "Joshua's going to challenge the King!"

"No," he shouted. "There has been fighting enough. I need to see him, not defeat him."

Armed Rats poured into the hall ahead of Joshua, but they hung back when they saw the crowd. "That Rat is a traitor," one of them called. "A Cat-lover. Turn him over to us, or it will not go well with you."

Joshua's escort mobbed the soldiers and pushed them aside like trillium blooms. They swept into the Hall of Mirrors, where the dozens of Rats became a hundred, then a thousand, real and imagined, physical and reflected. Joshua found himself at what seemed the center of the entire Rat nation, a horde of his people around him.

In one mirror, he caught the reflection of a single orange butterfly, fluttering above the crowd, but when he turned to see it, nothing was there.

Joshua's Rats burst into the Velvet Bedroom like an avalanche from the ultramontane, sweeping him in past guards and receptionists. The King stood, talking to two of his advisors, and they all froze at the onslaught of citizenry. Within seconds, the King found himself at the center of a small circle of worn carpet, hemmed in by Rats. Joshua stepped into that circle.

"Your Majesty," he said, with a polite nod of his head. Nowhere near the crouch that protocol required, but no Rat in the room was crouching at the moment.

"I see," said the King. "You look well, hero."

"Better than some." Joshua made circles of his fingers over his eyes, a brief mime of spectacles. "But I will make no issue of history, not now."

The King glanced at the wall of Rats around them. "It seems you would make whatever issue you want, hero."

"I go to the Dogs," Joshua said. He admired the King's cool head, standing proud before a crowd of subjects ready to strike him down and raise Joshua up in his place. "For us all."

"The Dogs," whispered the crowd, the words echoing outward like ripples in a basin. "The Dogs."

"All loyal Rats serve you and the pack against the Cats," said Joshua, then quietly: "Despite rumors to the contrary, I am and always have been a loyal Rat."

"Then go, with my blessing," the King hissed, sweat finally breaking on his face even in the blizzard cold of the House.

"I require your Dogskin cape and your feasting cup. As ambassadorial tokens to the Dogs."

"My ..." The King stopped himself before his voice pitched up into a threat. "And you will go, and trouble me no more?"

"Whether I return or not, I will trouble you no more," said Joshua.

"I do not know which would be worse," the King muttered, "but if it will take you from this place, have them with my blessing and good riddance." He raised his voice, calling out, "Fetch my regalia for the hero!"

"I have a name, Majesty," said Joshua.

"No, you do not." The King smiled sadly. "You belong to Rat history now, our hero in the last war against the Cats." .

The crowd began to chant as the regalia was passed hand to hand. "Josh-u-a! Josh-u-a! Josh-u-a!"

"May you die on their fangs," whispered the King as he hung the Dogskin cloak on Joshua's shoulders.

"May you live to see it," Joshua whispered back. He raised his hands to quiet the crowd. "Fetch me ropes," he called. "I will descend from the window in the eighth gable."

"In this storm?" someone asked.

"Life is a storm," Joshua said. "And I will weather it to bring us all to the Cheese."

The crowd swept him out of the Velvet Bedroom like a leaf before the wind.

On the end of the rope, Joshua spun in the blizzard. The snow plucked at the Dogskin cloak, at the skull tied to his belt. The crowd of Rats paying out his line wasn't being smooth or efficient about it—scuffling no doubt to touch the hero's last link with the Rat nation.

At the fourth floor, Rats crowded a window, staring out at him. Some prayed. Joshua smiled, flashing his fangs, then slid beyond their sight.

At the third floor, Joshua banged into a glass window. Within was a firelit room, occupied by a tortoiseshell Cat in a quilted jacket smoking a pipe and reading a book before the blaze. The Cat glanced up, waved the pipe at Joshua in a gesture reminiscent of Old Lenox's last salute, and resumed his reading.

The Rat lowered further, to the second floor. This window was shuttered, though dim blue lights played through the gaps. He was just as glad not to see through it. Whatever lived on the first and second floors of Jack's House was fearsome enough to keep the Dogs outside, and Joshua didn't care to meet them either. Getting the Dogs back in was a problem for another day, if his embassy ended in anything but sudden blood.

At the first floor, a pair of bloodshot eyes each as big as their framing window stared out at him. He shrieked and dropped away from the line to land in the snow as the great, slow lid dropped into a terrible wink with a sound like the rumble of thunder.

Gasping, Joshua stumbled into the driving snow, slogging through the drifts downslope toward the forest and the Dogs, his legs already numb with the chill. He didn't dare look back at Jack's House. The terrible regard of whatever lay behind the first floor window filled him with more fear than any Cat ever had.

"We don't usually bother to keep your kind alive," said the Dog as an orange butterfly looped past its right ear. The Dog was a big bruiser, dark, with mottled hair and one milky eye that rolled in time to unheard music. "But you brought such an interesting bonus."

"I thank you for my life," said Joshua, as he had every morning in the long weeks since his captivity began. "May I speak to the Dog King today?"

The Rat was in a cage of wood and bones, crudely lashed together by the fat, unfortunate fingers of the Dogs. His cage resided in a little clearing among a stand of spruces just below the tree line, the mountain looming above Jack's House to the southeast. The Dogs were obviously not accustomed to keeping prisoners, and it would have been the work of a moment to escape the cage, but where would Joshua go? Certainly not back to the Rat King, not yet. He was where he wanted to be, in the country of the Dogs. They just didn't seem to care.

"You're welcome," said his jailor, who then wandered away. Just like every morning.

Joshua stared up the slope through the trees, toward Jack's House and the mountain beyond. For all the gnawing despair and enforced lethargy of his odd imprisonment, he never tired of that view. Jack's House rambled with wings and towers the Rat nation had never suspected the existence of, like a giant nest made of timber, grown large enough to be home to the entire world. Every time he counted windows, he got a different number, but Joshua could see at least three hundred of them. There were people on the roof — Owls, maybe? The Mice had their legends, too, for all that the

Rats vigorously scourged their nests.

And the mountain beyond, its slopes a nearly perfect triangle, its gray-brown rocky bones just now appearing in the spring thaws, blue glaciers hanging impossibly high. The coy peak so often hidden behind plumes of snow and cloud would sometimes emerge to stab the sudden blue sky.

Snow farther up the slope around the House didn't melt until late summer, gone for a month or two before renewing, and some years never melted at all. Here downslope in the country of the Dogs, the snow was already melting. The Dogs liked to gambol in the ferns and grasses beneath the towering firs and spruce, even though they sometimes went to ground at the sound of distant growling.

Joshua would have wondered if the Dogs stayed away from the House for the sheer pleasure of the forest, except for that great heavy-lidded face he'd seen the night he left his old life behind. Even if the Dogs freed him, Joshua doubted he had the strength to confront those giant eyes. Whether it was only sorrow or some stranger emotion, those eyes were a pair of drowning pools to capture the soul of any thinking creature.

"Friend for you," called his jailor, returning unexpectedly. Dogs were creatures of habit — to the point of mania — so Joshua was most surprised. The Dog hung a leather sack from a nearby tree branch, popped loose the laces, and left again.

Old Lenox's piebald face popped out of the sack, one eye twisted shut, the other gleaming as bright as that day last summer.

"A Rat, I see," said the Cat. "I wondered where they'd gotten that mangy old skin they were all howling over."

Joshua dropped to a crouch, showing Old Lenox the same respect he had shown Benjamin. "I greet you, sir Cat," he said as he rose to his feet again, "though I thought you long gone to death."

"Close," said the Cat, "for these beasts smashed my limbs before they decided to spare me. It seems they use an occasional Cat as a divinatory aid. And you must be that young Rat who watched me from the attic window."

"Eighth gable was my duty station, back then."

"We call it the grouse gable," said Old Lenox reflectively. "They're all named after birds on our maps."

Joshua waited a polite moment to see if Old Lenox would say any more. "Benjamin spoke well of you," the Rat finally said.

The Cat frowned. "Is he dead?"

"Killed by an orange tom shortly after your departure."

"My son, I imagine. An agitator in the war party. What became of him?"

Joshua resisted the impulse to look down. "I stabbed him in the eye with a dart."

Old Lenox narrowed his remaining eye, his whiskers twitching as his lips curled back from his teeth. Then with a shiver, the Cat shook away his anger. "I suppose it needed doing," he said sadly. "And now what are you doing here?"

Joshua briefly considered, and discarded, deception. Old Lenox would probably see through him. Besides, Benjamin would not have approved.

"I've come to raise the Dogs against the Cats, to turn the tide of our war."

The Cat laughed, his bag shaking hard enough to threaten to fall. "You can't get three Dogs to agree on where the sun sets. How would you get them into the House and past the lower floors?"

"I have to try," said Joshua, slow and stubborn, "or you Cats will slaughter our females and eat our nestlings and drive us back until we are but bones in the attic."

"That is the way of the world," said Old Lenox in a prim tone. "You serve the Mice no better."

Joshua snorted. "Mice are our natural prey."

"And Rats are ours. What difference?"

The Rat thought about that. "We hunger for the Cheese, and await the Master. The Mice, they are just animals."

"Cheese. Only a Rat would hunger for Cheese, and so you believe everyone does. You have lost your memory of the Master, placing your faith in such a thing. It would only fatten Rats and Mice for us. And believe you me, the Mice hunger for it, too, despite their terror of you Rats."

"How would you know?" said Joshua.

Old Lenox leaned forward until he was at risk of falling out of the bag. "Because the Mice set us upon you last autumn, making an alliance to war upon the Rats so they could seek the Cheese in peace. How do you think the war party got such good intelligence of your defenses and domains? Mice are everywhere."

The truth spun in on Joshua, with the memory of a hundred throats torn out, heads smashed and nests destroyed. "They wish like we wish, and fear like we fear, and seek the Cheese like we do." The Rat stared at his hands as if they were newly grown upon his arms. "We are cousins, the Mice and the Rats."

"Fine time to discover empathy," grumbled the Cat, "you in that cage and me legless in this bag here. It's Jack's Cheese anyway, just like it's Jack's House."

"How do I stop this war of Cats and Rats?" demanded Joshua.

Old Lenox shrugged. "War is the way of the world. What's to stop?"

The Dog King walked into the little clearing. He was huge, with black and orange hair and a single cracked fang that left sores on his cheek. He wore a rough circlet of vines on his head, and carried the Rat King's old Dogskin cloak over one arm. He had a dozen Dog soldiers guarding him.

Joshua dropped to his crouch again. "Your Majesty."

"So, Cat," said the Dog King in a loud voice. "What says my oracle of this curious creature from the Master's House?"

Old Lenox squinted his good eye and thrashed his head around. In the middle of the fit, the Cat winked at Joshua, then banged his head backward against the tree trunk. "This one has been touched by the Bears," said the Cat, an impressive trail of saliva dripping down the leather bag. "He is sacred to them and through them to the Master. Set him on his course." The Cat screeched, then vomited forth a pile of gray, hairy goo, which the Dog King eagerly licked up.

"Does he speak truly?" the Dog King asked Joshua a moment later.

"Your Majesty," Joshua began, then stopped. He could deny being the Master's servant, but that might not even be true. The Cat could be an old liar and still tell the truth himself. What would Joshua do, if he were hung in a bag for the rest of his life? "I came from the House to seek your strength, that Rats and Cats and Mice might live in harmony."

"Dinner, all dinner," sniffed the Dog King. "I don't care if the pantry squabbles."

"It is not the pantry," said Joshua. "It is Jack's House. The Master's House. We are all his creatures."

The Dog King opened his mouth to speak, one finger tapping Joshua's cage bars, when a cloud of orange butterflies burst into the clearing, flooding the cage and surrounding the Dog King. Then, as quickly as they came, they were gone.

"Fire of the Master," said the Dog King. "The flames that do not burn."
He turned to the Dog soldiers, who stood quivering. "We go to the House.
This Rat will lead us to the Master."

Somehow Joshua found himself carrying the Cat. Strapped to the Rat's
chest, Old Lenox's bag was almost as big as Joshua. The Rat stumbled knee
deep across the snow banks that spread before Jack's House. The sky above
was a vast blue sea, without a wisp of cloud, so that Joshua felt as if one
missed step would send him sailing upward forever. The mountain towered
beyond the House, snow glaring with the afternoon sun. Around Joshua,
Dogs advanced in a ragged line, approaching the front of the House.

All the people of the House came forth to see such an unprecedented
delegation. The Owls on their roof, the Cats in their windows, the Rats in
their gables. Strange, sinuous people he had never seen threw open the
shutters two floors below the Rat nation, while others, heavy and slow,
appeared in windows elsewhere in the House. He glanced over his
shoulder, past the line of Dogs, to see great, hairy people who must be Bears
standing at the edge of the trees.

Overhead, the orange butterflies swarmed, some alighting on the snow
to spread their wings like wounds upon the earth, then flying again, around
and behind Joshua like a loose cape the size of the wind.

Joshua stopped a few hundred feet from the great front door, setting
Old Lenox's bag down before him so that the Cat's head emerged just below
Joshua's chin. Thousands of eyes glittered in the sunlight, the shadows of
the butterflies shifting on the snow. Around him, the Dogs breathed like so
many bellows, and the crisp snow crackled beneath his feet.

The entire world waited for Joshua.

"This is the House that Jack built," the Rat said. Even in his ordinary
voice, his words seemed to carry across the snow to every pair of ears. "And
all of us in it are His creatures."

The wind swirled around his feet as the butterflies in their thousands
came to light upon the snow. Joshua hadn't meant for it to come to this
point, not this fast. He wasn't ready. But he had to try, to trust that the
words would come to him, make the people see what he had seen—that
they were all one kind together in Jack's House.

234

"But the Master is gone. Jack is gone, and in His going He has given us all back to ourselves. We serve no one but each other, and the House that is our home. Jack is dead, and we are all Him." Joshua paused, his eyes stinging in the cold morning light. "Long live Jack."

Joshua's breath hung steaming in the crystal air, as if giving form to his words. The people stared at him, the Dogs, the forest. Then a window slammed shut. A Dog barked, laughing as if at some joke. A Mouse shrieked, then a group of Cats swarmed up a cornice to launch an impromptu assault on a window filled with Rats. Within moments, people all over the House were screaming and running. The butterflies leapt into flight, spiraling up into the sunlight, up and up until Joshua could no longer see them.

The Dog King walked over to Joshua and Old Lenox, urinated in the snow at their feet, then strode off without a word. His soldiers followed him, shouting at the Bears who still stood in the shadows.

Joshua sat down in the snow. He would have wept if he could have found the tears. "Some hero," he finally said.

"You did pretty well, for a Rat," said the Cat in the bag.

The Rat studied Old Lenox's single green eye. "I think I'm supposed to kill you now."

The Cat jerked his head toward the House. "Just because they don't listen to you doesn't mean you shouldn't listen to yourself."

Joshua stared at his paws again. He had set out to save the Rats, even the entire world. Could he only save himself? And perhaps one broken old Cat. He almost laughed. The two of them were still Jack's children.

"Fair enough, my friend," the Rat said. Grunting, he hefted Lenox's leather sack. "The House is before us, the forest behind us," he said. "Let us go somewhere else. Left or right?"

"Always with the empathy," said Old Lenox. "My right eye is the good one. Let's go that way."

As they crested a ridge a quarter mile past the last corner of the House that Jack Built, Joshua stopped and turned to look back. Balanced against his chest, the Cat looked with him. Great eyes stared back from a pair of ground floor windows. As Joshua waved, the right one winked back, a lid bigger than his body descending like sunset over the forest.

Joshua turned again and scrambled down the slope, out of sight of the

House, Cats, Rats, Dogs, any of the people. One last orange butterfly stuttered before them, leading the Cat and the Rat onward together toward undiscovered countries of the heart.

The Passing of Guests

The Passing of Guests

Hydrogen happened. The neighboring particle density doubled, then redoubled within seconds.

"Ahriman," Port said, interrupting a molecular-level simulation of oceanic behavior. It had been tweaking hurricanes at micro-erg energy levels for amusement. "There is hydrogen."

"What does that mean?" asked the electronic ghost of Port's first and oldest friend, cuing the conversation from its personality template. Ahriman's body rotted in a vat deep within Port's basalt keel.

"I have no idea. But it's the first spontaneous retrograde entropy in billennia."

"Something comes," Ahriman's ghost said with an inappropriate flash of insight. The template immediately initiated a self-diagnosis to correct the fault.

"What?" Port had long ago forgotten that most human of emotions, fear. "What comes?"

Ahriman's ghost was afraid. "Port," it said. "Something is wrong with me."

"No!" shouted Port. "Every time I restore you, you degrade further."

"Help," the ghost said. It slipped away from its interfaces, quantum handshakes with Port's systems dissolving like coastal fog on a billennia-vanished summer morning.

Ahriman's clone-worm stirred in its vat. Subtle errors across millions of generations of replication had reduced the ghost's body to a loose bag of lipids with calcium concentrations. Monitoring subroutines escalated queries to Port's consciousness.

Mourning its friend's ghost, Port allowed itself to be distracted by the emergent hydrogen. Fresh photons were emitted, in sprays of a few thousand at a time, but even that meager lightshow was dazzling in the darkness of the end of the Universe.

Inside the vat, the worm contracted, amino acids dissolving and knitting back together as increasingly complex proteins. The bony lumps arranged themselves in a longitudinal pattern with bilateral symmetry. A flash of scales, a bright black eye, a clawed finger, all bubbled like stew in a cauldron.

"I am here," whispered Ahriman, after a while. "But where is here?"

His claws found a large bar just beneath the lid. He pushed. The lid popped off to a jangle of alarms.

Port was finally distracted from the lightshow.

"Where have you been?" Port spoke on every wavelength, every frequency, up and down the audio and video channels, on quantum loopbacks. "I have been so lonely."

"For the love of life," Ahriman said, picking goo out of his finger webbing, "settle down. I've been dead."

"But *where*?" Port howled.

Ahriman winced. "Dead. It's not a where. It's not anything at all. Dead just is."

"People don't un-die."

Ahriman flexed his osteomuscular linkages, running through basic shapeshifting exercises. He tasted the air with his tongue—the atmosphere was brittle with the tang of a trillion of years of storage. "I did."

Port retreated to a more normal tone. "Oh, my friend. How did this happen?"

Ahriman surprised himself by saying, "God sent me." The answer felt right, the way breathing felt right.

Hydrogen continued to happen, at a prodigious rate, until a cloud of glowing gas enveloped Port. The cloud swirled like a boiling pot, agitated by the white fountain at its heart.

"Ahriman."

Pacing his tiny chamber deep in Port's basalt heart, Ahriman said, "Yes?" He had settled into the human form he had worn during the long millennia of his life with Port, back on Earth. He had been a cultural anthropologist, studying the history of the then-vanishing race of Man. Port had been a city, longing for and fearing its creators.

"Where is God?" Port asked.

"Everywhere."

"There is no everywhere, not any more. There's just here. Nowhere else."

"That will be true soon," said Ahriman, "but not quite yet."

"Far-infrared says the last brown dwarf has vanished. How could something millions of light-years away suddenly disappear?"

"Perhaps it died millions of years ago, just in time to disappear from our view now."

"I cannot believe in such a coincidence."

"Then you must believe that everywhere has become smaller," Ahriman said.

"Is God here?"

Ahriman smiled, seeing in his mind's eye the white fountain boiling outside Port's basalt walls. "He comes closer all the time."

"Ahriman, are you God?"

"Just His message."

"He sent you to me."

Flicking goo from a deep skin fold, Ahriman sighed. "Not exactly."

The cloud enveloping Port warmed to six degrees Kelvin, dangerous heat for Port's vacuum-degraded infrastructure. Port moved away, warping the cold, dead superstringlines underpinning spacetime. It was virtually free transportation, albeit slow, leaching only a minute amount of the energy Port converted from its finite supply of mass.

Port soon found itself orbiting the boiling cloud, a tiny planet around a peculiar nebula. Bits of frozen gas trapped in the crevices of Port's eroded surface infrastructure sublimated under the radiant energy of the cloud, sending free oxygen and nitrogen into space for the first time in hundreds of billions of years. Meanwhile, the roil of the cloud stabilized into a measurable spin state.

"The cloud appears to be condensing the remaining matter and energy in the Universe," Port announced. "It could have happened anywhere, but it happens here. The odds against this occurring in my proximity are incalculably small."

"So were the odds of me coming back from the dead," said Ahriman, "but here we are together again, at the end of everything."

"You said God did it."

"What is God but all the long odds that have ever been beaten?"

Port objected. "God or no God, there is no mechanism that could draw the Universe's matter and energy back together, even if simultaneity held any meaning."

Ahriman laughed again. "In these late years everything is simultaneous. These are just the last, longest odds He will play."

"You imply that through its own sheer improbability the Universe should never have existed."

"'There are more things in heaven and earth, Horatio, than are dreamt of in your philosophy,'" Ahriman quoted. "Think of all the Universes that failed to exist, missing their odds. We are guests of chance, Port, privileged to witness God's ultimate wager."

"I fear we shall not last that long. This white fountain grows at a pace that will soon overwhelm even my best maneuvers," said Port.

"As you said, all the matter of the Universe is gathering in one place. It would hardly be a quiet event."

"How do you *know* that?"

Ahriman wasn't sure. He looked inside his mind and found conceptual maps of spacetime, built from the forty-two balancing equations that solved for the net mass-energy budget of the Universe. "God said so," he said. "I think."

242

"Exactly what is God saying?"

"I am the message, not the messenger," said Ahriman. "What God means is for you to determine."

Port boiled with a panic not felt in billions of years, thoughts rolling in synch with the white fountain—which had definitely become a star of sorts, though unmatched in Port's vast astronomical records. The edges of the Universe continued to be missing from Port's instrumentation. Port needed to fight the protostar, or flee.

Fight with what? Flee to where? Port accelerated, trading orbital proximity for speed to set up a potential slingshot departure into…nothing.

The surface of the protostar seethed with images. At first they seemed to be noisome fractals, which resolved to chains of regular patterns, dancing themselves into larger forms like self-replicating biochemical molecules. Larger shapes arose, round and flat, blocky and elegant, rough and smooth.

"It replays the history of the Universe, I think," whispered Port, "as it grows denser." Even the light flooding from the protostar seemed pregnant with meaning, freighted with the significance of all the lost depths of time.

"Repent, for the end is at hand," said Ahriman, watching the show on one of the walls of his basalt prison.

"Repent?"

"An old human saying, long before our time my friend. I picked it up from the leading edges of the electromagnetic broadcast bubble when I first studied humans."

"*Them*," said Port. "Meschia and Meschiane, the last humans we ever saw, who came to shut me down. Somehow they have sent you back."

"Man as God?"

"No. But Man transcended reality in some fashion I have never understood, not in the trillion years since my creators vanished from the cosmos. Are you their message?"

"I am God's message."

"Is God the protostar?"

"I was here before that protostar," Ahriman pointed out.

"*With* it, not before it. And we will both end with it, as the protostar grows faster than I can escape. I can only radiate so much heat."

"Soon, Port, soon." Ahriman stroked the basalt walls the way he once caressed the ceramic tiles of Port's Earthly streets.

Port shivered, tumbling slightly in its orbit. "Gravitational waves from a disturbance in the protostar."

"Watch," said Ahriman.

On a timescale Port could no longer measure for lack of external referents, the protostar collapsed even as its density grew. Port pulled itself outward to avoid the tidal stresses of the expanding Roche limit.

The light was dying. Nothing was left in the observable Universe but Port and the protostar, now glowing with a dim and fitful spite. Port didn't orbit through anything that could be considered normal space.

Neither was the protostar normal matter anymore. "It seems to have become a giant...quark?" Port couldn't begin to measure the quark's diameter—it seemed impossible to correlate with the size of Port's own basalt keel, the only available yardstick.

"Ylem," said Ahriman with satisfaction. "Undifferentiated matter. The ultimate predecessor—and successor—to all the matter and energy in the Universe."

"Almost all. We're still here."

"Precisely God's point."

"How's that?" asked Port.

"We're here, together. Because you survived everything. Literally. Beating all odds."

"You didn't survive. You died."

"But you needed me. You've mourned me across the billennia, and finally, here I am for you. Again, beating all odds."

Port stared at the ylem, which still had that faint glowering sheen. Temperature in their little surviving pocket of the Universe had dropped back to a fractional point above absolute zero. "I loved you in another age of the Universe," said Port, "for you saved my life and set me on this long course. But that shouldn't be enough to bring you back."

"Would you follow Man into transcendence?"

"I..." Port could not answer. No fates were left except the ylem. Port realized its substance was already joining that ultimate end, that the ylem's faint sheen came from a growing stream of particles sublimating from Port's basalt keel and long-ruined surface structures, showering into the ylem in suicidal dives.

Ahriman traced equations on the basalt wall, then tapped the place where his finger had laid out the first. "I can show you how to open the way. You can return to them."

Port tried to imagine life on the other side of the veil of transcendence. Would its human masters welcome it after all this time. What would that mean, that life? What was paradise to a machine like Port? Unlimited energy. Purpose. Potential. Perhaps it took a soul to imagine salvation—electromechanical houris dancing attendance on endlessly recreated avatars seemed a hollow dream.

"Or I can orbit here," said Port, "and monitor the ylem until I erode away."

Ahriman tapped the second equation. "Which will restore the ylem to its original state, satisfying the equations. Then the game is over. All odds paid off, the betting window closed."

"'God does not play dice,'" quoted Port.

"We are but guests in His Universe," said Ahriman, "coming to death along with our host."

More of Port's substance eroded, making a delicate lace of its outer shell, opening tunnels into its body. Port's seat of reason, its computation cores, would be endangered soon, as would Ahriman's chamber. If the power converters did not go first.

"Your life, your choice," Ahriman said.

"I would not take you with me into death, and somehow I doubt you could attain even whatever transcendence is available to me." Port tried again. "Is there anything else?"

"A third way," said Ahriman, pointing to where he had traced the last equation. "You can ignite the ylem and make a new Universe. A sufficiently chaotic impact will destabilize the ylem, introducing the density variances required for eventual differentiation of matter and energy. Together we can give up transcendence to be the lightbringers, this time."

Port considered its life of service, and the astronomically longer life of independence that had followed. Port had played god in the lives of younger races, failures that still haunted it, then roamed the decaying Universe. It had collected data, by the petabyte. But had it learned truth? "After surviving these billions of years, I have earned transcendence. What does God say?"

Ahriman had no reply. Port would have to choose soon. The ylem continued to eat Port's density.

"Transcendence without the Universe behind it has to be a quiet sort of hell," Port continued. "There would be nothing against which to measure bliss. As you said, we are only guests of God in this place."

Port read the three equations Ahriman had traced on the wall, and chose one. Port then reeled in the very few remaining superstringlines inside the tiny allotment of spacetime that still survived, displacing its angular momentum to spiral inward.

"Together we will make a better light," Port said. It accelerated into the ylem trailing the tattered remnants of spacetime behind like a skein to disrupt the ylem's unstable equilibrium.

"Even God must talk to Himself," Ahriman whispered proudly. "Sometimes He also listens."

Port and Ahriman knew everything, for a moment, before they became everything new.

ABOUT THE AUTHOR

Jay Lake lives in Portland, Oregon with his family and their books. He can walk out onto his front porch and see a 11,200-foot volcano. This has no effect on his writing. Jay can be reached at http://www.jlake.com/

Jay's short fiction has appeared in many different magazines and anthologies both online and in print. He was a 2002 Writers of the Future Finalist and his story *Into the Gardens of Sweet Night* will appear in the Writers of the Future Anthology for 2002. Jay has been a reviewer for Tangent Online and is co-editor of the critically acclaimed *Polyphony* anthology series.

JAY"S ACKNOWLEDGMENTS

I want to thank Deborah Layne, without whom this collection would never have existed; Nina Kiriki Hoffman, for some of the best ideas about this book; Frank Wu for all the pretty pictures; and most especially the Wordos, the Fread list, Forteana and all my friends and family who read my work, prod me to be better and cheer me on when I finally get it right.

ABOUT THE ARTIST

Frank Wu is a strange alien creature sent to earth from Some Other Place, with twin missions to Love God and Love Your Neighbor. His secondary missions have included studying the molecular biology of bacteria and writing about giant space chickens and helping people get patents for DNA delivery devices. With additional side-trips into hanging with monks; and hunting for mastodon fossils in New Mexico and fish fossils and dinosaur bones in Wyoming and ammonoid fossils in Wisconsin. Frank has also ridden a banana-shaped moped, held Laura Palmer's diary in his own hands, and has touched sculptures in museums when the guards weren't looking. He also occasionally dabbles in art, said art having appeared in various magazines and books. He also won the Illustrators of the Future Grand Prize. Oh, and if your band is looking for a rhythm guy, he plays congas and is available for gigs in the San Francisco bay area.

FRANKS'S ACKNOWLEDGMENTS

First, I'd like to thank Deborah Layne for bringing me and Jay together and Jay for writing cool stories that were fun to illustrate.

The people I'd like to acknowledge fall generally into two categories: my friends, many of whom I've met in just last few years and many of whom are artists, authors and editors, who help shape my psychological universe and emotional and spiritual well-being; and my influences – mostly artists I've never met, but whose work has shaped my consciousness and aesthetic sense since I was born.

So thanks to my pals, in no particular order (no really, I love you all): James L. Terman of the famous Terman clan; Lori Ann White – don't worry, you're a fine writer and you will get your book published; the wacky Gary Shockley; Melissa Shaw; Kent Brewster of *Speculations*, who deserves to win the Hugo he keeps getting nominated for; Alan F. Beck; Nigel Sade; Patrick and Honna Swenson of *Talebones*, who've given me chance after chance to do art for them; Chris Garcia, who is always a delight; Sean Klein; Ken Wharton – whose first novel *Divine Intervention* I have the first autographed copy of – while he has my first numbered autographed business card; Rebekah Jensen – don't worry, you'll get your novel published, too; Lindsey Johnson, who always makes me happy; my pal Diana Sherman; Mary Anne Mohanraj and Jed Hartman at *Strange Horizons*, who helped me get off the ground; Ed McFadden of *Fantastic Stories*, who gave me my first chance to do a whole issue of art, and Warren Lapine and Angela Kessler, who published it; Matt Taggart, who's gonna be a Big Name Artist soon, just you wait; my Writers/Illustrators of the Future pals Mike Jasper, Dan Barlow and his wife Jennifer, Mark Siegel, and Ilsa Bick, whose works I've had the wonderful chance to illustrate, and Melissa Yuan-Innes, Paul Martens, Tobias Buckell, Leslie Walker, and William Brown – you guys are next; and to L. Ron Hubbard for starting the Writers/Illustrators of the Future Contest and everybody at Author Services for running it and treating us like royalty; Alison McBain, who may be yet the first to win both the Illustrators and Writers of the Future; Maia Sanders; Eric Witchey; Suzanne Robinson and Team EH – thanks for helping me show my art at cons – I love you guys; Michaela Eaves, for helping me polish and color-balance the pieces in this book; Mark R. Kelly of *Locus Online* for keeping me up-to-date on the really important stuff going on this world; Jae Brim, for your friendship; Derryl Murphy of *On Spec*, for making me controversial; Lillian Csernica, for being Lillian; Nina Kiriki Hoffman, who was there when we decided to call this *Greetings From Lake Wu* not *Guests and Other Disasters*; Rebecca Inch-Partridge – can't wait til your trilogy of trilogies is done; Ron Vick, for asking me to be GOH at WillyCon; Julie Czerneda, my fellow GOH there; Jerry and Kathy Oltion, who helped me find the perfect place to go fish fossil hunting; jim Van Pelt, who writes stories that are fun to illustrate; Magenta Brooks for posing for me; Bill Pierce – don't stop searching for yourself; and my pal Kevin O'Connell, whom I forgot to mention in the dedication for my Ph.D. thesis – sorry, Kevin; Paula Borden for friendship through the years; everybody at MoFo! and finally Lisa Bartsch, Mike Toy, Jim Morris, Eric and Belle Ettlin, and the folks at the Alpha Course and at the Vineyard Churches in Palo Alto and San Carlos.

I'd also like to thank Wah Ming Chang, who built the original *Star Trek* communicator, tricorder and phaser, the Salt Vampire, and the original Romulan bird of prey, plus the airship from *Master of the World* and George Pal's Time Machine; Eiji Tsuburaya, special effects genius behind Godzilla and creator of Ultraman; Martin Bower, who built the Mark IX

Hawk warship and a whole slew of alien ships and laser tanks (what could be cooler than laser tanks?) for *Space:1999*; and Brian Johnson, Derek Meddings and Reg Hill and the other technical geniuses Gerry Anderson worked with; Frank R. Paul, whose Martian war machine cover for the August 1927 *Amazing Stories* is IMHO one of the five best paintings done by anyone in the last century; Michael Whelan, whose painting of Joan Vinge's Snow Queen is another of the five; Ned Mann, who built art deco tanks for *Things to Come*; Fritz Lang, who directed *Metropolis* and *M*; Ralph McQuarrie, who designed C-3PO and X-wings; Al Nozaki, who built the manta ray-like Martian war machines in George Pal's *War of the Worlds*; Ray Harryhausen, who brought life to talos, the Ymir (whose name appears in each illustration), the Minoton, the Gwangi and so many others; Umberto Boccioni, who captured movement and destruction in canvas and bronze; Graves Gladney, who painted the July 1939 cover for *Astounding*, featuring A. E. Van Vogt's "Black Destroyer" – still one of the greatest magazine covers of all time; and Frank Kelly Freas, Frank Frazetta, Winsor McCay, Raphael De Soto, George Rozen, Ed Emshwiller, Vincent DiFate, Bob Eggleton, Paul Lehr, James Bama, Walter Baumhofer, Graves Gladney, Rubert Rogers, Alex Schomburg. Plus all the great artists whose work but not their names have appeared in books and magazines. Everything I do is an extension, a reiteration of what they have already done before me. As Newton is said to have said, If we see further, it is because we stand on the shoulders of giants. I'd also like to thank two imperfect men, Don Larsen and Simon Peter the fisherman, who showed that there is potential for greatness in the most humble of us. And, finally, of course, Praise God, from Whom all blessings flow; Praise Him, all creatures here below; Praise Him above, ye heavenly host; Praise Father, Son, and Holy Ghost. Amen.

Printed in the United States
16679LVS00006B/118-138